The *Little*
Christmas
House

BOOKS BY TRACY REES

Hidden Secrets at the Little Village Church

The Rose Garden
The House at Silvermoor
The Love Note
The Hourglass
Florence Grace
Amy Snow

TRACY REES

The Little Christmas House

Bookouture

Tracy Rees has asserted her right to be identified
as the author of this work.

ISBN: 978-1-80019-711-4
eBook ISBN: 9-781-80019-710-7

This book is a work of fiction. Names, characters, businesses,
organizations, places and events other than those clearly in the
public domain, are either the product of the author's imagination
or are used fictitiously. Any resemblance to actual persons, living or
dead, events or locales is entirely coincidental.

For Mum and Dad, with love and thanks for all our wonderful Christmases and for Teresa, who knows all about angels.

PROLOGUE

Last Christmas…

Holly

Holly Hanwell stood in front of the mirror, smoothing her festive, ivy-green satin dress over her hips. She'd gone full sparkles with her jewellery in honour of the occasion, outlined her brown eyes with a moss-green eyeliner and left her golden hair loose and wavy. The hotel-room door was ajar behind her and she could hear music wafting faintly up from the rooms below – the velvet tones of Johnny Mathis singing about the birth of a special child. Her hands drifted to her stomach and rested there. What did life have in store for her and Alex?

Behind her, the door opened wide. 'Wow, you look stunning, Hols!' It was Alex, coming to search her out.

Holly turned with a smile and they exchanged a quick hug. Alex was stocky, not much taller than Holly in her heels, with corn-blonde hair and a cheeky smile that belied his ambition and sharp corporate mind. He looked like an affable gardener or nanny but, in reality, he was a solicitor, who'd just been made partner at his new firm.

'You OK?' Alex asked. 'Everyone's dying to meet you.'

'I'm fine. Just making myself look pretty.' And taking a pause before launching herself into Alex's work Christmas party. After ten years together, she'd been to enough of them to know what to expect. He moved firms often – *If you can't move up, move out*, he liked to say – but although they were mostly a new set of people, they were usually very similar. They always found Holly, who was a primary school teacher, a 'refreshing novelty'.

'Well, I should say job done. You look very pretty indeed. Come on.' He held out his hand and Holly took it. They checked they had the key card to their room then descended the hotel staircase, which was vast and curved and perfect for a dramatic entrance – not that Holly wanted to make one, and not that anyone would have noticed, deep in conversation as they were in little knots of three or four. The banisters were thickly garlanded and a tall golden Christmas tree stood opposite a real, roaring fire. Gold candles and pine cones were heaped on the mantelpiece. No expense had been spared.

At the foot of the stairs, waiters stood by holding trays and offered them glasses of champagne. The music changed to Leona Lewis.

'It's lovely, Alex, really lovely.'

He grinned. 'Glad you approve. Come on – there's George. George? This is my partner, Holly.'

An hour later, Holly felt as though she'd met everyone in the entire firm. They were a nice enough bunch on the whole. They'd gone through the initial breaking-the-ice conversations about career, and Holly had several times explained that yes, she did love teaching and no, she wasn't looking to become a principal; she liked to be in the classroom with the children. Alex had caught her eye and winked – they often laughed together about how law-folk couldn't imagine doing anything but law and *certainly* couldn't countenance working with small, messy, noisy people for a living.

Now they'd moved on to personal chat: how long had various couples been together/married; how many children did they have;

where their next holiday would be and so on. Alex and Holly explained that they were planning a whale-watching trip in the Azores in April, that they'd been together ten years, and that they had no children yet but definitely would in the future. Holly squeezed Alex's hand each time he said 'definitely'. His positivity was one of the things she loved about him.

Holly felt tired but relaxed. School had broken up yesterday and Christmas term was always the busiest. Dean Court Primary, just outside the little town of Hopley in Kent, held a Christmas pageant every year and Holly had gone all out with her class's offering. She loved the creativity of it, the challenge of making festive magic that the children would remember for years, the joy of putting smiles on small faces… It was hard to explain things like that at a party like this, so she allowed herself to fall quiet and simply take it all in as the Christmas songs played on and the champagne glasses glinted and swathes of golden fairy lights glowed around the curtained windows.

Alex's colleague Rosa shouted for attention and proposed a toast. 'To Alex!'

Holly raised her glass and took another sip of sparkling champagne, super proud of her man. Alex made a short speech and then, while he was shaking hands all around, Rosa came to stand beside Holly.

'Let's hope we hang on to him for a while,' she murmured. 'I know he likes to go where the opportunities are. I think we can offer him plenty of scope, though.'

'Oh, I know you can,' said Holly. 'Alex is very excited about this position.'

'What about you? Do you move around a lot too?'

'Me? Not really. I've been at my present school five years now and I love it – bar the long drive from where we live in Maidstone. They have a strong emphasis on drama, which is my thing, so it's the full package for me.'

'That's great,' said Rosa. 'Sweet. You're bound to be a great mum when the time comes, with all that kiddie experience. Will you guys do it soon, do you think?'

Holly had to smile; even in this day and age, if you were a woman of child-bearing age, you always got asked these questions, even by another woman who was successful and career-minded. And if she had a pound for every time someone told her she'd be a great mum…

'We hope so,' she answered good-humouredly, raising her glass. 'Here's to the year ahead.'

CHAPTER ONE

This Christmas…

Edward

Sometimes in life there are those days when everything goes just right. You feel good, the sun shines and any worries just fade away. Days of ease. Today was not one of those days.

Edward paced the kitchen, reading a letter and tracking mud from his trainers across the length and breadth of the floor. When he was done reading, he folded up the letter and stuck it in his back pocket, then took two bowls from the kitchen cupboard and a carton of milk from the fridge. Empty. Irritated, he launched it across the room – an impressive overarm lob – where it bounced off the bin and lay on the floor.

There are some people who claim not to be able to cook. They say they 'have about five things', but when they list them, they're all Nigella classics with scallops and tahini and root galangal grown by the light of a full moon and picked on a Thursday. They have twenty-seven ingredients apiece and they involve braising and basting and a little light soufflé-ing for good measure. Edward wasn't one of those. He had one thing. Cereal. He'd found there was quite a knack to pouring just the right amount. But now they were missing one of the two ingredients needed. Could they eat it dry? *He* would eat it dry. But he wasn't the only one to consider.

It wasn't as if he could nip out to the corner shop. They'd moved just over a month ago from Leeds, the land of the corner shop, to this remote corner of the Kent countryside, and there *was* no shop, corner or otherwise. Their new house, Christmas House (they'd have bought it for the name alone!) was over two miles away from the outskirts of Hopley, their nearest town. So he had no milk, no shop and nothing for breakfast. What he did have was that damn letter in his pocket. Which he would *not* think about now.

From above his head came a thundering you would think could only be made by an alien, crash-landing his ship in an upstairs room. Or her ship – Edward wasn't the kind to make sexist assumptions about alien pilot gender. Footsteps drummed along the landing, came thumping down the stairs.

'No! Please!' cried Edward, crouching in the corner. 'I won't tell anyone you're here! I'll help you break into the bank. I'll defend you from the Men in Black! Only let me live! Let me live!'

'You're silly, Daddy.'

Edward sat on the cold lino floor, stretched his legs out and grinned. Not an alien but a small eight-year-old girl wearing black leggings, purple boots and a Spider-Man T-shirt. His Eliza.

'Oh, Lizzie, I'm so glad it's you. I thought it was aliens coming to abduct me and carry out more experiments!'

Eliza ran across the kitchen and took a flying leap, laughing, to land on her father's stomach. He winced from more than just the blow. She was so quicksilver and swift that he could never quite predict what her next move might be. His arms, instinctively, locked around her. Cold floor, jutting edge of worktop, metal drawer handles – there was endless potential for harm. But she was safe, perched on top of him, giggling into his trim six-pack. Or, in his less delusional moods, his slightly squishy stomach bulge. Safe. So he laughed too.

'How do you make that much noise getting up in the morning when you hardly weigh anything? You're as light as a feather. But you sound like a herd of elephants.'

'Spiders have to be light,' she said, jack-knifing off him and leaping onto a chair, then the table, then hurling herself at the wall. Edward winced again. She bounced and grinned. 'What's for breakfast, Dad?'

'Ah, about that.' He looked at his watch. Not much time before school. He wished he could tell her to play hooky, spend the day at home, but she'd been at her new school less than a week. *That* would not be responsible parenting. 'I have to be honest, Eliza, we're out of milk. As you know, there is only one meal I can reliably make, and that is cereal. Our options? Skip breakfast. Eat it dry. Juice. Or toast.'

Eliza frowned. Toast was not her favourite. 'Have we got any honey?'

'No.'

'Peanut butter?'

'No.'

'Daddy, what do you *do* all day while I'm at school?'

A fair question. Edward got to his feet with a sigh. Yesterday he'd spent the day waiting in for the plumber, who never came. Their shower didn't work. Just as well neither of them had long hair and they could manage in the bath. Still, it wasn't ideal. He'd used the time to clean up the living room and order some furniture so they'd have at least one passably cosy living space through what promised to be the deadliest winter that ever was, according to the weather forecast. Winter is coming and all that. He'd spent a good two hours hoovering up brick dust – last week, builders had knocked the two smaller rooms together – but he'd soon learned that brick dust has no end, and that it would be oozing from unexpected corners, carpets and the very fibres of his being for the rest of time.

Then he'd trawled various websites to try to find a housekeeper-slash-babysitter because his new job would start in just over a week and *someone* had to pick up Eliza from school and keep her company until he got home. But no success there either. Thus, the hours had slipped away and then it was time to go and get Eliza. To celebrate her fourth day of school, they'd gone to Pizza Hut and so hadn't noticed the sadly depleted state of the kitchen supplies until now.

'Don't you *shop*?' Eliza demanded.

'I don't, my darling, I'm afraid, no. I lounge about while a variety of beautiful ladies bring me ice creams and grapes.' Hang on, was that even child-friendly humour?

Eliza looked unimpressed. 'I'll write you a shopping list.'

Edward rooted around in the wasteland that was their kitchen and found a banana. Quite an old one. From the sniff test, he deduced it was fine, hastily peeled and mashed it, lacing it with sugar, spread it on toast and presented it to her with a glass of peach juice. *Peach juice* they had, for some reason. That old staple.

'It's quite nice, thank you, Daddy,' she wuffled through a mouthful. Edward threw back a couple of handfuls of dry Cheerios, pretending not to be hungry, and read her shopping list:

Honey
Peanut butter
Milk
Beans
Green nail varnish

It was at times like these that Edward wondered if *certain people* were right and he really had bitten off more than he could chew. If he had made a huge, wildly disastrous mistake, in fact. Single parent; small daughter; new home; said home under renovation when he had never done up a house before... Sometimes Edward felt like an overgrown kid himself, barely managing to racket through the motions of adult life. When, in fact, not only was he a grown-up; he was a *parent*.

Eliza was nearing the end of her toast and staring through the window with an expression of rapture. As he followed her gaze, he dared to hope that maybe he hadn't done such a stupid thing after all. The new house in Kent was as different as could be from their old home in Leeds. Christmas House sat in the most perfect spot: woodland to its left, fields stretching to its right. *It's the middle of nowhere*! said an appalled voice in his head, but he wouldn't listen to it now. They had moved in early October, when the woods had been orange and gold, full of crunchy leaf drifts perfect for jumping in, and the fields had been bare, brown and peaceful. Even now, as November took hold, it was still beautiful: all sepia and silver and rainbows. Most important of all, it wasn't Leeds. It was somewhere new.

Then he remembered the time. 'Lizzie-Loops, school. Hurry! Brush your teeth, get your things and let's *roll*.'

Eliza's delight faded and her slim shoulders curled over just a little bit. *Oh God, I can't bear it*, thought Edward. It was like her full weight landing on his stomach all over again.

'Lizzie-Loops? Your new school's alright, isn't it? It's not so bad going there?'

'It's OK, Daddy. It's just… new.'

'I know it is, sweetheart, but remember what we talked about. New isn't bad, new isn't nasty; it's just unfamiliar. And the only way to make it become familiar is to keep going and to keep smiling.'

'I know. It's just… What if it's going to be like my last school?'

'Has anyone been nasty to you? Has anyone said anything?'

'No. No, they haven't. But what if they do?'

Edward sighed again and gathered her into his arms. He'd shut out the world, the future and especially the past if he could, and keep her here with him every single day. But that wouldn't be right. He generally considered himself fairly crap at single fatherhood but even he knew that. 'They won't. I promise.' Of course, he couldn't possibly promise that. It wasn't within his power to ensure that every child and every teacher at her new school would be kind and sensitive or, failing that, just blissfully ignorant of who her mother was. But love makes you do lots of stupid things, and rash promises are the least of them. 'It's a new school. You were very unlucky at your old one, that's all. Now, you said you sat next to a nice girl yesterday, didn't you?'

She nodded. 'Fatima.'

'Right. And you like your teacher, don't you? Miss Hamster?'

She giggled. 'Miss Hanwell.'

'Excellent. So that's two people you like already and it's only been four days. You didn't meet two really nice people in three whole years at Eddington, did you?'

'No.'

'So it's *already* better. And it'll *keep* getting better, and the house will get organised and be a real home for us. Then you can have your friends over for parties and we'll forage for holly and ivy at Christmas and fill the house with them, and do the same with flowers when spring comes…' He stopped just short of promising her the moon, set in pride of place over the mantelpiece.

'I love you, Daddy.'

'I love you too, Eliza-Bean.'

Eliza's natural demeanour was silly, jokey and madcap – at least, when she felt safe and happy. But now she looked at Edward with a solemnity that could make a grown man weep. Again, he reminded himself, he *was* a grown man, the whole unit responsible for this fey little marvel before him.

She planted a kiss on his cheek and went off to find her school bag, which was about as big as she was.

When Edward reflected that all his assurances may or may not be true, that he was sending her into the unknown alone, guilt speared him. But staying optimistic was the only way to make sure that Eliza stood any sort of chance of a normal life. Then he realised that she was ready and he wasn't, so he pulled on a fleece and a bobble hat and they ran out to the car. He would deal with the letter later.

CHAPTER TWO

Holly

Holly Hanwell loved her classroom at this time of day, when the only sound was the creak and hiss of the old central heating pipes stirring themselves to life. The Victorian school in Hopley was now equipped with all the mod cons – tablets, projectors, whiteboards and the like – but, in quiet moments such as these, Holly always imagined she could smell chalk dust on the air and hear the faint ringing of hobnail boots. The ceilings were high and cobwebby; the windows were leaded and cranky. Soon, twenty-five eight-year-olds would burst in and it would be a snowstorm of energy and laughter from the start to the end of the day. With a few scrapes and tears thrown in.

Now that November was well and truly here – Diwali and Halloween were behind them and Bonfire Night was past – Holly could turn all her attention to Christmas, her favourite festival of them all. At least, it was *usually* her favourite, but she wasn't at all sure she could love it this year. She wouldn't think about that now. One of the great things about being a teacher was that it fully absorbed all her attention all day every day, leaving little space for melancholy thoughts. Term would carry her to just before Christmas, then there would be the two weeks of Christmas itself to get through, but surely by *next* year things would be better?

She set out all her notes and lesson plans for today neatly on her desk then started taking down the artwork from this week's display. Bonfire Night had been a Sunday this year, kindly timing for displays and parties. On Monday, she'd set the children to work painting either a scene from the history of Guy Fawkes or their favourite firework. As a result, the walls were papered with outlandish Catherine wheels, speeding rockets or glitter-doused fountains, punctuated by grisly depictions of the gunpowder plot – exploding heads and the like.

It had been a good week for Eliza Sutton to start. Not too serious; no tests in her first few days. She was an enchanting child: pretty, clever and quirky. But she was very quiet. It was something more than shyness; *haunted* was the word that came to Holly. She hoped it didn't signify a troubled home life; those instances always broke her heart. But Eliza's grey eyes had brightened when Holly had asked the children to talk about what they'd done for Guy Fawkes Night; she'd talked about her father's firework display in the garden of their new house, followed by a movie and popcorn. She'd chosen black paper as the backdrop for a bright pink fountain and asked if there was any glitter; she was artistic too.

Children were like fireworks, Holly thought as she took each picture down carefully, using a knife to prise the staples free, so that she could return them to their artists undamaged. Noisy, colourful and explosive, demanding your full attention, taking your breath away the whole time they were there in front of you. When the classroom emptied again, and the quiet returned, the peace was like a velvety night sky, restful and conducive to reflection. Holly's before- and after-school hours were the most creative of her day.

Eliza was like a damp squib, she thought, continuing her analogy; something with all its potential doused, subdued and forlorn. Strange, when she clearly adored her dad. Holly hadn't met Mr Sutton. Mr Buckthorn, the principal, met all the new parents, doing the introductory talks himself and only passing on information to the class teachers as and when it was strictly necessary. He called it discretion, but several teachers, including Holly, suspected it was just a way of making himself feel more important. Either way, Holly preferred not to know too much in advance. That way she could get to know the children without preconception. Already she could sense that this snuffed-out version of the new girl wasn't the real Eliza Sutton. She just didn't know why yet.

When the whitewashed brick walls were bare again, she laid out a Christmas image on each child's desk from a folder she had compiled over the last months. It was a nicer welcome than the maths test they would need to do later. Then the hordes descended, shedding anoraks, flinging bags to the floor, chattering and laughing. Holly couldn't help laughing too. They were so shiny, so full of mischief and startling ideas. The thing she loved most about her job was that it allowed her to see the world through children's eyes, and that made it eternally a magical – and often very odd – place.

'Miss Hanwell, is this going to be me?' asked Lily Orton, waving her Christmas picture in the air. 'Am *I* going to be the angel in the Christmas pageant?'

The class quietened, ears pricked at the mention of the pageant, and sparkled with anticipation.

Holly had distributed the pictures without any thought as to which desk was whose, which she now realised was a mistake. She saw that Lily had a picture of an angel bathed in a golden glow. With her long, white-blonde hair and enormous... self-esteem (it seemed harsh to say 'ego', referring to a child), it was an obvious leap for Lily to make.

'No,' said Holly firmly. An expectant hush had fallen. Even the Simmons twins, who had ADHD, were listening. 'The pictures are discussion points only. But I *will* be talking to you about the pageant today' – cheers erupted around the room, although Eliza, Holly noticed, sat quietly, biting her lip – '*after* we've finished today's maths test.'

The elated children drooped immediately; cheers gave way to boos and yawns. Holly laughed. 'It's not so bad. You should all be prepared *if you've done your homework*!'

Javai Anand looked at the ceiling, the floor, out through the window, anywhere but at her. Homework and Javai – Jai for short – were not well acquainted. Every class had the archetypal naughty boy, it was often agreed in the staff room, and Holly's was blessed with four: Jai, Jason Tillwell and the twins. But she didn't get wound up about it. Not every child excelled at school; it didn't mean they didn't have their own special light to shine through life. Holly prided herself on nurturing that. Yes, she had targets to meet and it was *her responsibility* – Mr Buckthorn was fond of repeating – to help them navigate the school system so that they could eventually get the qualifications they needed to be effective in the world when they grew up. But other things were important too for Holly, like making them feel that they each had talents that didn't need to fit a mould to be valid, and making school a warm, welcoming place for them – a magical place, even, when possible.

She remembered her own childhood, a dreary primary school in Manchester, being bullied by Deborah McGinty and her pals, years of staring at the window panes, watching the rain wriggle its wandering worm tracks, not participating, not doing well, all because she'd been bored and unhappy. Holly's love of learning had developed late, not till she was fifteen, and then only because of a wonderful drama teacher who saw Holly's talent for the creative arts and encouraged her all the way. He showed Holly what school *could* be like, and she tried to channel him through every challenge of her job, keeping a gimlet eye on her small students; she wanted each and every one to feel safe and be receptive to learning. She made the days as varied as the curriculum and Mr Buckthorn allowed, because every child was interested in *something*. Lighting sparks they could carry with them; that's what it was all about.

The maths test, though, was necessary. She handed them out, pointed to the clock and told them they had twenty minutes. Then she sat at her desk and made a show of reading but in reality, she was watching them all. She learned so much about the children when they didn't know she was looking. She saw David Kanumba pass something into Matt Simmons' outstretched palm. She narrowed her eyes but whatever it was went straight into Matt's mouth. A sweet then. OK.

Evie Greavey (what had her parents been thinking?) stared all around her, looking lost, a little tearful, then leaned over until she was almost at a forty-five-degree angle and had a good view of Indira Khan's test paper. She glanced up at her teacher; Holly sat motionless, head angled towards her book. Evie started scribbling. Interesting. So she was struggling with maths and she cared about it. Mr Buckthorn was fastidious about cheating. 'Name and shame!' was his rule. But they were eight, for heaven's sake. Holly couldn't see what good shaming could do for any of them. She would think about how to deal with Evie in due course.

Jason Tillwell was labouring raptly over his paper, tongue sticking out of his mouth, pen clutched inelegantly in his fist. Unlike Jason to be studious. Vicky Myers, in the back corner, was chewing up paper and shooting spit balls out of an empty biro husk, into Lily's shining golden hair. Holly made a spit ball of her own – she had learned certain skills during her misspent youth – and aimed it carefully. It landed on Vicky's desk and she looked up in shock. Holly raised her eyebrows meaningfully and Vicky turned beetroot-red and started scribbling. Holly smiled, her eyes drifting over to Eliza Sutton.

Eliza's focus was absolute. She worked steadily, chewing her lip from time to time, and finished the test with minutes to spare. When Holly gathered in the papers, she could see at a glance that her mark would be a good one.

Vicky's had a note on the bottom: *Sorry, Miss*. Holly patted her shoulder. Jason's paper had very few answers on it but was graced with an elaborate drawing of a zombie, which he parted with reluctantly. Evie sat up very straight and handed her paper in with a saintly air but didn't meet Holly's eyes.

Holly put them in her drawer to mark later and got down to the exciting business of talking about Christmas. For Eliza's benefit, she explained that Dean Court Primary was famous for its Christmas pageant. All the staff, children and families got involved – and everyone was always very excited about it. Each class worked on a different play or performance, and they were always put on one after another to make an all-evening extravaganza. Holly's class always finished the show. Although all the teachers threw their hearts into the pageant, Holly's background in theatre and the arts made her productions extra lavish. She didn't say that to the children, of course.

'We even get the local newspaper coming along,' she said. 'They always print a photo and give us a write-up. But that's not the important bit. The important bit is that it's great fun – right, guys?' The children whooped in agreement. 'It's something we all work on together in our class groups. *Everyone* gets involved, whether it's being the star of the show, or singing in the chorus, or helping with the sets. In terms of parts to be played and jobs to be done, there really is something for everyone. So welcome again, Eliza, and I hope you'll enjoy your first Dean Court pageant as much as we all do. Now, would anyone like to guess what our class will be doing this year? I bet no one will be able to.'

'Nativity!' shouted Dean Corwell, who claimed the school was named after him even though it had been standing for a hundred and fifty years before he was born.

Holly shook her head. 'You know Year Three always do the nativity.'

'Oh yeah.' Dean scowled. 'Stupid little kids.'

'*A Christmas Carol*?' suggested Fatima Jefferies.

'Brilliant guess, Fatima, but no.'

'*The Grinch*?' yelled Javai, but Holly shook her head.

'I told you no one would guess.' She couldn't help laughing at their frustrated expressions. She'd have only herself to blame if they got wound up past all sense, but it was so funny. Then Eliza raised her hand.

'Is it something completely new, that you've written yourself?' she guessed.

'Wow. Yes, you've hit the nail on the head,' marvelled Holly. 'That's exactly it. Aren't you clever?' She was pleased to see Fatima give Eliza a congratulatory nudge. She was sure Eliza would burst back into life once she had some friends. 'It's called *A Christmas Wish* and it's a play I've been writing especially for all of you. That's why it will be extra special this year. We'll be making something *completely* original and no one will have seen it before. So I'm relying on all of you to bring it to life for me.'

The children cheered again. 'Will there be space monsters?' Griff Heaton wanted to know.

'Ah, that well-known symbol of Christmas, the space monster,' said Holly. 'Er, no.'

'Can there be loads of fake blood?' demanded Jason.

Holly grinned. 'Because nothing says peace and goodwill like a massacre.'

Holly laughingly answered all their questions and started the process of democratic discussion about who would do what. There were six weeks until the pageant and a lot of work to do. It really would keep her too busy to ponder the disappointments of her life *outside* work until it was all over and Christmas was well and truly here.

CHAPTER THREE

Eliza

When Eliza left school at 3.30 p.m., her dad was waiting at the gate. Her heart lifted when she saw him and she ran to give him a hug. He was the most comforting dad in the whole world – tall with curly brown hair and grey eyes just like her own. His chin was always scratchy because he kept forgetting to shave, and he was dressed in ancient jeans and an old sweatshirt. He wore them a lot since Mummy left, and Eliza liked him best like that because his scruffy clothes meant that he wasn't at work – they meant that he was all hers.

'Lizzie-Loops! You're a sight for sore eyes. How was your day?'

'Alright thanks, Daddy.' She could see his smile fade a bit so she tried again. 'Really good actually!'

'Hmm,' he said, not believing her, she could tell. 'Let's get you home, and then what do you say to a walk in the woods before it gets dark?'

Eliza cheered up even more. She loved the woods. Last week when they were out walking, she'd heard a rustle and whipped her head around just in time to glimpse a red bottle-brush tail, tipped with white, vanish into the brambles. A fox. Eliza thought wild animals were so magical; she wanted more than anything to see it again.

Nearby, Fatima was getting into a glossy red car. 'Bye, Eliza, see you next week,' she shouted and Eliza smiled and waved. She was wary of making friends, but school would be very lonely and boring if she *didn't*, and Fats was so pretty and nice. Her dad waved too, and Fatima's parents, who were sitting in the car, waved back. Her mum stuck her head out of the window.

'Welcome to Hopley,' she called. 'We're in a hurry or we'd stop to say hello. Meet you properly next week.' Their car pulled out into the stream of vehicles leaving the school.

'So that's Fatima. She looks nice,' said her dad as they drove off when their turn came.

'She is. I ate lunch with her today. She likes Spider-Man too.'

'A sensible girl, then. And what's on your mind? I can tell you're not operating on 100 per cent Eliza power.'

'We're doing a Christmas pageant.'

'Ah.' He reached forward and turned the radio down, then switched it off.

'We spent quite a lot of time talking about it at school. It's a big deal, Daddy. *Everybody* goes to it. There's going to be a picture in the newspaper.' Her father made a face. The two of them didn't like the newspapers. 'And Miss Hanwell's written our very own special play for us to put on. She's so excited and she's so lovely. But…'

'But,' said Daddy. 'I know. Did anyone say anything? About… you know?'

Eliza shook her head. Then she said 'no' out loud so that Daddy could concentrate on the traffic.

'Well,' he said, 'you know the score, Lizzles. You don't have to do anything you don't want to. You won't be letting anyone down, and Miss Hanwell will understand. So there's nothing for you to worry about, OK?'

'OK. Miss Hanwell did say that anyone who didn't want to have a part could even help out backstage.'

'There you are then.' They reached a straight bit of road and he reached out to pat her arm.

'But she *really* wants us all to be onstage, you can tell. She doesn't want anyone to feel left out. I've got a letter about it for you in my bag.'

'Tell you what. Don't worry about it now. Why don't you have a think over the weekend? And then if you really don't want to do it, you can tell her next week and explain that you'll help out backstage and it'll all be fine. Absolutely *fine*. Whatever you like, darling, I promise.'

'OK, Daddy.' Eliza looked at her dad as he drove. He was saying all the things she needed to hear and he meant them, she knew that. He was the best dad. But he looked sad, and she knew that he was worried about her, and, really, he had enough to stress about with Mummy gone and the house empty and half-finished. Eliza didn't mind about that, but *he* thought she did, so he worried about it. And he knew, and she knew, that if Eliza Sutton wasn't onstage in a Christmas pageant, it meant things still weren't right, and he worried about her most of all. She imagined his face if she decided to be in it after all and it was almost enough to make her decide to do it. Almost.

They reached the house and turned in through the stone gateposts topped with two stone... somethings. They were so old and chipped that they could have been anything really. Lions were most common, Daddy said, but for all that was left of them, they might have been griffins or dragons, or even sheep! Eliza loved that she lived in a house with stone guardians on the gateposts – even blobby ones.

The car crunched over the gravel and Eliza thrilled. She loved that she lived in a house surrounded by gravel. She loved that her home was called Christmas House; how could it fail to be magical with a name like that? She loved that they had a big garden, even if it was a bit of a tangle at the moment. A wilderness, Daddy called it, and he sounded worried about that too.

The house was big and square and grey, with some pointy bits on the roofs, and it reminded Eliza of a hotel they'd once been to in Cornwall, except that it was all theirs.

They ran inside and found the house was cold as usual; Daddy hadn't quite got the hang of the central heating yet. That was yet *another* thing that worried him, but Eliza couldn't care less. That's what jumpers were for! And hats. And mittens! She was already wearing all of those things and ready for their walk. She dropped her bag in the hall as her dad grabbed a scarf and hat, and out they went again.

At first, they chatted. Daddy had had a busy day plastering the bathroom, painting Eliza's bedroom in the pretty shade of butter yellow she had chosen and taking delivery of a washing machine, which meant they could do laundry at home instead of always having to go to the laundromat in Hopley – though Eliza had quite liked their trips to the laundromat. She liked watching the clothes sloshing round and round in the suds and trying to follow one thing with her eyes until her eyeballs were rolling and she had a headache. He'd even been food shopping and remembered her green nail varnish. She wondered if he'd let her wear it to school.

Eliza made him laugh with stories of the boys in her class and their ideas for the pageant. 'Aliens and blood,' he said, chuckling. 'What did Miss Hanwell say to that?'

But as they headed deeper into the woods, they fell silent, walking hand in hand. It was nice just to listen to the trees whispering and the cawing of rooks. Every now and then there was the pretty song of a robin.

The woods were like magic to her. They were *just* like Enid Blyton's Enchanted Wood. They found chestnuts and red spotted mushrooms. There were little paths that wound through the trees and unexpected grassy clearings that were thick with fallen bronze leaves now. As they explored, she kept her eyes wide open for the fox, but there was no sign of him or her. Her biggest wish in life at the moment was that they would see it before Christmas.

Daddy worried, she knew, that moving here was too big a life change for Eliza after all the other changes. He thought he had to fix everything to make it right for her, but she wished she could make him believe that it already *was* right and she was fine. She loved everything about being here, with him. The day they'd moved to Hopley had been the best day of her life.

CHAPTER FOUR

Edward

Once Eliza had gone to bed, Edward sat alone in the living room on a beanbag, in the glare of a shadeless light bulb and the glow of an electric heater. It really was cheerless, he thought, looking around. As Edward, he could look past the flaws to the potential of the place: the pleasing proportions of the room, the stunning view from the long windows, cloaked now in darkness and stars. But as a father, wasn't it his job to fix it all? Immediately? What sort of a home was this for a little girl? They were living like squatters.

A mug of tea sat steaming beside him on the floor. He'd have loved a glass of red wine but he hardly ever drank these days. It was the thought of Eliza upstairs asleep, the fear that she would need him in the night. Not that he'd ever been the sort to drink himself into uselessness, but still. The sense of responsibility was paralysing sometimes. He unfolded the letter and read it again. He'd read it three times already, but this time he needed to decide what to do about it.

It was from his mother. He knew she meant well, so what was it about her, wondered Edward, that produced this haze of resentment in him, encouraging him to want her to be wrong, even when it seemed likely that she was right?

Dearest son, she wrote, in her impeccable flowing handwriting. *Won't you and Eliza come to us for Christmas, you stubborn pair? You know you'll never get the house organised in time, and it's very large for just the two of you. You'll be rattling round in it like gimmicks in a cracker! Not very nice for a little girl. Come to us and she can be spoiled by her granny and grandad, have a good healthy dinner that hasn't been microwaved or burned, and play with her cousins. Darling, you must know it makes sense; it's an age since Cressida left and high time you both started living a normal life. Eliza deserves a proper Christmas.*

Edward scowled at the letter. Personally, there was nothing he would like less than a Christmas with his parents and all their insufferable friends, but he would do it for Eliza's sake. It was true that he wasn't a gifted cook and he struggled with domestic niceties. Their new house certainly was big and felt completely unmanageable at present. He hadn't had time to put up a single decoration or buy a single present. 'Festive' was hardly the word. Yet to him, perhaps bizarrely, this house suggested Christmas, and it wasn't because of its name. He didn't know if it was due to the high hopes for a new life with which they'd moved there or because of the faint, cold smell of pine that hung over the garden at night. Certainly, its charms were intangible to the impartial eye and he could hardly expect Eliza to feel the same. It probably *would* be better for her at his mother's.

He'd always maintained that a single parent could manage Christmas just as well as a couple, but it took a lot of confidence – and a lot of *time* – and this year, for the first time, he wasn't sure he could pull it off. He'd be starting his new job in a week and *then* where would he find time for home-making, let alone for Christmas? He hadn't even organised care for Eliza yet, though he was interviewing some people over the weekend.

As much as he didn't want to concede defeat and miss their first Christmas here, it would solve a lot of problems if they went to stay in his parents' large, suburban house in Bexley. It had no character, smelled of air freshener and would be filled with his parents' materialistic neighbours, who would gossip about his ex-wife and make personal remarks about Eliza right in front of her as if she couldn't hear them. He would spend the whole time grinding his teeth, tense as a rock, counting the minutes till they could leave. But there would be good food, central heating and a widescreen TV. His mother would take care of all the presents and gift-wrapping and little child-centred surprises; in fact, she'd love doing it.

When he and Cressida had married, they'd been a pair of young dreamers. Alright, he'd been twenty-seven, but everyone knew that men didn't get any sense until they were forty. He hoped to acquire some himself when he got there. Cressida had only been twenty-one. They'd been dating a year; it was an instant infatuation and no one could talk them out of it. He'd been smitten; Cressida was a beautiful young actress, playing small parts in theatre, struggling to make ends meet. She was passionate and full of life and he couldn't imagine what more he could ever want. Cressida's big dream was stardom, but she was always self-deprecating about her talent and beauty, always realistic about her odds of success in an overpopulated, punishing industry. They'd been really happy for a while.

He shook himself. Their lives had moved on. That first Christmas, three years ago, six months after Cressida had dropped her bombshell and moved away for good, had been… interesting! But Eliza had been a good sport. She didn't mind about things like burned turkey and microwaved vegetables. Edward wasn't gifted in the arts and crafts department either, but he had made up for his lack of skill with scissors and paste by taking Eliza on extravagant sprees in Leeds's shopping arcades, delighting her with a superb disregard for taste or moderation. They'd spent a small fortune on cards, glossy gift wrap and shimmering ornaments. The new Edward and Eliza traditions sprang up swiftly: McDonald's on Christmas Eve; the *Top of the Pops* Christmas party on Christmas Day; football in the park on Boxing Day.

On the whole, Edward thought he was doing pretty well. He knew Eliza loved him and that they had fun together, but he lived forever in hope that he wasn't missing anything.

One day at the swimming pool back in Leeds, a young woman had started chatting.

'How old is she?' she'd asked, watching Eliza kicking solemnly back and forth in her purple and yellow swimsuit. 'Five?'

'She's seven!' Edward had been a little offended.

'Oh, isn't she small for her age?' the woman had exclaimed, as if being small were the best thing ever. She'd batted her eyelashes, making tiny chlorine droplets tremble. 'Her mother must be very petite?' It was a good way of establishing whether Edward was available, he'd conceded, but he hadn't been in the mood for flirting and had swum off after Eliza.

That afternoon he'd taken her clothes shopping in a department store. He'd wanted to know what women in shops would say about Eliza – sensible motherly types, not flighty youngsters in Rihanna-style swimsuits. A city leisure centre wasn't St Tropez, for heaven's sake! Also, he'd wondered if he needed to update her wardrobe. The most difficult thing about parenting Eliza was that she was a girl and he wasn't. If she was a tomboy because she wanted to be, that was fine. But not if it was only because he was failing. What about things like jewellery and make-up? Should they be on the agenda or was she still too young?

He'd steered her to a rack of pretty dresses but Eliza had been having none of it. She'd wanted blue leggings and Spider-Man T-shirts and a yellow bomber jacket with Bart Simpson on it. All the clothes that fitted Eliza had been age 5–6 and he'd had to quash a rising terror that when her mother had left, she'd stopped growing. Was it trauma? Was it his fault for being a rubbish cook? Was she malnourished? But the shop lady had told him the sizing was always very approximate anyway.

'It's just to give people a starting point,' she'd said. 'She looks fine to me. Lovely skin and sparkly eyes. I think she's fine.' Edward had wanted to kiss her.

The thing that had prompted their move away from Leeds was that Eliza had become horribly unhappy in school. Once a gregarious, popular child, her mother's leaving had changed everything for her. Her friends had proved not to be real friends at all.

Edward's office in Leeds, through sheer good luck, had been two minutes down the road from Eliza's school. He would pop out to meet her after school and take her back to the office for the last couple of hours of his day. She would sit doing her homework, or reading, or pretending to be a hotshot advertising executive. His colleagues would come in for a 'consultation' and she would dispense advice like, 'You need to nail this one, Jackson – we've got a lot riding on it,' or, 'Try and think outside the box. What do the customers want – what do they really *want*?' She obviously listened a lot when Edward was on work calls. Edward was never so popular at work as when Eliza was there.

Even though he'd never once forgotten to collect her from school, never once been late, she'd started running like a bullet to Edward's office every day, arriving just as he was leaving, once somehow passing him on the way. He would never forget his cataclysmic fear when he got to the school and found her gone. It was as if she couldn't get to him soon enough, as if she were afraid that he would suddenly disappear too.

The final clincher was the fact that Eliza had suddenly stopped taking part in the school plays. She'd inherited her mother's passion and talent for inhabiting other characters and adored having an audience, make-believe her own personal realm. But that was something Eliza and her mother had always, always enjoyed together, and Eliza wanted nothing more to do with acting after Cressida's departure. The teachers were unsympathetic; if anything, they were narked that they had lost their star turn.

Edward didn't care if Eliza no longer wanted to be onstage. She could be an astronaut, a builder, a refuse collector or anything she wanted when she grew up – fine by him. But this introverted, clingy child just wasn't her, and she wasn't happy. Too many months went by with Eliza crying in the night, dreading going to school.

Edward had always dreamed of doing up a slightly ramshackle house. Leeds, with its gritty, grungy streets and exciting energy, had lost its allure without Cressida to light it up, and it didn't feel like the sort of place to nurture two poor lost souls back to happiness. Eliza had forever wished they could live in the countryside; all her favourite books were about children swimming in rivers, climbing trees, entering gymkhanas and so on.

Together the two of them spun castles in the air about a new life and gradually the dream turned into a plan, and when Edward was offered an amazing job with an ad company in south-east London, they'd moved to this big old house near the small town of Hopley in the middle of Kent. They'd found the house quickly – love at first sight for both of them.

He'd enrolled Eliza in a new school with a good reputation and a reassuring atmosphere. The headmaster assured him that confidentiality would be tantamount and that if anyone started being unkind to Eliza, it would be dealt with swiftly. It didn't matter at all that she would be joining them halfway through the term. They had a strong reputation for dramatics; if Eliza did rediscover her love of performing, the avenues were there, but there would be absolutely no pressure. It was perfect. When Edward started work the week after next, it would add an extra forty-five minutes to his commute to take her there and get to work on time, but he would undertake it cheerfully if Eliza could only be happy.

It had been such a joyful September. When Eliza had learned that instead of preparing for a new term at Eddington Primary, she never had to go back there again, she'd lit up like a house at Christmas, excited at the prospect of leaving Leeds and making a new start. They'd spent their last few weeks in a whirl of preparation and decided not to take much with them. Their Leeds things wouldn't suit the new house; the style was all wrong. And besides, they wanted to leave it all behind. Everything.

That had been all well and good when they were in the throes of an emotional cleanse. But now that they were here, it did mean that there was an awful lot to do and nothing to sit on.

Edward felt a tight band around his chest whenever he thought of it. Another theoretical advantage to their new location was that it was the perfect distance from his parents; not so close that they could drop round every day uninvited, but close enough that Eliza could see her grandparents more often. He would have liked to think that his parents would be a support network, excited about his choices and willing to help out in small ways now and then. But it was tricky with his mother. She was one of those endlessly competent people, and she knew it. On the two occasions that he'd asked if she would mind being here for furniture deliveries while he was out sorting other things, she'd been very willing but had taken it as proof that he'd bitten off more than he could chew. He'd be better off moving to a smaller semi just down the road from them, she'd stated with great certainty. So he'd stopped asking her, and now he was paying extravagant sums to ensure the essentials were delivered before he started work.

It would be like that all over Christmas if they went, he knew. He *did* wonder if he'd made a huge mistake – several times a day – but he didn't want his mother reminding him of it at every turn. He wanted to give this life that he and Eliza had dreamed up together a chance. It felt out of control now, but they'd only been here a few weeks. Once there was furniture, once Eliza had settled at school, once he'd found a housekeeper/childminder to plug the gaps, then surely it would all feel better?

Though what if it didn't? Was living here a rural dream – or was it isolated and impractical and the source of countless unnecessary problems? Was the house a real home in the making, worth all the teething problems – or was it a white elephant that would be the ruin of them? The bottom line: what was best for Eliza?

Edward looked around, suppressing his own feelings and trying to be objective. It didn't even look habitable, let alone Christmassy. Perhaps Eliza did need a hearty family Christmas. She'd certainly eat better than she would here.

Well, I'll ask her, he decided. *Just because she's only eight doesn't mean she doesn't know what she wants. I'll tell her about the letter and she can decide. I'm happy with that.*

CHAPTER FIVE

Holly

Holly was deep in thought as she came home after work on Friday. The simple act of turning the key in the lock released a complicated spate of emotions in her: grief (it was not too strong a word, even now) for all she had lost; disbelief and delight that this charming little place was *hers*; pride that she had bought it all on her own; and melancholy – that home was now an empty house. She kicked her boots off in the hall, turned the lights on and hung up her coat. The heating had already kicked in. Even after eight months it was still a little strange to see only her coats on the hooks, only her shoes on the rack, but it was getting less so.

Hers was the first in a little terrace of converted oast houses, five in all. They all had pointed black roofs, red-brown brick walls clad with timber around the upper storey and circular living rooms. Holly loved that room – it made her feel as if she were living in a hobbit hole. She'd moved here back in March and hadn't yet seen the seasons make their full cycle in her neighbourhood and garden.

She threw herself onto the curved, saffron-coloured sofa; she'd had it made specially to make the most of the smallish living space. It was wildly expensive but it had been her only extravagance, and it was the right thing for the room; Holly was a great believer in getting things right. A shame she had been so spectacularly wrong about all the important matters.

This year, Holly was in the unusual position of feeling more Christmassy at work than at home. At school, the pageant would keep her busy, and the children would make the whole thing magical; whereas at home, the full impact of her recent life changes was hitting her hard. What on earth would Christmas be *like* this year? Before Alex, she'd spent every Christmas with her parents. Wherever she was in the world, she would always go home to Cornwall for at least a week. Once she and Alex were an item, they'd always spent Christmas together, alternating between his parents and hers, and their flat in Maidstone. But now, there was no Alex. And her parents were going to India for a month; it was their trip of a lifetime, long-awaited and determinedly saved for. Of course, when they'd booked it, this time last year, Holly had still been with Alex. And Holly had been so happy for them; no one deserved a special treat more than her parents after recent spates of ill health and a few financial wobbles. She still *was* happy about it. Only, it left her very alone.

Once everything changed, they'd offered to postpone their trip, but she refused to let them. She'd actually caught her father on his laptop with his finger hovering over the cancel button and had to pull him away. Then they'd begged her to go with them, but Holly's job made it impossible. She had two weeks off for Christmas. Term dates weren't negotiable, and she knew that if she tried to get to India and back within the time, she'd start the January term like one of the zombies Jason Tillwell was so obsessed with.

'Look,' she'd argued, 'Christmas is months away. I'll be *fine* by then. I'll be all sorted and back on my feet. You'll see.'

'You still need your parents,' her mum had worried.

'Of course I do. But not every single minute. I'm thirty-five years old. I can manage one Christmas on my own. That's what being an adult *is*.'

'But you shouldn't be on your own for *this* one.'

'So maybe I'll go skiing with Carla or something, or to a country cottage with Izzy. It won't do me any harm to do something completely different for once. It could be our whole family's year for an adventure.'

But Carla was spending Christmas in Paris, with a newly discovered relative. The joys of ancestry.co.uk! The invitation hadn't included one all-at-sea best friend. And Izzy, for the first time in living memory, was in a serious relationship. Now she was all loved-up with Alyson, which probably explained why she'd failed to find happy-ever-after with any of her boyfriends. Holly knew that if Izzy realised how much her friend was dreading the holiday this year, she would invite her to spend it with them in a trice, but she couldn't do that to Iz. Crash her first Christmas in a really-properly-in-love relationship? No, she wasn't such a sap as all that. People bounced back from break-ups all the time and she would *not* be pathetic. There *was* a bit more to it than that, but even so. No, she just had to face the fact that it would be a quiet one this year – very quiet – and get on with it.

She looked around at the space. It was sweet. Pretty. Filled with small luxuries and old treasures from different times in her life. But not many from the last ten years. It wasn't that she was trying to erase Alex from living memory; she couldn't do that, but she didn't want to see reminders all around her every day. This was a new start. A blank slate.

Her pal Penny was coming over this evening for a girls' night: bolognese and wine. Holly hauled herself up from the sofa, flicked on some lamps and found some music. Then she took herself to the pretty kitchen with its fitted oak cupboards and brightly coloured pinboard on the wall and began halving mushrooms, her mind drifting back over the day. She was thrilled that the children liked her idea for the pageant. They hadn't done any proper work for the last part of the day, just brainstormed and tried things out and generally exhausted themselves having fun. But wasn't that what Friday afternoons were for? The only disappointment was that Eliza Sutton had looked absolutely terrified the moment Holly had announced her plan, and her little pointed face, pale at the best of times, had stayed whiter than paper all afternoon.

Holly hadn't pushed her; it was only Eliza's first week at the school after all. It must be very daunting, knowing no one and then having everyone else go crazy about something you'd never experienced and couldn't avoid. But she prided herself on making a welcoming atmosphere in her class. She was watching them all like a hawk and she hadn't seen anyone being anything other than friendly and relaxed with Eliza. They were a good bunch on the whole. Energetic (Holly's favourite euphemism for completely wild) at times, overfond of gory imaginings in a couple of cases and certainly Jason Tillwell would end up in jail at some point – but they weren't unkind children. Though Eliza had still looked as if she were gripped by a private terror.

Some children were shy – Holly knew that. But she'd found over the years that with the right environment and some gentle encouragement, their natural exhibitionism won out. She wasn't sure it would be that way with Eliza. There was something about that child; she was so quirky and bright, yet an air of tragedy clung to her. It tugged at something in Holly, made her feel protective, even maternal. She wondered where Eliza's own mother was.

By the time Penny arrived, the bolognese was simmering, the spaghetti boiling and two glasses of red were waiting on the kitchen counter. Holly whipped open the door to see her friend standing on the doorstep with her nut-brown hair in two long plaits, a woolly purple bobble hat perched on her head.

'Hi, Pippi,' said Holly.

'Oh, the plaits? It's getting so long now it's driving me mad. How are you, my friend? How are the short people treating you?' Penny shuddered theatrically. She wasn't a kiddie person.

She and Holly had very little in common, in fact, yet they got on fantastically well.

'The small people are brilliant. How's life on the commune?'

'It's not a commune; it's a community. And good thanks. I spent the day helping to build a composting toilet. We do need another.'

'And you prefer that to playing make-believe with a bunch of kids?' marvelled Holly. 'Wine?'

Penny was Holly's newest friend and it was good to have one fairly nearby. Holly's older friends were scattered across the UK and there was something so nice about Penny dropping in for dinner, or Holly driving out to the community for a meditation class or a walk in the woods. Penny seemed just a little bit subdued tonight, though, Holly thought, as the evening progressed. Mostly her usual feisty, irreverent self, but slightly dimmed.

'Are you OK?' she asked at one point. 'You seem a bit… concerned.'

Penny frowned. She wasn't the sort to beat around the bush. 'I was doing a bit on the community website today. Hate computers as you know, but compared to the others I'm a tech whizz, so… Anyway, are you still on Facebook?'

'What? Yes.' Holly was thrown by the change of subject. 'I know, I know, I keep meaning to come off it but I never get around to it. It's nice to look now and then and see what people are up to.'

'I feared as much. That's why I need to tell you something. So I was checking the links to Facebook and Insta were working and I saw something. About Alex.'

Holly put down her wine glass. 'Oh?'

'His new girlfriend's having a baby.'

The whole world spun. For a moment, Holly's stomach surged violently and she ran to the kitchen, the sink being the nearest full-sized receptacle. She leaned over it, breathing heavily, clammy.

The window pane was steamed up from cooking, the air scented with the rich, cosy smell of food.

She heard Penny's moccasins come softly into the kitchen. 'Mate, I'm sorry.'

Holly nodded and was relieved to find the nausea was passing. 'Urgh!' she groaned. 'I can't believe I reacted like that. Yes, it was a huge disappointment. Yes, the future I always wanted has vanished. But it's been *months*! When am I going to be really OK again? When am I going to accept it for real, instead of just saying the right things?'

Penny put a hand on her shoulder. 'It takes the time it takes, yeah? And this is a big bit of news – the biggest you've had in a while.'

Holly nodded and returned to the sofa, sank into the soft cushions and curled up her legs. She wasn't going to throw up, thank God, but she wanted to cry.

'I didn't want to tell you,' said Penny. 'But I spend all of about five minutes on Facebook in a month, so if I can stumble across Alex's posts and see the news, then you're going to see it the second you go on there, right? And I thought it might be better to have some company when you found out.'

Penny was kind. Holly appreciated her friend being so considerate. Although… was it better to howl now or howl later?

'Want to talk about it?' asked Penny. 'Or radical change of subject required?'

Holly sighed. What was there to say that could possibly help? 'Radical change of subject.'

CHAPTER SIX

Edward

Breakfast on Saturday morning was a resounding success. After driving to the big supermarket outside Hopley yesterday, Edward not only had milk and four kinds of cereal, but bacon, eggs and pancakes that were ready made, needing only to be warmed in the oven. Providing he didn't forget about them and leave them to burn, even *he* couldn't ruin them. Giddy with choice after yesterday's famine, Eliza opted for all three, and though the bacon was a bit dry and the eggs were all bashed up and somewhat too greasy, it was a breakfast of kings.

Despite the vast plethora of things that needed doing, buying, fixing and organising, they took their time. They had a big afternoon ahead – interviewing three candidates for a weekday carer for Eliza. They needed to conserve their energy. And they needed to have a serious talk.

A steady drizzle fell outside, but the bleak light somehow made their kitchen appear more inviting, perhaps because it was warm and filled with the smell of breakfast. The steamed-up windows and the trees nodding in the wind outside, the background hiss of light rain against the windows reminded them that they were indoors, cosy and dry. Their kitchen was far from beautiful; the cupboards were rickety with ugly handles, the floor was lino-clad and shabby, the single-glazed window let in a myriad of draughts. Decor-wise it hadn't been touched since 1968. But when the two of them were together in it, it glowed with peace.

'Eliza,' said Edward. His daughter sat up straight. He rarely called her sensibly by name, so she would know right away that it was something important. 'I need to talk to you, man to Spider-Man.'

Eliza nodded gravely, eight going on sixty. 'I'm listening.'

'Right, well, it's about Christmas, and I want you to be completely honest with me, alright? Promise?'

'OK.'

'Good. Well, as you can see, Lizzie-Loops, this place is not very homely yet.'

'It feels like home to me,' she said.

Edward searched her face. Did she mean that or was she just trying to make him feel better? She was like that, his Eliza, always looking out for his feelings, always trying to look after him.

'It doesn't *look* especially homely,' he ventured, gesturing at the bare light bulb, the horrible old kitchen units, the general lack of any adornment whatsoever. How *could* that seem homey to a small girl?

'But it *feels* it,' she said with a shrug, 'and that's more important, isn't it?'

'Well, *I* think so,' he said carefully. Oh God, had he somehow brainwashed her? 'But I want you to be aware, Lizzles, that it's likely to look like this for quite a while. I'm afraid that in all the excitement of moving here, I kind of underestimated how much there was to do. I start work in a week and then there'll be no time at all. So whatever doesn't get done before then won't get done for ages, realistically. Understand?'

'Yes.'

'Good. So the question is this. Where would you like to spend Christmas? Your grandparents have invited us there. Your granny would be over the moon to have you; I think she's bursting for the chance to spoil you rotten. She pointed out – and she's right – that I can't cook, we live in a bare, uncomfortable house and that I have very little time to organise treats, presents, decorations and so on. So if we spend it here, it'll be a funny sort of a Christmas. Whereas if we go to Bexley, you'll have warmth and comfort, endless amazing home-cooked meals, cousins to play games with and no end of treats. So please tell me truthfully, what would you prefer?'

Eliza went pale and sat chewing her lip. 'Honestly?' she asked. 'Like *honestly* honestly?'

'Complete, uncompromising honesty is what I require.'

'Then I don't want to go, Daddy!' she burst out. 'I'm sorry, I don't mean to be ungrateful or hurt your feelings. I know Granny's your mum, and I do love her. But I won't enjoy a Bexley Christmas half as much as being in our house with you. I'll have to be good all the time and everyone keeps falling asleep in front of the TV and I don't like the cousins and they cheat at games. And there'll be neighbours dropping in all the time and talking about council tax and cheap flights to winter sun and I'll be *bored*! And I want to see the fox and it might come on Christmas Day,' she concluded in a mutter.

Edward couldn't help laughing. She had just summed his own feelings up in a paragraph. Out of the mouths of babes. 'That's fine, Lizzie-Loops. I'm happy to do whatever you want to do. The only thing I want for Christmas is for you to enjoy it. I want you to know that.'

Eliza nodded. 'I know, Daddy. Are you sure *you* wouldn't rather go where there's proper turkey and central heating? You're not getting any younger, you know.'

Edward snorted. 'I'm painfully aware, my darling. But don't worry, I think I can survive one more Christmas living rough. But what about our dinner? What about decorations?'

'I like dinner,' said Eliza thoughtfully. 'And decorations. But I don't *have* to have them. I can *feel* Christmas here, can't you, Daddy? That's all I really need, and to be with you, and to be silly. Anything else is just nice and extra really. Perhaps our new helper person can make it a bit Christmassy. But it doesn't matter if they can't. Why are you looking at me like that, Daddy?'

Edward was looking at her in wonder. What a precious child she was. Sparky, funny, sure of her own mind and in possession of an inner compass that most adults would envy. What a huge mistake Cressida had made in leaving her behind. But her loss was all his gain. 'Because you are a very, very special person, Eliza Sutton. And I am so lucky to have you as my daughter.' He was filled with an enormous, ballooning warmth, that he and Eliza were so alike, that being together was so important to each of them that it even trumped presents and crackers. Despite all the scrabbling around chaotically, all his mistakes and inadequacies, he'd obviously done *something* right.

'*Did* you want to go to Bexley, Daddy?'

'About as much as I want to spend Christmas in a war zone, my darling.'

While Eliza went outside to look for foxes, or evidence of foxes, Edward phoned his mother. It didn't go so well.

'Darling, I firmly believe you are both complete lunatics!' exclaimed his mother when he told her. 'That *can't* be what Eliza wants. It just can't. You're influencing her, Edward; you're being selfish.'

Edward's blood began to boil but he forced himself to speak evenly. 'Mum, that's a horrible thing to say, if you think about it. I promise you I sat Eliza down and explained the whole situation – what it'll be like here and what it would be like with you. I was brutally honest and I told her I was completely happy with whatever she wanted to do. And this is what she chose.'

'But, darling, there was your mistake. She's *eight*. It was your job as her parent to make a good decision in her best interests. That's what parents do.'

'Mum, sometimes I think you don't know Eliza at all. She knows her own mind, always has. I promise you, she doesn't *want* to—' He paused and bit back the rest of the sentence: he didn't want to hurt her feelings. 'She doesn't want to miss her first Christmas here. We'll visit, I promise. We'll bring presents over before Christmas and we'll come for a day sometime after. But this is our decision. We're both very grateful for the invitation, by the way.'

'Oh yes, I'm sure,' she scoffed. 'I can feel your gratitude and enthusiasm all the way down the phone line. It's heart-warming, really.'

'Mum!'

'Edward, I have to be honest, I'm worried about Eliza. Now don't take offence, but a girl needs a mother, or failing that, a mother figure. I know you do your best but you're a man and you have to work full-time…'

Edward started pacing up and down the hall, past the coat stand and the stairs, past the other rooms, to the back of the house, then back again to the kitchen and the front door. 'My job isn't going to be full-time. It's four days a week. You know that, Mum.'

'Oh, same difference. It's still the *majority* of the time. And what *about* those four days? I know you plan to hire someone, but what if you can't? Besides, what kind of an upbringing is that, leaving her with a total stranger? You just don't understand the business of parenting. She's running wild and she's still not back on track at school. Your father and I have talked about this a lot and – don't fly off the handle – but I want you to consider something.'

'What?' asked Edward warily.

'I think we should take Eliza.'

'Take her where?'

'Take her *in*! Have her to live with us. Custody, if you like. It would be so much better for everybody.'

Edward felt the blood drain from his body. 'You want custody of my daughter?' he checked, unable to keep a certain menace from his voice.

'Now, now, Edward.'

'Don't "now, now" *me*! I'm in rude health, capable of earning an excellent wage and perhaps most important of all, I *love* Eliza! I love looking after her, being with her. I'm a willing father. For God's sake!'

'Now, Edward, I did say not to fly off the handle. I really don't want to upset you. I just want to help.'

'I appreciate that. But, Mum, employed single parents do bring up children, you know. All the time. And sometimes, those are fathers! And people do move to houses in need of work. It's a fixer-upper, not a ruin! Eliza is fed—'

'Barely.'

'… clothed, housed and loved. She's happy. Her mother left her, we've moved here; that's quite enough change for one small girl. I'm keeping her with me, and I never want to hear you mention this again. It's insulting and it's inappropriate and it's… it's…' For once, Edward was out of words. The sense of outrage was overwhelming. His parents had always been strait-laced and conventional, but *this*! That anyone would suggest that he wasn't what was best for Eliza was hurtful in a way he couldn't find the depths of. 'I'm going now, Mum. I'm interviewing for our home help this afternoon.'

His mother sighed. 'Alright, darling. Good luck with that.'

Edward hung up quickly, hands trembling. His parents had been discussing whether Eliza should go and *live* with them. What on earth had possessed them? Were his life choices really that terrible?

The biggest problem was their conviction that because Eliza was a child, she had no right to contribute to their decision-making. They only wanted Eliza's happiness; he knew that. But if they had their way, she wouldn't *be* happy; she was too free-spirited to thrive in such a regimented environment. But he doubted he'd change their minds now. It had been the same when he and his brother were young. Until they were eighteen, they weren't old enough to know what was best. Even then, their parents insisted on choosing their universities and courses for them. His brother Adam had acceded, and it had worked out well for him, Edward had to admit.

Edward had brazened it out and gone where he wanted to, travelling, then veterinary college, but his parents hadn't been happy. And there had been further ructions when, eight months before qualifying, he'd dropped out to start earning money because he'd met Cressida. Young and foolish didn't even begin to cover it, but at least they'd been *his* choices – the good, the not-so-good and the slightly deranged.

He remembered a childhood with all the basics in abundance – money, a large house, good schools and so on, and love, too, expressed in an old-fashioned way. But in that life, he had felt squeezed between two narrow tracks that made him want to burst out on either side. No wonder he'd fallen for Cressida, who was lively and wild and imaginative. They'd made a wonderful, colourful life for themselves, and he'd been truly happy for a while.

Since he'd acquired sole care of Eliza, he'd questioned himself every step of the way. He tried never to impose on her the way *he* wanted to live. Or *was* that a parent's job? It wasn't like he gave her a choice about the fundamental things, like going to school. But whether to stay in Leeds or move away; town or country; Christmas in Hopley or Bexley… those were things that had to feel good to her, surely? Or was he kidding himself? Was he too ready to accept what she told him because it was what he wanted to hear? Only his mother could make him second-guess himself like this.

Well, he thought, checking the time and seeing that the first candidate was due to arrive soon, *let's just see how we get on this afternoon. Maybe we'll get someone absolutely perfect, and everything will fall into place, and it will prove that this life can work – that it's meant to be.*

Quickly he washed all the dishes and even dried them and put them away. Usually they left them on the draining board to drip-dry but he wanted the candidates to feel he was at least a little bit on top of things. They had to interview in the kitchen because it was the only room with enough chairs. And one of those was a garden chair.

'We really did make an interesting choice when we decided to leave everything behind,' said Edward, looking around him.

By 6 p.m., his spirit was broken, and even Eliza was drooping. The first candidate, Elizabeth Reynolds, had looked around her with flared nostrils as though offended by a nasty smell. There wasn't one. Whatever flaws Christmas House might have, it didn't smell. It was a trifle damp, perhaps, because of the erratic central heating and the steadily dropping temperatures, but it was clean and hygienic. Yet Ms Reynolds looked at them as if they were squatters pissing it up on Newkie Brown every night. Clearly, she didn't want to work for them and the feeling was entirely reciprocated. She only stayed ten minutes.

'We could've left the dishes,' observed Eliza.

The second candidate was Robbie Brass, a young man with shoulder-length curls and a sweet smile. Eliza took to him immediately, her pointed face covered in smiles. Come to that, Edward liked him too, but Robbie reeked of weed. It floated off his hair, his skin and his dungarees. Edward had nothing against stoners, per se. A spaced-out flower child was more pleasant company than a revved-up, angry boozer. But not in charge of his daughter. He didn't want anyone under the influence of anything stronger than fresh air around Eliza. No way.

When they showed Robbie to the door, Eliza shot a hopeful, excited glance at Edward. 'Thanks so much for coming, Robbie,' he said. 'I'll be in touch.' Then, once the door was closed, he turned to Eliza and shook his head. 'No, darling. I'm sorry.'

'But I thought he seemed nice,' said Eliza woefully.

'He was nice. But I could tell that he likes doing some things that make him not the right sort of person to be in charge of young children.'

'What things, Daddy? And how could you tell?' And then he had to explain to his innocent angel about drugs. He kept it brief. Need-to-know basis and all that.

'Why?' wondered Eliza, frowning. 'Why would anyone want to do *that*?'

The third candidate broke their hearts. Right away, she seemed perfect and they both warmed to her. Her CV was the best of the bunch, she had great experience and a qualification in childcare. Appearance-wise she was a dead ringer for the singer Jamelia, with long, swinging braids, a wide smile and a hint of mischief lurking in her almond-shaped eyes. She made Eliza laugh and shot Edward a couple of looks as if to say 'Oh my God how adorable' about Eliza. A sure-fire way to Edward's heart. They talked for an hour and a half, drank several cups of tea and it felt like a match made in heaven. Until one small detail came up that had somehow escaped discussion before: that the job was for four days a week.

It was what reconciled Edward to the whole scheme of going out to work and leaving Eliza in the care of strangers: that at least it wouldn't be *every* day; that at least on Wednesdays, he would be there to meet her from school, bond with the other parents at the school gates, chat to her teacher, the famous Miss Hanwell. The salary in his new job was such that it allowed him to have that one day at home, to tilt the balance in favour of reasonable parenting.

'I'm so sorry,' said Chrissy. 'I really hadn't picked up on that – how stupid of me. I need a full-time job. I *really* need a full-time job. I'm saving to go to drama school. I would have loved to work here – sorry, not that I'm presuming – but I may as well say straight away that I can't do it. I hadn't realised the pay was pro-rata.'

'If I up the pay?' tried Edward, desperate.

'I need the five days' pay. You couldn't offer that for four days, surely?'

Edward slumped. 'I'd want to, but I can't.' He wasn't skint by any means, but moving had been expensive and sorting out the new house was costing an arm and a leg. It made no sense to overpay someone to that extent; he had a daughter to raise, after all.

Regretfully they said their goodbyes and wished each other luck. 'Bye, Chrissy,' called Eliza, waving forlornly as she walked down the drive.

Edward groaned. So close! He was on the verge of running after her and offering her all the money she wanted but he had to plan ahead, had to think of contingencies.

'Don't worry, Daddy, there's still one more person to see tomorrow,' said Eliza, slipping her hand into his.

CHAPTER SEVEN

Eliza

On Sunday evening, it was a sorry dinner that they pushed around their plates. They had tried roasting a chicken as practice for Christmas, but it didn't go very well. It was dry in places and slimy in others and Daddy said more than once that he didn't even know how that was possible. The vegetables were greyish and tasteless, and the gravy was thin and boring, nothing like the delicious, velvety sauce that Granny made. After a few listless mouthfuls, her father swept up both their plates and took them straight outside. A wash of cold air swept into the kitchen through the back door, and Eliza heard the sound of the bin lid being lifted and their dinner dumped.

Eliza sighed. Perhaps she should learn to cook. But Daddy said he refused to perpetuate gender stereotypes and that since he was perfectly intelligent and reasonably practical, there was no reason his eight-year-old daughter should have to cook their meals. But Eliza didn't think he found cooking hard because he was a man – lots of the top chefs on TV were men – she thought it was just because he was naturally very bad at it. You couldn't be good at everything.

They were extra glum tonight because the fourth person they'd interviewed had turned out to be the worst of the lot. Agnes Pertwee had had icy blue eyes in a greyish-white face, a fleshy neck and a cold air. She hadn't said one word to Eliza, and Eliza's skin had crawled from the moment she'd arrived. Her father had obviously felt the same because he'd shown her out eight minutes later, saying afterwards that she'd put him in mind of a serial killer. The moment she'd gone, Daddy had grabbed his phone and called Chrissy. 'I'll offer her five days' money after all,' he'd muttered while it was ringing. 'Six, if I need to.' But Chrissy had already said yes to another job.

Eliza watched as he busied himself heating up two tins of tomato soup and burning toast, throwing it away and filling a toast rack with new slices. She could tell from the shape of his shoulders that he was feeling really, really bad. When it was all ready, he set it in front of her with a glum expression.

'I'm sorry, Lizzie-Loops. It's not exactly a feast.'

'It's good!' Eliza shrugged and cut some cheese into her soup. She loved it when it melted and went all stringy.

'Doesn't bode well for Christmas dinner.'

'It doesn't matter, Daddy. We've talked about this.'

'But, Lizzicles, what are we going to *do*? I don't have someone to look after you while I work and I can't feed you.'

'This is food.'

They finished their tea in silence and Eliza wished she had a magic answer for him, but she didn't. She was only eight. She knew, somehow, that everything was going to be alright. She wished she could make him see that too but grown-ups needed explanations for everything if they were to believe it. They didn't seem to just *know* very often.

It wasn't until they'd made hot chocolate that Daddy seemed to cheer up a little. Hot chocolate would do that to you, every time. They started to laugh about Agnes – that was one of the good things about Daddy: he could always see the funny side in things – when an almighty crash outside made them both jump. Eliza clutched the table. 'Is it robbers?'

Her father looked worried for a minute then relaxed. 'Four-legged robbers,' he said. 'Foxes, I bet. Cheeky sods.'

Eliza flew across the room, wrenching open the door. Sure enough, the bin was on its side, the lid some way away, spinning, and their disappointing chicken dinner was strewn across the grass. But of the foxes there was no sign. Eliza *thought* she saw two shadowy shapes disappearing into the deeper shadows at the edge of the garden but she couldn't be sure; her eyes were adjusting to the dark night after the bright light of the kitchen.

'They were here, but they're gone,' she called over her shoulder, bitterly disappointed. 'They've made a bit of a mess, though, Daddy.'

Edward joined her on the doorstep and sighed. 'I suppose we can't blame them when I just put almost a whole chicken out. It's winter, after all. You go and get ready for bed, Lizzie-Boots; you've got school tomorrow.'

Eliza sighed. Much as she liked her new school, she wasn't ready for the weekend to be over. She wanted them to stay up late watching films together and spying for the foxes' return, but she was never allowed to on a school night so there was no point asking.

She went upstairs and brushed her teeth. From the bathroom window she could see, in the glow of light from the kitchen, her father scooping up the chicken and bagging it several times over before putting it back in the bin and putting a heavy stone on the lid. The foxes would never come now.

CHAPTER EIGHT

Holly

Holly had only one goal for the weekend: not to think about the news that Penny had told her. The trouble was, she didn't have a lot to occupy her. First, she sat up in bed, reading, but her book wasn't working the escapist magic she was looking for. Around the edges of its imaginary world, she was all too aware that she was here in bed alone, that the house was too quiet, that there was no Alex with her, reading the papers and chatting. The bedroom was pretty, decorated in pink and peach; Holly had a flair for interiors, and a plus of having no partner was being able to indulge in feminine colours. But... her future was so unimaginably different from what she had always wanted that she felt it might crush her...

So she got up and made a coffee and stood looking out at her small garden. It was a square cottage garden that owed its splendour entirely to former owners. Much as Holly loved nature, she had no clue how to cultivate her own patch of it; her thumbs were so far from being green they were practically puce. Despite her neglect, there had been colour somewhere in the garden ever since she'd moved here in March. Even now, with the borders and bushes a wistful palette of sepia, umber and plumy cream pampas grass, a ruby-red acer still blazed. Its leaves were falling, though – scattered on the lawn beneath. Holly had taken to counting the number of leaves that were left on its slender boughs. Currently there were thirty-seven. The garden could be a project, occupy her weekends. She could buy a book, start watching Monty Don. But winter wasn't really the time for that, was it?

Standing still wasn't helping. She headed for the shower then dressed in jeans and her favourite red jumper and blow-dried her wavy blonde hair. Self-care, taking pride in your appearance, that was important, wasn't it? Just because she was alone didn't mean she should sit around in sweats with unbrushed hair all day. She had to feel ready for good things and then good things would happen. Holly prided herself on being brave and positive and putting on a good face.

But after breakfast and a cursory tidy around, it was still only half past ten. She was all dressed up with nowhere to go. She decided to do laundry, but when she looked in the basket, there was next to nothing in it. She was too organised through the week, she decided; no chaos to catch up with on the weekends. She'd always been that way.

Speaking of being organised… she spent a couple of hours drawing up lesson plans and brainstorming lists of the stage decorations that the children could make in class. It always gave them such a sense of purpose to see the sets coming together over the weeks, and made them so proud, when parents exclaimed over the final effect, to know that they had contributed to it. Time passed more quickly when she was working but, at the back of her mind, she knew that it wasn't the ideal solution. The whole point of weekends was *not* to work, to have time for your personal life. Working because you really, really had to get something done was one thing. Working because there was literally nothing else to do was quite another.

She made lunch then decided to go Christmas shopping. It wasn't too early, not with her parents leaving England on 1 December. She could look out for inspiration while she was at it for her own Christmas – a solo Christmas. It had to be faced – if possible, embraced.

It turned out to be a terrible idea. Walking into Hopley was nice: the rain had stopped and she enjoyed the quiet lanes, the soft November colours, a smoky lilac and grey sky. But once she was there, it only served to emphasise her isolation. Hopley wasn't the most picturesque of places. The outlying bits were charming and the countryside around was gorgeous, but the town centre was one of those where small businesses kept closing and pound shops kept opening and, as the younger folk had moved away and the sense of hope and spirit were eroded, the cafés had grown brassier and the pubs edgier. She'd seen some small signs, recently, that it was coming back to life, but on the whole, shopping in Hopley wasn't the most uplifting experience.

But usually, when she went to town, she would see two or three of her pupils at least. The parents always waylaid her, glad of a chance to have her to themselves for a few minutes and talk about their precious darlings. Even though her parents and many of her friends lived far away, her job always made her feel part of a community. But today, through some malign fate, she saw *no one* she knew, only eager Christmas shoppers: families, gangs of friends and, worst of all, mothers and daughters, which made her miss her own mum *and* think all the more sharply about all that she'd lost.

She started to lose it in the middle of the high street, panic coming in towering, dark waves that rolled over her, deafening, disorienting. She stumbled around a corner onto a quieter street where there would be fewer people to see her; embarrassment was a problem she didn't need to add to all her others. She leaned against a wall, forcing herself to take deep breaths and gradually, gradually, the fear receded. Slowly she came back to herself and could feel her feet on the ground again.

'Oh God!' she said aloud, looking around in confusion, as if a gale had picked her up and put her down again somewhere entirely new. She looked at her phone. Should she call someone? No, she was OK now. A bit wobbly, but OK.

She looked down the street and saw a lovely little antiques store with a pale blue sign. *Varden's Antiques* was etched on it in black script. That was new; it would be a nice place to explore one day, but not today. She wasn't in the spirit for shopping after all.

She braced herself to return to the busier main street. The sensible thing would be to go and have a hot chocolate somewhere, rest a while, make sure that the funny turn had passed off. But coffee shops had always been one of Holly's greatest pleasures – something to enjoy with Alex, or her mum, or a friend. In her current state of mind, she really thought that sitting in one alone might finish her off altogether. She just wanted to get home.

So she set off, taking her time, taking deep breaths when she remembered. How had this happened to her? She'd always been popular, always had friends and a boyfriend and too many offers on a weekend to fit them all in. It was pure circumstance that other people had moved on, moved away, at a time when her own life had imploded. She would get through it, she told herself sternly. People started over *all* the time. It was hardly impossible. She had a job, a house... it was a strong start.

When she got home, she did a double-take on the doorstep. There was a wreath on her navy front door. Holly hadn't put it there. It was tied to her door-knocker with thick red ribbon, a traditional swirl of holly and fir, studded with pine cones, little golden bells and jewel-bright berries. Absolutely beautiful. But who had put it there?

She looked up and down the street, which yielded no clues. Did she have a secret admirer? Was it a Christmas elf? Some kind of neighbourhood scheme? Perhaps Penny had done it, to cheer her up. But if this were Penny's doing, it wouldn't be so full and glossy. It would be wilder and more homespun, something she'd thrown together from ivy foraged in the woods. For a crazy moment she thought that maybe Alex had changed his mind and decided to come back to her, that this was his opening gesture. But Alex was having a baby with someone else.

She went indoors – no explanatory note on the mat – and threw herself onto the sofa where she cried and cried. She hadn't let herself go like that for months. She'd thought she was getting better, moving on too. Obviously, she was cut far, far deeper than she'd allowed herself to admit. But what to do about it? Holly wasn't a fan of wallowing. She didn't want to feel as if her life had ended. She wanted to cheer the hell up and get a grip. Apparently it wasn't that easy. What if it never *became* easy?

She sat up and pushed her hair, now damp from tears, off her face, and wiped her eyes with the heels of her hands. She took a deep breath and went to make hot chocolate, then resumed her seat in the corner of her sofa. What was the point of a big squishy sofa when there was no one to cuddle up with on it?

Before she knew it, she was crying all over again. Terrible. Now it was somehow five in the afternoon. The light had faded and the room was growing dusky and cool. She closed the curtains and switched on the light to beat the glooms back into the corners. What a dreadful, desolate day.

CHAPTER NINE

Edward

It was a cupboard that saved Christmas. Just an ordinary unassuming cupboard in the hall, with an unattractive plywood door. Opened, it smelled musty and revealed a couple of chipboard shelves festooned with cobwebs. In a rather unlovely touch, the door was fitted with a hasp and staple so that it could be padlocked. Edward remembered the previous owner saying it was where he'd kept his weedkillers and that he hadn't wanted the dog or grandchildren getting in there. There was no padlock now, but that would be an easy buy. And once he had somewhere that could be locked, he could start storing Christmas presents. He could do a bit of shopping this week while Eliza was at school and that way, when the time came, he wouldn't be totally unprepared. He would start today.

Edward found that he couldn't face the drive to the shopping centre and the mall itself. It was too brassy and frenetic there and he was *tired*, he realised, deep down in his bones. The last two months had been a lot of upheaval, hard work and worry. The disappointment of the weekend had been the last straw; starting another week with no idea how they were going to cope from next Monday was just exhausting.

It was a beautiful day and he needed to go easy on himself. He cleaned out the cupboard with lemon disinfectant and left the door open so it could air – he didn't want Eliza's things to get damp. Then he pulled on his coat, found his wallet and headed out; he would walk into Hopley. His only exercise of late had been cleaning and hammering and painting. Hoovering had become his resistance workout. He needed fresh air. Hopley wasn't thriving in terms of shops, but it had a few and at the very least he could buy the padlock and some wrapping paper.

But he never made it into Hopley that day. He hadn't appreciated, in their brief visits so far, how pretty this side of the town was. Hopley wasn't the *best* place in the world, they'd decided. A bit short on character, a couple more pound shops than anyone really needed. But they'd always gone in by car because two miles was a long walk for Eliza's little legs. That meant they'd always parked in the car park on the far side of town, where there was a lot of concrete. By walking in, Edward got to see Hopley's more charming side.

Country roads, their hedgerows bristling now in winter starkness, winding between bare, stubbly fields. Larger, more lovely houses, with whimsical gardens and welcoming facades. A pretty little pub called The Swan, which sat on the edge of a stream that bubbled right underneath Edward's feet. The road rose up gently to bridge it then sank down again, like an old man into an armchair, to carry on its way. A coot paddled madly through the cold green water.

Then on his left he saw a gorgeous old church. Norman? Medieval? Edward wasn't too hot on architecture. Either way, it looked very inviting, even though it was currently braced by a fretwork of scaffolding – a new roof was evidently underway. It was built of soft grey stone with a square tower and a trio of spectacular stained-glass windows. A huge old yew tree stood to one side, its boughs sweeping the path like a doorman ushering in guests. Edward hesitated. He wasn't a church-goer, but for some reason, just now, it called to him. He was tired. He was heartsore. He needed to get a padlock, but mostly he just wanted to sit down and have some peace. If those weren't good reasons to visit a church, he didn't know what were.

He walked towards the lych-gate, lifted the latch and stepped into the graveyard. He'd always liked graveyards. He liked to read the names and dates and inscriptions and wonder about the people buried there, the lives they had lived. Had any of these guys been such an inept father as he was? he wondered, wandering between the headstones. Honestly, lining up someone to look after Eliza should have been the first thing he did, not painting and plastering and the rest. He'd just been so desperate to make the house habitable. But after-school care was the lynchpin on which this whole endeavour depended. Stupid. He thumped his forehead as he picked his way between mossy tumps, feeling the cold in a whole new way. Had Eliza worn her gloves this morning? He couldn't remember.

After a circuit of the graveyard, he tried the door of the church. It was open. He loved that. He went inside, treading softly, and looked around. The vaulting roof was patched with canvas while the work was being carried out, but it did nothing to detract from the church's overall attractiveness. It had a wide nave, old, well-polished pews and those windows, spilling colour over the floor. Impressive fountains of white flowers spilled from stands on either side of the pulpit. Christmas hadn't come to St Domneva's yet.

On a huge shelf to his left lay a visitors' book, opened to its current page, with a biro next to it. Edward went further in and stood in front of the stained-glass windows, absorbing the elaborate scenes they depicted – presumably, the life of St Domneva. Then he sat down and closed his eyes.

He wasn't a praying man – apart from the impromptu prayers of an ever-anxious parent – an inarticulate *please, please, please* – whenever Eliza fell over or had a nightmare or burst into tears, which wasn't often, really. But the last two days had drained his usual resources. The failure to find a home help, Eliza's anxiety about the Christmas pageant and most of all, that phone call with his mother on Saturday. On Sunday evening she had texted him. *How did you get on? I hope you found the perfect person to take care of our precious girl.* A stab in the heart because he hadn't. A painful reminder of just how hard it would be to find the right person to take care of Eliza.

He hadn't replied yet, although this morning he'd been on the verge of texting her to say she was right about everything and he needed her help. But then the cupboard had distracted him and now he was here. He breathed deeply. *Please, please, please let me do what's best for Eliza. Please give her everything she deserves. Please let my little girl be happy, and please keep her with me. I don't want to be selfish, but I don't know what I'd do without her.*

He didn't know how long he sat there, but he was roused from his reverie by soft-soled footsteps. He opened his eyes and saw the vicar, a friendly-faced man in his forties with sandy hair. 'Don't let me disturb,' he stage-whispered.

Edward gathered himself. 'No, you're not,' he said, his voice sounding strangely loud in the empty church. Those acoustics! 'Hello, I'm Edward Sutton – new to the area.'

The vicar came over to his pew. 'May I?' He took a seat and shook Edward's hand. 'David Fairfield. Vicar here, as you can see. I thought I hadn't seen you before. How long have you been in the area?'

'Only a few weeks. My daughter and I have bought Christmas House. I must admit, it's more of a project than I'd anticipated.'

Reverend Fairfield frowned. 'Christmas House. Is that the old place with the gateposts and the gravel, a couple of miles out?'

'That's the one.'

'The owners didn't come to our church so I didn't know them, but I understand they'd been there a long time.'

'Yes. And they didn't do much to it. It's sound – the roof's not leaking or anything like that…'

The vicar gestured upwards. 'That's a big thing to be thankful for!'

Edward smiled. 'It is. I know. But we came with such high hopes for a new life and now it's all feeling rather unmanageable. Eliza's only eight. I start a new job next week. Christmas is coming…'

Suddenly he found himself telling the vicar everything. Cressida's departure, the bullying in Leeds, their dream of a new life in the country, the pressure from his mother to be a perfect parent when he was floundering to master the toaster – her insistence that he wasn't enough to care for Eliza.

'I hate to admit she has a point,' he concluded, scowling. 'I really, really hate to admit it – but I'm not coping. We need a new *shower* put in! Basics! I can't find anyone to look after Eliza when I'm at work and it can't be just any old person, can it? It has to be someone really, really special to take care of her. I don't know anyone here – I don't know what I was thinking. It was a great dream, but I can't make it work.'

The vicar listened, nodding, and then they sat in silence for a while. Edward waited for him to offer some God-style comfort: God works in mysterious ways; despair is an opportunity for faith; we each must suffer a dark night of the soul, etc. Surprising, really, how much philosophy was lurking around in his own brain. At last, Reverend Fairfield spoke.

'I think I have a solution,' he said. 'Can you be at home this afternoon?'

Edward stared at him. 'A solution?' Not a perspective, a comforting piece of scripture or an invitation to church. An actual *solution*?

'Yes.' The vicar looked thoughtful. 'I have a parishioner who's looking for some work and honestly, she'd be perfect for you. Pam Dixon. A lovely woman. She's in her sixties, she and her husband have both retired and they're driving each other mad at home together all the time. Well, she can tell you, if you're interested in meeting her. She's brought up four children so she knows her onions, shall we say. She'd be able to help you out with all the domestic stuff too. Shall I put you in touch?'

Edward looked at him as though he were Jesus. 'Yes please!' he said faintly. His and Eliza's dream was teetering on the brink – might it just be saved? And was it *very* wrong that he already couldn't wait to let his mother know? 'This is so very kind of you,' he added, recovering himself. 'Sorry if I'm a bit… It's just, I was resigned to having to give up on it all, but if this works out, then it's all doable again.'

'I'll get going.' Reverend Fairfield clapped his hands to his thighs and stood up decisively. 'I'll go and see her now and tell her to call on you. What time? Two thirty?'

'Perfect. Thank you, Reverend Fairfield. I can't tell you how much this means to me.'

'It doesn't help, being new to the area and not knowing anyone, does it?' he said. 'There's nothing like a personal recommendation for these kinds of things – gives you more peace of mind. And once you meet Pam, well, she knows everyone. It'll get better – you'll see. I have a daughter too. For what it's worth, you sound as if you're doing a great job to me.'

He left, and Edward rubbed his hands over his face. Had that really just happened? All along he'd imagined some whizzy young nanny type, probably from New Zealand, with Montessori training and certificates, but perhaps what they needed was someone older, motherly, calm. He had every faith in Pam Dixon without ever having met her. And it was because he trusted Reverend Fairfield. Not so much because he was a vicar but because he was so obviously a good person. To-the-point, sympathetic and practical.

Edward wandered home, seeing the world anew. In the bare hedges he could imagine spring; on the winding road he could imagine happy journeys. He thought, too late, that he should have given his phone number to the vicar in case Mrs Dixon needed to contact him. What if she was busy at 2.30 p.m. and wanted to come earlier, or later, or tomorrow? Now he just wanted to get home and be sure he didn't miss her. But perhaps this was the way things were done in village life.

He got home and looked around, wondering what Mrs Dixon would make of them. It was only then he realised he'd forgotten to buy a padlock. But there would be other chances for that, and he patted the cupboard door in thanks when he passed it.

CHAPTER TEN

Holly

Holly was glad to be back at work on Monday. She was always better when she was busy. And work was the one area of her life now where she felt truly fulfilled and happy, as if she were in the right place, doing the right thing.

By lunchtime, she'd given out the first assignment for the pageant and things were in full swing. She was having the children make patchwork angels that would all be arranged on the stage in the final production. It was a way of emphasising how each individual contribution would add up to something spectacular and wonderful. It was also a way of challenging common assumptions about what angels should look like. Lily Orton had been adamant on Friday that she should be the lead angel (there wasn't one, only five all-equal angels) 'because I have long blonde hair and blue eyes'.

Lily didn't mean to upset anyone else but Holly had noticed how Fatima, with her brown skin, dark eyes and glossy blue-black hair, had slumped when she said it. So Fatima wanted to be an angel too – good to know. Holly didn't blame Lily. Her mother, in Holly's opinion, placed far too much importance on her daughter's beauty – as if she thought it was Lily's passport to whatever life she wanted, as if Lily didn't have anything else to offer. Not a good message for a little girl to absorb. Holly wasn't bothered about being PC – the impulse to challenge assumptions and give the children new perspectives came from deep in her heart. She never wanted a single one of her children to feel inadequate or wrong or barred from something that they really wanted to do. So instead of asking them to make angels out of white material and silver foil, they were going to be patchwork – every one different, every one colourful. Lily would certainly be an angel in the pageant – she wanted it so badly and Holly would never deny her that – but so would four others and they would be whoever wanted to the most.

'Angels are magical beings,' said Holly. 'They can protect you, they can work miracles, they can answer prayers and make you feel loved. Who can you think of that makes you feel like that?'

The answers came thick and fast. 'My grandfather.'

'My cat!'

'Mrs Brown in the bakery.'

'And what do they look like?' asked Holly, laughing.

'Whiskery!'

'Furry and ginger.'

'Fat.'

'There you are then. You'll know an angel when you meet one, never mind what they look like.'

The children piled out for lunch, chattering excitedly, all except for Eliza, who hung back. 'Could I talk to you please, Miss Hanwell?' she asked, looking nervous. Her grey eyes were huge in her thin little face.

Holly felt a pang in her heart, a longing to sweep Eliza into her arms and smother her with love. But she was only her teacher. 'Of course you can. What is it, darling?'

Eliza bit her lip and leaned against Holly's desk, then stepped away and stood up very straight. 'I'm very sorry, Miss Hanwell, but I can't be in the Christmas pageant,' she said in a rush, looking all jittery and upset.

Holly knew she must tread very carefully, and not just because Mr Buckthorn had told her to. 'Alright, Eliza, thank you for telling me,' she said as calmly as she could, trying not to let her huge disappointment show. She felt as if she'd failed Eliza, but this wasn't about her. 'Remember I said last week that no one has to take part? No one has to do anything they don't want to.'

Eliza nodded gravely. 'But I feel bad,' she burst out. 'You're making a lovely play, Miss Hanwell. It's going to be beautiful – I can already see it in my mind's eye. I think you're very clever. And it feels ungrateful to say no. But I'm not ungrateful, honestly.'

'I can see that. Please don't feel bad. I'd love you to take part, but if it's not right for you, that's fine. Do you want to tell me why? You don't have to, but if you want to talk about it a bit, I'm happy to listen.'

'I'm too scared,' said Eliza. 'I get really bad stage fright. Once I was sick in front of everyone. I used to be really good at things like that. But then it changed and the last few plays in my old school were really, really horrible. I couldn't be in them anymore, and I can't be in this one.'

'Do you know what changed?'

Eliza nodded, looking everywhere but at Holly. 'But Daddy and I agreed that we wouldn't tell anyone,' she said quietly. Holly felt a lurch in her stomach. Parents getting their children to keep secrets always rang a warning bell. But then, Eliza hadn't said that he'd *told* her not to tell anyone. It sounded like a joint decision. What *was* the story there?

'Darling, you don't have to tell me anything at all. But you *can* tell me, if you think it would help. Does that make sense?'

Eliza nodded again. 'Thank you, Miss Hanwell. I'd better not tell you yet. But maybe one day I will.'

'Alright. And don't worry about the play. You'll make a patchwork angel for me, though, won't you?'

'Oh yes! I'm looking forward to that. I think it's a brilliant idea. I want to call mine Guinevere.'

'That's a good name. So there'll be a bit of you up there onstage along with everybody else after all. And you'll help out backstage, won't you?'

'Yes please.'

'That's wonderful. I'll have my hands very full managing that lot; it'll be good to have a second in command. So you'll still be involved, you see?'

'Thank you. I'm so pleased. I didn't want you to think I don't like the play.'

'I don't think that, Eliza. And if you change your mind, even the week before, I can always find room for another angel onstage. But it's completely fine if you don't, OK?' Suddenly Holly could see Eliza as an angel as clearly as if she wore wings and a robe.

'OK.'

'Good. Now go and find some friends and enjoy your lunch. And remember I'm always here if you need me.'

Holly watched out of the window as Eliza walked outside into the wide concrete yard. Children were running across it, screaming, anoraks streaming cape-style from shoulders. A pair of bare chestnut trees beyond the wall sketched dark lines against a grey sky. The child still wasn't happy, she could tell. She was relieved not to have to do something that terrified her, but that wasn't the same thing. Holly had been warned that there was an issue, but she'd hoped to inspire Eliza and put her so at ease that it would wash away whatever had happened at her old school. Well, she hadn't done it *yet*. But there was still time for everything to change. Really, whether Eliza was onstage or not didn't matter in the slightest. But she had to be happy. Happier than this.

CHAPTER ELEVEN

Edward

At 2.30 p.m. exactly, a red Mini turned in to the gateway of Christmas House. Edward watched as it parked carefully next to his own car, then the door opened and out stepped a stout woman with curly brown hair, shot through with grey, and a navy quilted jacket.

He hurried to the door. 'Pam Dixon? I'm Edward Sutton. Thank you so much for coming; it's lovely to meet you. Come in, come in.'

She paused on the doorstep and smiled. 'What a lovely place you've got here. So spacious and so close to the woods.'

He felt a wave of relief pass through him. The first test passed: she liked the house. 'It's rough, I have to warn you. We've had so much to do since we arrived and had to get Eliza settled in school. But yes, thank you, we love it.'

'Of course you do,' she said comfortably, rocking past him on stiff hips, holding her large handbag before her in both hands. 'Where are you having me, Mr Sutton?'

He stifled a smile at her wording and gestured at the kitchen. 'I thought in here for a cup of tea and a chat – it's the room we use most at the moment, though it's not very attractive. And then I could show you around the rest of the house so you can see what's what.'

She nodded and settled herself on a chair in the kitchen, creaking a bit. 'No milk or sugar for me, Mr Sutton. Just teabag and water, I always say. I'm cheap to keep, not that Mr Dixon would agree. Always on at me about buying new things for the garden. But I tell him, some women spend a fortune in the beauty salons. I've only ever had two manicures in my life and they were both gifts. I think a lovely garden contributes more to the world than shiny nails, don't you?'

'Well yes – yes I do!' said Edward, filling the kettle. Then he turned to her and grinned. 'Though I have neither.'

She smiled back, a nice moment of accord between them. 'I don't suppose you have Earl Grey, Mr Sutton?'

'I'm afraid not. We're woefully underprepared for guests.'

'That's fine. Regular tea will do. I'll bring some in if you decide you want me.'

'You'll do no such thing,' said Edward, who had already decided that he did. 'I'll get some for you, and anything else you like. Can I tempt you with a Hobnob?'

Time flew by. First, Mrs Dixon told him her story – bored stiff in retirement, missing the kids, in danger of murdering Mr Dixon with his new passion for ham radio. ('I'd hoped for fishing,' she confided wistfully, 'such a nice, tranquil hobby, and out of the house.') It would be best for everyone if she could find some enjoyable occupation. Then Edward told his and Eliza's story, and for the second time that day he found himself oversharing to a complete stranger.

'I know what you've got,' she said when he eventually finished, several Hobnobs later. 'That millennial burnout, that's what it is.'

'Millennial…?'

'I read about it in the magazines. Millennial burnout, they call it. Well, you're a bit older than these so-called millennials, I suppose, but I don't see why we can't all have it. There are all these solutions, aren't there, on the internet and what have you, and we're all supposed to avail ourselves of them. If you're fat, you can learn about healthy eating, and if you sit down too much, you can do yoga, and if you're stressed, you can do meditation. Life hacks, they call them. They've got those podcast thingies and all sorts. There's no excuse anymore just to be ordinary, just to be struggling along in an ordinary life like we always have. You feel like you should be the best father *and* the breadwinner *and* a good cook *and* a home decorator *and* a project manager and it's just too much, Edward – no one could do it. You're not failing; it's just too much.'

'It does feel a bit much,' he admitted.

'Course it does. I've brought up kids. I've worked a job. I've renovated a house and I can cook a superb Sunday roast. But not all at the same time. You stick to the two things you *have* to do, that no one else can do in this scenario. That's being Eliza's dad and doing that fancy advertising job that'll bring the money in. Leave the rest to me. And the things I can't do, like give you a new shower, I'll sort out for you. I know a good plumber. Reliable, not scatty like the rest of them.'

'Really? Truly?' Edward was starting to feel increasingly as if he were in a dream. 'I hadn't expected… I mean childcare for Eliza is the main thing. The *main* main thing. And I'd hoped… a bit of housework, being here for deliveries, perhaps a meal once a week or so… I don't want to ask too much of you.'

'Write me a list, Edward. Put *everything* on it. I'll work my way through slowly. Don't worry, I won't tire myself out. I'm done with exhausting myself for everyone else's benefit. But I'll do what I can when I can and you'll soon see a difference. Now, I should meet Eliza today, shouldn't I? To make sure she's happy with this arrangement, before we make it all official.'

Edward looked at his watch and groaned. 'I've lost track of time *again*!' It was talking to Pam Dixon that had done it. It was such a relief to have someone to talk to at long last – someone who wasn't his mother, questioning his plans at every turn, wanting the best for him and sure that *her* way was best. 'Yes, you're right, and I need to leave now. Will you come or would you rather stay and explore the house?'

'I'll stay here, have a quick look around. You can tell Eliza about me on the way home.'

Edward raced to the school, heart bubbling. He wasn't that late, but he was afraid that Mrs Dixon would disappear like a genie while he was out of the house. He wasn't in the least bit worried about leaving her alone there. For one thing, they had nothing whatsoever that anyone would want to steal, and even if they did, hell would freeze over before Mrs Dixon would steal it.

Here came Eliza, dressed all in red today, like a little Christmas pixie. Elf. Whatever. She was swinging her school bag as she crossed the yard and talking to a little girl, not Fatima, with blonde hair in two stringy plaits. Then Fatima exploded through the door and ran to catch up with them, throwing an arm around their shoulders and telling them something that made them laugh. It lifted Edward's heart and he got out of the car.

'Hi there!' He turned to see Fatima's mum beside him, her long dark hair hanging in glossy waves. She had a kind, tired smile. 'I'm Firoja. It's lovely to meet you properly at last. Sorry we had to rush off last week. It was Fatima's tennis lesson and that coach is *strict*!'

He laughed. 'No problem. I'm Edward. I'm afraid *I* have to rush off today. I've got someone waiting at the house to meet Eliza – I'm hoping we've got childcare sorted at last for when I start work next week.'

'That'll make all the difference – good luck. What about tomorrow? Tuesday is the one day Fats doesn't have anything after school, if you can believe that. If you're free, we could take them for a hot chocolate. I remember being the new family and not knowing anyone. It's horrible.'

'We'd love that. Tomorrow then. Thanks, Firoja.'

'I'll see if my husband, Liam, can join us. His working hours are all over the place so I never know if he'll be around or not.'

Eliza waved goodbye to the others and threw her arms around him. 'I had a good day, Daddy!'

'I'm glad, Lizzie-Loops, and I bet you I've had an even better one. I've got two bits of good news for you.'

'You do? What are they?'

'Tomorrow after school we're invited to go for hot chocolate with Fatima and her mum. Maybe her dad too. Would you like that?'

'Definitely! Fun! What else?'

'I think I've found our helper. She's waiting at the house to meet you. It all depends what you think of her, of course, but I have a feeling you'll like her.'

'That's amazing, Daddy! Where did you find her?'

On the drive home, Edward told Eliza all about his visit to the church and Reverend Fairfield and Mrs Dixon. As they turned into their crunchy gravel forecourt, he was relieved to see the red Mini still there. Eliza hurtled over the gravel and he followed. They opened the door to two unfamiliar sensory greetings. Number one, the air was filled with the smell of cooking. Number two, the house was warm. 'What did she do?' whispered Edward.

'It's like magic!' gasped Eliza, her eyes wide.

Mrs Dixon, now very red-faced, came to the kitchen door. 'You must be Eliza! Well, aren't you a bright little thing? I'm Pamela Dixon and I'm very pleased to meet you.' She held her hand out and Eliza shook it heartily.

'I'm pleased to meet you too, Mrs Dixon. Are you *cooking*?'

In the kitchen, a glass of milk and a biscuit waited for Eliza and another mug of tea awaited Edward. 'I took the liberty of having a poke through the fridge and there were a few veggies that weren't going to last much longer. I found some chicken, so I've made a casserole. I'll turn it down to simmer before I go. Give it ninety minutes and it'll be all ready for you.'

'Wow!' whispered Eliza. '*Casserole.*'

'That's very good of you,' said Edward. 'I'll pay you for today, of course.'

Mrs Dixon snorted. 'Indeed you will not. Nonsense.'

'Have you… have you done something to the heating?'

'Yes, it's your rubbishy old thermostat that was giving you the bother. We used to have one like it, that's how I know, otherwise I'd have been clueless. I've got it going now, so all you have to do is press off when you're too hot and on when you're too cold. I thought that simplest. But if I were you, I'd get a new one when you can. Put it on the list.'

Edward glanced at Eliza, raising his eyebrows, and she nodded happily, a milk moustache resting above her wide smile. 'Mrs Dixon, if you come and work with us, will you take me for walks in the woods after school sometimes?'

'Well now, I like a nice woodland walk. I'm not too fast on my feet, on account of my bad hips, but if you're prepared to take it slow, I think I can promise you that.'

'I think slow is better sometimes. You get to see more things, like mushrooms and interesting plants. I could take photos of them and take them to school for nature hour. And are you very good at telling stories?'

'Not very good, if I'm honest. I don't have an imaginative bone in my body.'

'Oh, I don't believe that!' said Eliza. 'Everyone does!'

'Well, be that as it may, I've never thought myself as the creative sort. But I can *read* you stories, if you've got some good books.'

'That'll be lovely. And will you mind if I tell *you* stories? Or will I annoy you with my chatter?'

'Gracious, I love a story. I should say your chatter will be the biggest perk of the job!'

And, in just such a series of negotiation and compromise, the deal was sealed.

CHAPTER TWELVE

Holly

It was the end of the day. A high, pale blue sky was studded liberally with clouds, mostly dark like amethysts, with one bright pinkish-white one like a diamond set in the centre of a crown. Only half past four – so many hours of the day still ahead – yet all Holly wanted to do was go home and sleep. There was something so restful about this fading light, the hiss and gurgle of the school's elderly heating system. Since her meltdown at the weekend, she'd admitted to herself how the events of the year had left her feeling shipwrecked, and now all she wanted to do was sleep. Sleep was healing; perhaps that was why.

But this evening her car was booked in for a service. So she stayed at school, marking some English comprehension tests, until it was time to go. The school car park was cold. Although there was no frost, the surrounding fields somehow *looked* cold for the first time that winter. The clacking of the crows sounded newly urgent as they flew back and forth in squadrons on preparatory missions, and smoke puffed out from the chimneys of the surrounding suburban streets. Holly jumped into her car, shivering.

She waited on-site while the service was carried out. The waiting area in the corner of the showroom was brightly lit and Christmas songs were already playing on the speakers.

Oh no, don't start, thought Holly as Mud sang self-indulgently about a lonely and cold Christmas. There was a tea and coffee machine – she helped herself to a coffee – and a plate of mince pies. She took two of those as well (might as well make a pleasure of a necessity) and grabbed a couple of magazines and leafed through. They were the kind of magazines she only ever read in two places – the hairdresser's and the car showroom. The rest of the time they didn't interest her much, but somehow, at the hairdresser's and the showroom, she liked nothing more than to find out who was dating whom in the world of celebrity nuttiness and which famous actors were making a film that marked a departure in their career.

She skipped over an article about Jake Weston, star of the action-film world. She'd never really gone for that blonde, blue-eyed, muscle-bound type. She spent a while reading about Gerald Smithson, an older actor who often appeared in arty, literary adaptations. Her mother had always thought old Gerald was dishy and Holly rather liked his quirky, ultra-English style. Then she came across an article about Cressida Carr. The photos were stunning, commanding the eye and refusing to let go – Cressida Carr had often been called the most beautiful woman in the world – but Holly had never been a massive fan. Certainly she was talented, and fabulously lovely to look at, but there was something a bit cold and remote about her, Holly had always thought (her mother felt the same). They preferred Julia Roberts, Reese Witherspoon, Jennifer Hudson… women with character, who you could imagine sitting down and sharing a pizza with.

She was about to skip the article but from the headline it looked as if Cressida was making a new period drama, and there was nothing Holly liked more than a good period drama. She read the piece. It began with the summary of Cressida's career to date, a few outings on the British stage, an acclaimed West End performance, then a small but life-changing part in a British film in 2014. So determined had Cressida been to seize every chance, Holly read, that she'd taken the part while pregnant and persuaded the director to adjust the filming schedule so that her scenes could be shot before she started to show. Wow, and she hadn't even had the clout then that she had now. She must be a *very* determined woman. Holly admired that. What must that child of Cressida's be like, after floating in the womb on a film set? she wondered. Was he or she steeped in acting magic, a little performer in the making? Or were they completely different – grounded and practical rather than creative? Where was that child now? In Hollywood with Cressida, presumably. What must *that* be like?

Holly read on, learning how the call from Hollywood had come out of the blue one day and how Cressida had leaped onto a plane to make the audition. Now she was dating Reuben Mason – good grief, now *he* was gorgeous – and this upcoming film would be her fourth in just the last three years. Her work ethic must be astonishing. She was one of the most photographed women in the world, Holly read; she'd been voted into the *Maxim* top ten sexiest women three years running. Holly rolled her eyes. Good to know that objectifying women was still going strong. Oh, and her new movie was being filmed in Britain in December. In London. She was 'in equal measure nervous and excited' about returning to home soil.

It would be a challenging role, Cressida said. Her character was a runaway wife, fleeing an abusive marriage. 'She is not obviously beautiful but full of inner strength.'

Holly snorted to herself. So it would be challenging to play someone not beautiful? *So* hard to look like an ordinary person, darling! She grinned, returning to her original opinion of Cressida, which was that she was probably a bit of a cow. She looked at the date on the magazine – June. Filming would be about to start any minute. Well, good luck to her. Holly started the next magazine, which had a feature about Susan Sarandon. Holly loved Susan.

When she arrived home, her head was still full of Hollywood and drama, which made a pleasant change from her recent thoughts. She parked up, fetched her work bag from the boot and walked to the door. Outside, in a metal stand, was a small Christmas tree. It was a real one, with that beguiling smell floating off it, and whispered of magic and dreams. Holly looked all around. Was it for her? Or had someone just set their own tree down there for a minute to rest? But there was no one about. Once again, her little close was quiet. It was a pretty tree, full and symmetrical. Should she take it inside? What if a weirdo had left it and it was seen as encouragement? At least the wreath could stay outside the house. Speaking of which, it did look ever so pretty there. The gold bells winked at her in the light from the street lamp.

Holly waited a few minutes, frowning, then walked up and down the close in case she saw someone she could ask, but all the houses were in darkness. In the end she shrugged, unlocked her door and hefted the Christmas tree inside.

CHAPTER THIRTEEN

Edward

Winter was coming, but Edward didn't care. Mrs Dixon had arrived in their life in the nick of time like a Christmas angel come to save them. If ever there was proof that angels came in all shapes and sizes, thought Edward as he drove home from work on Friday evening, Pam Dixon was it. Things had improved from day to day since she'd joined them. The plumber had come to do the shower on Monday. She'd taken delivery of a dishwasher on Tuesday and shown Eliza how to use it; Eliza was to give him a lesson this weekend. A sofa, two armchairs, a rug, a coffee table and a bookcase had also arrived throughout the week, so now the living room was one more or less fully furnished room. And yesterday a man had been to service the log burner and clear it out, so now they could have a fire in there on chilly evenings. What could be more Christmassy than that? They'd had home-cooked meals four days that week and hadn't once heard the sound of foxes knocking the lids off the bins. Altogether, they'd made enough progress that he could relax and enjoy this weekend with Eliza.

He'd missed her hugely during the week, but having Wednesday at home helped, and he had to admit, it was good to be back at work. In the domestic realm, he felt he was winging it, all the time, forever one step away from disaster. In the office, he knew what he was doing, he was good at his job and there was something very calming about that. The pace was fast, especially because he was only working four days, but so far, he'd been able to get away on time every day and be home with Eliza by seven.

This week had been mostly about learning the ropes, getting to know the staff and clients – endless meetings – to get him into the swing of it. He had a feeling that next week he'd be fully submerged. Bring it on. He loved thinking creatively again, finding the exciting angles for even the dullest of products, being able to enthuse people when no one had been able to before. He felt like a grown-up, clever and buzzed, and it was a good feeling.

His phone rang on the passenger seat and he glanced down to see his parents' number. There was a lay-by up ahead so he swung into it and answered the call. He didn't want to talk to them with Eliza around, not after last time. And he wanted to boast about how well things were coming together.

'Hello, darling, how was your first week at work?' asked his mother.

Edward filled her in and asked after them. Then she got to the point. 'I know you asked me not to bring this up again, but I *just* wondered, have you thought any more about what I mentioned last time? You know, about Eliza coming to stay with us?'

Edward sighed and resisted the urge to knock his head against the steering wheel. 'No, Mum, for the simple reason that I don't need to. It's not going to happen. Please stop talking about it.'

'But, darling, I *worry* about our dear little girl. We could give her so much. I know you have this Mrs Dixon now for the weekdays, and I'm certain she's an excellent woman, but really, Edward, I'm her *grandmother*. Surely no one could do a better job for her than me?'

'It's not about which of you can do the best job; it's about Eliza staying with me, her dad. Mrs Dixon allows that to happen, and Eliza adores her. They're great friends already. We're getting organised in the house at a rate of knots, thanks to Mrs Dixon, and Eliza is as happy as a bird.'

'Ah, so she's decided to be in the Christmas show then?' Despite her obvious efforts to be conciliatory, his mother's tone held a detectable note of one playing a trump card.

'No. But it's early days for her at school. She loves it there but she's still touchy about the stage stuff. Which is understandable, I think, given her reasons.'

'That woman should be hung, drawn and quartered for abandoning her daughter like that.'

Now there he agreed, but he knew from experience that blaming everything on Cressida and seething in bitterness didn't help – tempting though it was, and he'd done his fair share of it. It certainly wouldn't help Eliza. 'I know how you feel. But it was a long time ago now.'

'And Eliza's still suffering by it.'

Cars swooshed past the lay-by and Edward looked to the dark sky for patience. 'But getting better, steadily. We're moving on, Mum, both of us. And that's all you can hope for after something like that.'

Edward heard his mother sigh. 'Have you got a shower yet?'

'Yup.'

'Any furniture?'

'The lounge is completely plush. And we've got more on the way. Mum, this is actually none of your business, you know.'

A wounded silence followed and Edward kicked himself; he hadn't wanted to hurt her. But really, he wasn't a particularly remote person. He'd probably tell her everything quite happily if it wasn't always such an interrogation, if he didn't always feel he had to defend every single life choice he made. No one could possibly know better than Sarah Sutton – so thought Sarah Sutton.

'Well, I can see you're quite set on your course of action,' she said in a bruised voice.

'You mean caring for my own daughter, in our own home? Yes, strangely enough, I am. Now I'm ten minutes from home and I want to get back to Eliza so I'll head off and catch up with you next week.'

He hung up, shaking his head. His bloody mother. She'd always been demanding and bossy. But suggesting he should just hand over Eliza was ridiculous. He'd lost sleep over her outrageous suggestion when she'd first made it, ruing through the dark night his dearth of culinary skills, the impulsive steps he'd taken without thinking them through to the nth detail. She made him worry that he was a terrible father. But terrible fathers didn't make their daughters happy. He couldn't believe his mother was still thinking about it; persistence was that woman's middle name. He gave an expressive growl then started the engine and went on his way.

His mother's comments made him think about Cressida – which he did rarely these days – where she was and what she was doing. He knew in general terms, of course, but not in specifics. What on earth must her life be like? He found it hard to equate with the young woman he had loved. It took him down a spiral of memory to a time when she was full of dreams, tousle-haired and always barefoot around the house. Always clutching a sheaf of paper as she learned monologue after monologue in preparation for auditions for parts that she fervently prayed would come her way. Always with a mega-watt smile for him.

She was twenty-four when she got pregnant. Too young, for Cressida. And it was a surprise. Edward always used the word surprise, rather than accident, when referring to Eliza. 'I'm not ready,' Cressida had said at once. 'I can't do it.'

Edward had been astonished – not at *her* reaction, which he found perfectly understandable, but at his own; out of nowhere, he wanted the baby desperately. That came as a bolt from the blue! But he wouldn't force Cressida into anything; it was too huge. When she'd asked him if he wanted the baby, he was honest and said yes. When she'd asked him if he could ever forgive her if she didn't go through with the pregnancy, he was honest again – yes;

it must be her choice. She'd thought about it hard for two weeks and announced that she would keep the baby. He'd checked and double-checked that she wasn't just doing it for him, that she really felt she would be happy, and she'd reassured him, laughing and crying. 'We're having a baby, Edward!' He'd been over the moon.

CHAPTER FOURTEEN

Holly

Another weekend rolled around and Holly woke with a feeling of trepidation on Saturday morning. Was she strong enough to try Christmas shopping again? She'd have to be, basically. She only had this weekend to get everything for her parents if she wanted to wrap and post it all before they left for India.

Once more she walked; it was one of those rich winter days with sun and cloud in rotation, one swelling into the other and turning the sky purple-grey, the hedgerows a luminous mass of copper and aubergine. Hopley was busy again but this time everything felt a bit more normal. She bumped into Dean Corwell and his dad, Lily Orton with her mum and sister and David Kanumba with his parents and a scowl the size of Kent. There had been an incident with an ice-cream sundae, she learned. David was one of those boys who could eat ice cream whatever the weather – the more the better. The large-sized dish hadn't met expectations and his parents wouldn't let him order another since they didn't want their son in a sugar coma for the rest of the month. They all stopped to talk and Holly felt a small sense of belonging and purpose to offset the new aimlessness at the heart of her existence.

She visited the little antiques shop she'd noticed on her last visit – a charming place in a quiet side street, with the only bow window in Hopley – and found a wonderful ornament of a bird with a sweeping tail, studded in brightly coloured stones and bearing no resemblance to any actual species she was aware of; early twentieth century Russian, apparently. It was at the same time tacky and beautiful. Her father would love it. It was also ruinously expensive, but he was worth it.

She found a Victorian opal pendant for her mother and couldn't stop beaming while the dapper, quietly spoken owner packed them carefully into blue boxes for her. Hopley wasn't Regent Street, but you only really needed a couple of interesting, different shops and you were all set.

'Christmas presents?' asked the man as she pushed her debit card into the machine.

She nodded, smiling. 'For my parents. This shop is new, isn't it? I'm so glad you're here – you have such treasures.'

'Thank you; I'm pleased you like them. Yes, I opened back in October – moved down from London. James Varden.' They shook hands.

'Holly Hanwell. Well, I'd better get on. I need to shop for my friends now and much as I'd love to treat them all to gifts from here, I'd be bankrupt, so I need to find somewhere else.'

'Do you know Namaste? My friend Mahira runs it. It's a little esoteric shop with crystals, books and jewellery, that sort of thing. If you're looking for something a bit different, it might suit.'

'Thank you, that sounds great!'

James gave her directions and Holly set off. As she re-joined the high street, with its well-used Christmas lights in the shape of tipsy Santas and corpulent penguins, she saw Eliza Sutton and her dad walking down the opposite side of the street.

'Hello there!' she called out, pleased to see Eliza and curious, she had to admit, about the father. Mr Sutton was paying rapt attention to whatever Eliza was telling him. He was tall and brown-haired, but unlike Eliza's shiny dark crow's wing, his hair was curling and unruly. He was smiling but stressed-looking, like most parents at this time of year. That was all she had time to observe before they stopped outside a hardware shop. 'Eliza, hello!' she called again, but they didn't hear and disappeared inside.

Holly didn't need anything in the hardware line. She hesitated for a minute, then went on her way; she wasn't in the habit of stalking her pupils or their rather attractive fathers. As she walked off, Holly pictured how Eliza had looked up at her father, her face shining with joy; how she had hung off his hand and chattered with abandon to him. It couldn't be the father who had caused this fracture in his child's spirit; she was sure of it.

Recent events were such that when she got home, she half expected to find another mysterious Christmas development – lights around her roof, perhaps, or an outdoor Santa planted in her lawn. But there was nothing. She really would have to try to find out who had brought the tree and the wreath, she thought, unlocking the door. As she pushed it open, she felt resistance and heard something brush across the floor. A long, narrow box lay on the mat, with no address, just her first name written on the outside. She picked it up and opened it. Inside were five lengths of silver tinsel and several flat, colourful ornaments made from paper: birds, fairies, bells and stars. They were absolutely gorgeous but who was *doing* this? It was too bizarre. She absent-mindedly pushed the door closed behind her and wandered into her lounge where the little tree still stood bare before the window. She could decorate it now but again, should she? What if she had a stalker? Did stalkers *give* you Christmas ornaments, as a rule?

She was just wondering whether to go and ask the neighbours if they knew anything about it when there was a tap at the door. Holly found her next-door-but-three neighbour, Phyllis, standing outside with a cardboard box. They'd only spoken a handful of times since Holly moved in, but Phyllis, an older woman with snowy hair and lively brown eyes, had always been chatty.

'Phyllis! How lovely to see you. What's up?'

'Well, my dear, I haven't seen you in a while and you're new – quite new anyway. I just wanted to check you're alright.'

'That's really kind of you. Do you want to come in?'

'Only if it's not a bad time. I don't want to hold you up.'

'I've no plans. Come on in. Can I get you tea? Coffee? Hot chocolate? Baileys?'

'Cup of tea for me, dear. If it's no trouble.'

'It's not a bit. Take a seat. It's lovely to have a visitor,' said Holly, and it was. It was part of what made a home, wasn't it, having people dropping in and out of each other's houses, the rituals of tea-making and welcome and cheery farewell. Holly had been missing that.

'That's a pretty tree. A lovely shape. Where did you find it?'

'I've been meaning to make some enquiries with the neighbours actually. It just appeared on my doorstep a few days ago. And the wreath a few days before that, and a box of tree decorations through my letter box today. No note, no explanation, nothing. They're lovely things, but it's a bit odd, don't you think?'

'*Very* odd! Maybe you have a secret admirer,' said Phyllis hopefully.

'Wildly unlikely. I hope it's not a stalker.'

'Do stalkers *spread* Christmas cheer, generally speaking?'

'I was thinking the same thing. So you haven't seen any clues? It's not some sort of neighbourhood scheme or anything?'

'I've never heard of such a thing. Sorry to be no help. Oh, but I've brought you a cake,' added Phyllis, handing her the white box she was carrying. 'Just to be neighbourly.'

Holly opened the lid and breathed in. 'Lemon. I love it. We'll have some now.' She busied herself making Phyllis's tea – and a hot chocolate for herself – glancing into the lounge at intervals. She saw her neighbour perusing her bookshelves. It *was* an irresistible thing, looking at another person's books. She carried the drinks and then the cake through.

'You have a lovely selection of books,' said Phyllis, coming to join her on the sofa. 'Some lovely old classics and some brilliant new ones too.'

'You like books?'

'I was an English teacher.'

'No way! I'm a teacher too. Primary.'

Phyllis beamed. 'How lovely. So how are you, dear? Our little close is mostly elderly folk; I hope you're not finding it too lonely.'

'Not a bit. Well, maybe a *bit*. I'm single… my friends are all over and my parents are in Cornwall so sometimes life feels a bit… quiet. But I love my job – I'm lucky that way. The children are amazing so I'm happy at work. I just need to work on my personal life now.'

'I had a feeling something was up.' Phyllis hesitated then continued with a confessional air. 'I came to say hello a week or so back but then I saw you through the window. Crying your heart out. I wasn't snooping – your curtains were open and you know how the inside of someone else's house always draws the gaze. Anyway, I could see it wasn't the moment to call so I went away. That's why I've brought the cake.' She gently removed one of the cream china plates from Holly's hand and took a generous forkful of lemon drizzle.

Holly looked at her, touched and embarrassed. 'God, I can't believe you saw me bawling. I spend my life putting on a brave face. I'm mortified. But it had been… a bad day.'

'Pish,' said Phyllis, and Holly grinned. How could you not love someone who said *pish*? 'Nothing to be embarrassed about. We've all had those days – or those patches of weeks or months – where everything feels insurmountable. There's not a one of us exempt. It's none of my business at all, but if you'd like someone to talk to, I'm a pretty good listener.'

Holly got up to draw the curtains then sat down again. She'd been feeling totally and deeply alone. To feel the hand of friendship reaching out to her from so unexpected a source was disorienting. It was like being guided from eclipse to a glimmer of light.

'I'm not being nosy, I promise. I just want you to know I'm here if you need someone,' Phyllis added.

'You don't seem nosy at all,' said Holly, 'just lovely. Thank you, Phyllis, perhaps I will tell you. I don't want to bring you down, though.' And she wasn't used to telling her story to anyone who didn't already know her history with Alex. She had told Penny and thought that was enough of an unburdening, that there was no need to talk about it anymore. Clearly that hadn't worked out as well as she'd hoped.

Holly and Phyllis sipped in silence and Holly let her gaze drift to her bookshelves. The sight of them filled her with bittersweet feelings because they were laden with her old children's books. She'd kept them because she treasured them so, and because she had always dreamed of sharing them one day with her own children. She heaved a deep sigh, reflecting that yes, Alex's desertion was sad, but the reason for it was much, much worse.

'Back in January, my partner left me. Alex. We'd been together ten years and we'd been trying for a baby for four.'

'Oh, my dear, I'm sorry. A break-up is a great heartache.'

'It is. But that's just the tip of the iceberg. We weren't engaged, officially, but we always said that once I got pregnant, we'd have a small wedding in a registry office. We'd always dreamed of being a family. All the conventional trappings: a big house, the school run, a nursery we'd decorate ourselves... that was our dream. We wanted the same things and I thought that made us rock solid. At first we just let nature take its course, assuming it would happen at some point, but, as time went on, we started to wonder. Towards the end of last year, we did all the tests, to see if anything was wrong, and if so, what.' She glanced at Phyllis, who nodded.

'We spent Christmas in Cornwall with my parents, then we went back to Kent in the new year and the phone call came. The results. There *was* something wrong, and it was me. Alex checked out completely fine.' Holly looked down at her hands, still unable to believe fully what she'd learned that day.

'I have a septate uterus. It's something you're born with apparently; it's pretty rare. I had no idea. I never had any problem with my periods or anything like that. A bit of pain during sex sometimes, but not often enough for me to think there was a particular reason for it. Sorry – is that too much information? A septate uterus doesn't even mean you can't conceive. It does put you at a higher risk of miscarriage, and repeated miscarriage. And obviously I hadn't even *conceived* in all that time, so it wasn't looking promising for our chances.

'The medical team were supportive, said never to lose hope, that IVF could help. But I was devastated anyway. For the next week or two, I struggled to come to terms with the fact that we had a really hard road ahead of us, with no guarantee of success at the end of it. Turns out Alex's thought processes were quite different. He left me. He didn't put it quite like this but the gist of it was that I wasn't a good enough bet. He really, really wanted children – well, I already knew that – and he thought that with me, his chances weren't high enough. We already knew the statistics. Even without a misshapen womb, if you've been failing to get pregnant for over three years, the likelihood that it'll happen naturally is low. He… he wanted to "let me go" – those were his words – and try to find someone else who could give him a greater chance.'

'Good heavens,' said Phyllis in a small voice.

'Yes. I didn't want to hold him back – of course I didn't. I *hated* the thought that I very likely would be the cause of him never having something he wanted so much. He deserved a chance at fatherhood. But I couldn't help feeling… rejected. Like I was defective, you know? And once he found out, he wanted to trade up, get a better model. He didn't mean it like that but…'

'Hard to feel any other way, I should imagine.'

'Very hard. I still do, if I'm honest.' Holly sighed, feeling the tears brew. She took a deep, determined breath while Phyllis patted her shoulder. 'And… I would have stayed with Alex if it had been him.'

'Because you loved him more than the idea of having children?'

Holly considered. 'In all honesty, no. I did love him. But not *more* than that – it was all bound up together. We weren't married, but we were planning to be, so in my mind that's what a relationship like ours *was*. You know, for better, for worse. Whereas he just *went*! Ten years of shared history, of knowing each other *so* well… he was prepared to let all that go for the chance of placing a better bet. It made me feel so unimportant as a human being.' Suddenly she remembered his work Christmas party last year. Someone had said to her, about Alex, 'He likes to go where the opportunities are.' Wasn't *that* the truth?

'Oh, my dear. He didn't want to consider adoption?'

Holly shook her head.

'Then in my view you are entirely better off without him. If you didn't mean more to him than all of that… but I suppose others have told you as much and it's cold comfort.'

'I suspect you're right, but it's not just the loss of Alex. I think if it was only that, I'd be lots better by now. It's the loss of the *me* that I always thought I was, the me that would just get pregnant and be a mother. When you saw me howling the other night, I'd just heard that his new girlfriend is pregnant. We only broke up in January! So there *he* is, carrying on, living *our* dream with someone else and I feel… like a boat washed up and stranded on the shore. I had a panic attack in the middle of Hopley! Then I came home and lost it all over again. That's when you saw me.

'I don't know how to think about my life now. Everyone says there are plenty more fish in the sea. But I can't get excited at the prospect of new love now. Whoever I meet, I'll have to tell them there's a good chance I can't have children and it'll be difficult either way. The only men who'd want to take it further would be men who don't *want* children and they wouldn't be right for me. I'm a primary school teacher. I *adore* children. So I don't know how to make anything that's ahead of me feel… right.' Then the tears did come again, and she buried her face in her hands while she sobbed.

Phyllis didn't rush in with soothing words or inappropriate hugs. She just sat there while Holly cried, occasionally breathing, 'Oh my word. Oh my word.'

Eventually Holly wiped her eyes and blew her nose then looked at Phyllis with a wry smile. 'So there we are,' she said. 'That's me. Tragic story.'

'Well, you know, it really is,' said Phyllis. 'It's very sad, my dear, and I'm sorry to hear it.'

'I keep counting my blessings,' Holly hastened to explain. Phyllis's generation were so stoic; Holly didn't want her to think that she was a self-indulgent loser. 'I work with children, after all, and that's just a delight. I have wonderful parents and friends. I have this lovely house, I'm healthy…'

Tauntingly healthy. Holly was blessed with a slim but curvy figure, a fast metabolism and had never had so much as a palpitation in her life until last weekend. Once, during a smear test, the nurse had told her that her cervix was the perfect shape for child-bearing. Ironic. She was pretty and the word people most often applied to her was 'glowing'. Ironic again that it should be a word most often applied to pregnant women when Holly's glow would probably never envelop her own little baby. She looked and felt like the picture of health; she could run and dance and touch her toes – but she couldn't do this one thing that she had always taken for granted, that she had always longed for.

'I didn't drift into my job because I couldn't think of anything else to do. I *chose* it. I love children and I'm good at working out what they need, good at making them laugh, good at helping them to learn. Everyone's always said it's my gift in life. I try to tell myself that's enough, but I always wanted my own. It feels so old-fashioned to say that these days. My friends tell me that children are lovely, yes, but they're not the be-all-and-end-all. To me, they are. I saved those books' – she waved at her childhood books on the shelf – 'to share with my own kids. I had so many plans...'

Phyllis nodded. 'It's good to look on the bright side, of course. But you know, Holly, you can't *really* look on the bright side until you've looked the darkness full in the face – and that's not easy to do. I suppose that's what that panic attack of yours was telling you. What you're dealing with isn't an easy thing to come to terms with. Not every woman wants a child, but for those that do, it's such a strong instinct. Not to be able to fulfil it... well, I can't imagine.'

'It's like being forever hungry and not being able to eat.'

'Horrible. I think you had the panic attack because it's the only way you'll come out the other side. By admitting that it really *is* that bad. And once you do, life will start to reassert itself. It always does. It won't be exactly the life you always dreamed of as a younger woman, but it will take another form and you'll be happy in a whole new way, because you'll be stronger.'

Holly felt a shiver, as if something deep inside her recognised the truth of Phyllis's words. 'Since the weekend I've been taking things much slower, thinking a lot. Feeling sadder, and *so* tired, yet somehow better. Everyone's been kind, they really have, but hearing that I can adopt, or that I'll get to keep my figure, or that I should have enough of kids at school doesn't actually help.'

'I can imagine. You know, once you've properly mourned all that you've lost, and you start opening up to a new sort of happiness, you'll see that there are possibilities. You *could* adopt. On your own or with a partner. You might meet someone who's willing to try IVF with you. Or someone who already has children, and you could become a stepmother. But you can't swap one dream for another, just like that. You need time to let go of the old one and then there'll be a period where everything shifts around before you're ready to think about things like that. Meanwhile, just know you're in a strong position. You have a career you love, a good income and a home of your own. Women of my generation hardly ever had that. Those are invaluable treasures, my dear. Well done, you.'

Holly reached out and switched a lamp on, reflecting that Phyllis's words, like the lamp, had shed an extra glow on her situation. She'd been in too much of a rush, she realised, to be brave and cheerful. It wasn't going to be nearly as easy as that. But that didn't mean she couldn't do it.

CHAPTER FIFTEEN

Eliza

It felt like time was whizzing by. At school they were busy working on the scenes for *A Christmas Wish* and Eliza watched with fear and envy as her classmates rehearsed and forgot lines and fell over and laughed. At home, the rooms were steadily taking shape under Aunty Pam's formidable project-management skills. Eliza's room looked like a proper bedroom now, with pretty bedcovers and blankets, a carpet and a lampshade and a mirror. Steaming showers were no longer a forgotten luxury and they could have central heating whenever they wanted it.

Her homework – to make a patchwork angel – was so far just a series of ideas she'd drawn and a pile of old clothes her father had found for her in one of their boxes, but she was going to get started today and if it was too hard, Aunty Pam was going to help her next week.

On Sunday morning, Eliza woke to cold, clear darkness and a feeling of excitement. December wasn't far away now! She scrambled out of bed, pulled on her dressing gown and climbed onto the window seat in her bedroom, where she was greeted by the sight of the first frost, sparkling on the lawn. She gasped with delight. Everything looked so mysterious out there, silent and shadowy and glittering.

Eliza loved this new home, with its creaking beams that talked to her at night and its broad window seats, which meant

that anything she wanted to do could be done curled up next to
a window pane, as if she were floating on a cloud. She said her
daily prayer for a white Christmas. Her breath made a curtain
on the pane and she drew absent-minded shapes on it with her
finger, deep in thought. There was nowhere like a window seat
for sitting and dreaming.

She was trying to come to a decision about something. It
would be a pretty grown-up decision, she thought, even though
she was only eight and three-quarters and the thought of it made
her feel excited but also scared. She hadn't told Daddy yet. Just
in case. She was thinking of telling Miss Hanwell that she would
be in the play. But just thinking about it made her stomach fold
over like a pancake.

When Eliza was younger, she'd been in every concert her school
had ever held. She'd grown up with Mummy playing make-believe
with her, encouraging her to sing, dance and act, and Eliza had
loved it. It didn't frighten her; it just made her happy. When she
was three, she'd been a dolly mixture in the local pantomime – the
youngest person to take part. At four, she had been in two school
plays. At five, she was the head of the caterpillar in the Autumn
Almanac. But since her mother went away, she found the stage a
terrifying place – those big echoing boards and the sea of strange
faces staring up at you, assessing you. Knowing your mother had
left you and moved far away. It was all too easy to imagine people
watching and saying, 'She's not like her mother, is she? She was
so talented and so beautiful. No wonder she left.' During Eliza's
last attempt in Leeds, she had been so scared she was actually
sick onstage during a performance. She had never got over the
shame – and promised herself she would never do it again.

But the pageant was all anybody ever talked about in school.
They had ordinary lessons, of course, but some part of every
day was spent making things for the play, rehearsing bits of it or

learning songs from it. It was impossible not to be infected by it, and Miss Hanwell had the *most* wonderful ideas.

The play she'd written was about two children, a brother and sister, who rescued a reindeer and hid it in their garage. They lived with an unkind uncle who would be very angry so they had to keep it a secret. They were helped by various different angels, and all sorts of magic happened. Miss Hanwell had a friend who provided the animals for local nativity scenes, like at the Christmas tree centre, or the church, and he was going to lend her a real reindeer! That alone made Eliza want to take part. *A real reindeer!*

The first scene was going to be a Christmas tree coming to life. The floor of the stage would be strewn with boughs of fir; fir branches would be hung from the ceiling too. The backdrop would be green, transforming the whole stage into a big Christmas tree. The patchwork angels, as well as the huge paper balls, horns and drums that Eliza and the others were making, would be the decorations for the tree, hung all over the backdrop. There would be little platforms of different heights, painted green so they'd be invisible, for the children to stand on. Dressed as angels and snowmen, they would look like decorations too, hanging in the tree. They would have to stand very, very still, as if they *were* decorations. Then when the music started, they had to climb down slowly and stiffly, as if they were just coming to life.

Eliza thought Miss Hanwell was amazingly clever. It would be more spectacular than anything she had ever done in Leeds. She could just imagine the excited rustle of proud parents in the hall as the curtains drew back on the scene. And what about the gasp of disbelief when the reindeer, who was called Skydancer in the play but whose real name was Bob, walked onto the stage, led by Sophie Lewis, who was playing the little girl? In the end, Eliza's imagination had got the better of her and she'd started to imagine that perhaps she wouldn't be afraid in Miss Hanwell's pageant – that she *had* to take part. And *then* she'd thought how much her father would love it – especially if she was actually in it.

The other reason she wanted to be in the pageant was to do something wonderful for him. He seemed happier now that Aunty Pam was with them, but she knew that Granny and Gramps were still nagging him about Christmas and Eliza really, really didn't want to go. She'd got up for a drink late one night and had overhead him on the phone, arguing. Eliza knew it was wrong to eavesdrop but it was so rare to hear Daddy cross that it gave her a horrible lurch in her tummy and she hadn't been able to stop herself listening.

Her father had been saying that he *could* hold down a job and be a proper dad. Well, *obviously*! At least four of the children in her class lived with only one parent, and one of those was a dad. And three of them – Jinny's mum, Kyle's mum and Grant's dad – all worked full-time. How dare Granny make Daddy worry like that! It was true that when Grant fell off the roof of the school toilet and his dad couldn't be reached, his mum turned up to rush him to hospital. Eliza didn't have that because her mum was so far away and almost never talked to them. But they had Aunty Pam. They had Granny and Gramps. And Eliza wasn't going to fall off a roof – she wasn't that stupid. So they were just making Daddy upset for no good reason.

She was pretty sure that she'd convinced him that home was the best place for them over Christmas. Still, it wouldn't do any harm to show him, once and for all, that she was happy and fine and this new life was doing her the power of good. And to prove it to Granny and Gramps too. If she took part in the pageant, they'd know for sure.

As Eliza gazed into the garden, the sky slowly lightened. Her eyes narrowed. She wiped the mist off the window with her sleeve and sure enough, there was something she hadn't seen before. The grass was pale with frost but there was a delicate line of black running right across the middle of it from the woods to the house, like the beads of a fine jet necklace her mum had owned and left behind. Eliza forgot all about the pageant and decided to investigate – she flew downstairs and through the kitchen, blowing kisses to her dad on the way.

Her father had set out a huge weekend breakfast. Eliza was so excited she wanted to tell him right then that she was going to be in the play. But she didn't want him to be disappointed. She would give herself another few days to think about it. She pulled on her wellies and rushed into the freezing outdoors in just her nightie and dressing gown.

'Er, Eliza!' called her dad behind her. 'Where are you going?'

'Just a second,' she called back, bending over with her hands on her knees like a miniature Sherlock Holmes. Sure enough, the black marks on the lawn were paw prints in the frost. Two sets. Foxes!

Eliza straightened and squinted into the corners of the garden, but they were long gone, vanished into the woodland. They were so secretive and clever. Why didn't they ever let her see them?

CHAPTER SIXTEEN

Holly

There were twenty-two leaves left on the acer tree that Sunday morning. The weather had been soft and steady, with a fair bit of drizzle but no lashing rains or leaf-stripping gales. Colder weather was coming apparently. The weekends were the only time Holly had to check the unrobing of the little tree, since it was dark when she left for school in the mornings and dark when she got home, and she'd forgotten to check it the previous day. She stood at the window, cradling a coffee in her hands and staring at the tree. She couldn't help feeling that it reflected her own shedding – of hopes and dreams and what she'd always thought she'd known about herself.

But for the first time, it didn't feel like a melancholy reflection. Remembering what Phyllis had said and facing the bitter depths of her disappointment, Holly had realised that what she'd been trying to do – put a brave face on, keep her spirits up, focus on the positives – was not what the situation demanded. She'd skipped a step or two in the healing process, and how could that work? She'd gone to bed early every night this week, sleeping from nine till six like a log. She'd never slept so much. Life was reduced to working, eating and sleeping, and somewhere in the simplicity of that, the non-expectation of it, was comfort. She'd cried a lot too.

Now she looked at the tree and thought, *When those last leaves fall, it will be bare and naked, nothing but a scribbled shape against a wintry sky. That's what I'll feel like when I've finally said goodbye to all my old dreams. But that tree is going to come back to life. Leaves will bud and they'll light up the garden with ruby flames again, brand-new leaves every bit as splendid as the old ones that right now are struggling to hold on for dear life.*

Holly wanted to flame and be ruby-bright too. It didn't feel possible right now, but if happiness depended on getting everything you wanted, then no one ever would be, would they? Holly was determined to find a new road to happiness when the time was right.

She turned away from the window. Her guest-room floor was a blitz of tape, ribbons, rolls of paper and gifts. She'd done well in Namaste; who knew that Hopley had such lovely shops? She'd bought a glinting, sugar-white piece of quartz for Penny. Holly knew nothing about crystals but she'd heard Penny talk passionately about their different properties and 'energy matrices'. If nothing else, this piece was completely beautiful so she figured she couldn't go wrong. She'd bought a book about nature for Carla, who was fond of the great outdoors, and pretty crystal bracelets for Izzy and Michelle. She hadn't found anything for Phyllis yet, but it would have to be something special; inspiration was needed. If she'd thought of it, she could have gone to the newsagent and bought boxes of chocolates for her colleagues at work; maybe she'd go after work on Wednesday, which was late-night shopping in Hopley.

Her parents were leaving for India shortly so she'd pulled out all her Christmas things and wrapped and posted their gifts, but she hadn't felt enough Christmas cheer to want to wrap the rest. Normally it was a job she loved, but every year before, she'd daydreamed whilst doing it about a time when she would be packing baby clothes, then toys and stocking fillers for her children. So the job was suspended, the floor a mess, until she could face it. She picked her way between gift boxes, bows and bags of presents and shut the door firmly on the Christmas chaos.

The next morning, before school, she was in her quiet class-room as usual, writing a to-do list, when Eliza walked in. Just the sight of her made Holly smile. Eliza had straight black hair cut in a deep fringe that stopped just above her eyes, which were big, grey and serious. Black eyebrows and lashes gave an uncompromising look to the top half of her face. But a turned-up nose and a pixie chin gave her a dainty, almost otherworldly appearance. Holly loved each and every one of the children in her class, but there was something about Eliza... She felt a tug of recognition every time she saw her, as if they were old souls together. If Holly could have a daughter, she'd want one just like Eliza.

'Hello, Eliza, you're early. What have you got there?' Eliza was toting two large carrier bags, as well as her giant school bag, like a diminutive pack donkey.

'It's for my patchwork angel,' she said, emptying the bags onto the floor. Holly's eyes widened as a fabric rainbow lit up the room. 'Daddy and I went through all our boxes and you said the patchwork should be full of special memories and we found some wonderful things. Shall I explain them to you?'

'Er... yes please.'

'Well,' began Eliza, in a didactic tone, 'this was one of Mummy's dresses but she left it behind and she hasn't come back for it in three years so I don't think she needs it anymore. The material's so pretty it did make me think particularly of angels.' It was a flowing apple-green chiffon evening dress that looked as if it had cost more money than Holly made in a month. Good grief. So her mother was still alive, then.

'Are you sure your father doesn't mind you cutting that up?' she asked, a little faintly. 'It's very beautiful.'

'Oh no, Daddy doesn't want it,' answered Eliza. 'He gave me this too.' Her tone suggested that 'this' was much more important that any silly dress. She pulled out a man's silk shirt, with turquoise and red spirals, silver buttons like soup plates and impressively flared collar and cuffs. 'This was Daddy's dating shirt when he was sixteen,' Eliza explained. 'He was into the sixties, even though it was the nineties. He can't wear it anymore because he got too fat, but when he was young he used to wear it whenever he wanted to impress a special girl. Daddy used to have lots of girlfriends.'

'Gosh, that's nice.' Holly tried not to laugh. If parents only knew what their little darlings innocently said about them at school, they'd never be able to hold their heads up here again. It was the kind of information she had to be determined to forget for parents' evenings or she'd never be able to keep a straight face.

Eliza had brought gleaming rosy-pink ribbons from a pair of outgrown ballet slippers, a soft white lace scarf from which she planned to make the wings and a red velvet doll's dress. 'It was Suki's, but I've lost her. Now I know it doesn't look very shiny,' she admitted, 'but I can put some glitter on when it's finished, can't I? Is it alright to put glitter on patchwork?'

'You can do whatever you want,' Holly assured her. 'Goodness, what a treasure trove. I think your angel will be wonderful, Eliza.'

She couldn't help it – her heart twisted at the thought that someone, somewhere, had walked away from Eliza. What she wouldn't give for a daughter like that: sweet and funny and thoughtful. It was a dream that had faded almost into non-existence. She bent down to help Eliza put all the things back in her bags and wondered if she'd ever feel normal again. There were still leaves left on the tree, she reminded herself. There was more letting go to happen.

CHAPTER SEVENTEEN

Edward

Since Edward had started work, the days were flying by, faster than rockets. November had started with long, dragging days of questions – where should they spend Christmas? Would they find a home help in time? Was he doing the right thing? But now time was passing in a flash and December was almost upon them.

Work was exciting. He'd found out on Monday morning that his team was being given the opportunity to present to a prospective new client – a huge client – just before Christmas. A top-brand cosmetics company were launching a new fragrance – it would be a lot more creative a campaign to work on than bathroom cleaners and mobile phone plans. The biggest opportunity, in fact, that he'd had to do something really ground-breaking in the whole nine years he'd worked in advertising. He'd already had to put in a couple of late nights in the office, and he knew it wasn't ideal. It was what his mother had said from the start, that you couldn't keep a job like that in a box.

But Eliza didn't seem to mind. She and Mrs D were as happy as clams together. Eliza was busy with projects for school so, in the evenings, they sat together in the lounge in front of the crackling fire, Edward with his laptop, Eliza sprawled on the floor with paper and pencils. And glitter. That child loved glitter – he kept finding it everywhere. This morning he'd felt something gritty in his shoe, and when he'd picked it up to investigate, a shower of glitter had poured out all over his trousers. It had taken ages to brush off. And now there was a silvery track in the men's loo at the office. He found it in their hairbrushes, on the sofa and in the toilet. She was a glitter fiend.

This week he couldn't have his Wednesday off. But he was being paid overtime and that was no bad thing; the cosier the house became, the emptier his bank balance. Work was busy. He had lunchtime meetings every day with existing clients, whom he was determined not to alienate in case the fabulous big new deal fell through. Not that it would – Edward had the bit between his teeth – but still he wanted to keep all the balls in the air. He wouldn't get his big break at the expense of long-term, loyal clients.

As well as all this, he'd been helping Anita, the finance director, choose a motorbike for her son; he was going to get seriously spoiled this Christmas to make up for his father having walked out in April. And he was chatting to Dilip, the company's legal adviser, about his mother's wild suggestions – just in case. His parents would never take him to court, he knew that, but his mother was still making pointed comments now and then and he wanted reassurance wherever he could get it. Dilip had worked in family law before he'd turned corporate.

'If every parent who couldn't cook lost their children, Edward, I for one would never see my three. Your mother is an annoyance, nothing worse.'

Edward had felt so much better hearing that.

The result of all this frantic activity was that Edward still hadn't bought Eliza any presents. Lindy, his secretary, and Anna the temp had both offered to shop for him but he was damned if he was going to be the kind of father who let women from the office shop for his daughter. He'd do it all online before it came to that. Already he'd ordered a couple of things he knew she really wanted: a basketball; an ice-cream maker. As if anyone else could possibly guess what kind of quirky, Eliza-type things his daughter would like anyway. So he hastened into Hopley for late-night shopping after work.

It was a crisp, Christmassy evening. Had it suddenly started to feel more festive because it was almost December now, and the weather had grown colder, or was it just that he'd been too preoccupied to notice before? His footsteps rang out on the frosty pavements and the stars glittered above the orangey haze of the street lights. It was also bitingly cold. Over the last couple of days, the temperature had plummeted and sales of hats, gloves and scarves had soared everywhere. Of course, with his endless daily rushing, Edward had brought none of these with him, so Lindy had loaned him her scarf for the evening, which happened to be a long, shocking pink woollen one. He wound it around his neck and ears and sunk his hands deep into his pockets as he jogged from the car park into the town centre.

The constant juggling involved in having a career *and* being a parent made him think of Cressida again. He'd been doing it more and more since his mother had mentioned her the other day. It was funny how things worked out. Cressida had no sooner decided to continue with the pregnancy than she was offered a small part in a British film – a romantic comedy set in the sixties. She'd never done film work before; it was an amazing opportunity. Amazingly, the film schedule had worked: they'd agreed to shoot her scenes before she showed; she was very persuasive. Cressida had been exultant. 'In this day and age, we really can have it all,' she'd said and Edward had hugged her, so proud.

Of course, it hadn't been so easy after Eliza was born. Edward had seen how Cressida had deflated after tasting the one thing she'd wanted all her life. There was no more film set, only life at home with a baby. He'd sympathised. His own dream of going back and finishing vet school had been put on hold indefinitely. The only difference between Edward and Cressida had been that for Edward, Eliza made it all worthwhile.

Now, in Hopley, his breath puffed out in clouds before him and the cold seared his nostrils. A Salvation Army band played carols in the town centre, the familiar refrains gaudy and golden thanks to tuba and trumpet, their message of hope travelling the streets. On a super-fast and inspired shopping spree, he bought several stocking fillers: a set of *Star Trek: The Next Generation* writing paper, a crystal angel for Eliza's bedside, a wildlife calendar and some ridiculous chocolate novelties. He went to a shop which sold children's clothes but became utterly stuck so headed to WH Smith and buried himself in various lavish editions of treasuries, Narnia box sets and pony stories.

'Do you think she'll make it?' asked an amused voice behind him. He turned to see a pretty woman with curly blonde hair; it took him a moment to recognise Eliza's teacher, Miss Hanwell. 'In the pony book,' she continued, laughing. 'Do you think Chloe's going to make it to the gymkhana in time?'

'Oh!' He grinned. 'All I know is that she'd better give that snotty Victoria what for in the egg and spoon race or I shan't be buying any more of these.'

She laughed. 'Impressive. How many fathers know the ins and outs of their daughter's pony stories?'

'Believe me, I know *all* about it,' said Edward, dropping the book into his basket. 'Eliza likes to share with me. Edward Sutton,' he said, holding out his hand. 'It's nice to meet you properly at last instead of quick hellos across the playground.'

'Likewise,' she said, shaking his hand. 'Goodness, your hands are cold.'

'Impromptu shopping trip – not really dressed for it. But I'm so behind with everything this year.'

'It's always chaos for ages after moving house. I moved in March and I'm only just starting to feel organised.'

'Exactly. And I've started a new job too. Chaos doesn't begin to cover it.'

They chatted while Edward queued for his books then wove their way through the throngs of Christmas shoppers to the door. Outside, the cold seeped in through their layers of clothes and Edward unthinkingly wrapped Lindy's scarf once more around his neck. Eliza's teacher burst out laughing. 'Hot pink is definitely your colour, Mr Sutton,' she told him. 'And very in this season.'

'Like I said, ill-prepared,' he told her, feeling embarrassed. 'My secretary lent it to me to save me from dying of frostbite. Look, you're probably busy but if you've got any time, would you like to get a coffee and tell me how Eliza's getting on at school? If it's good news. If it's not, then please will you lie?'

Miss Hanwell smiled. 'I've got some time. Make it hot chocolate and you're on.'

'Great. Let's go.'

As they hurried from the shop to Veronica's café round the corner, Edward, acutely aware of the ridiculous pink scarf he was wearing, hoped he hadn't come across in any way that could be misconstrued. It was surely natural to want the chance to get to know her a bit, given that she was one of the most important people in his daughter's life right now? There were conversations to be had about Eliza, he was sure, and school wasn't the place to have them with so many people always around. But was it OK to notice that Eliza's teacher was really pretty?

CHAPTER EIGHTEEN

Holly

Veronica's café was fuggy and crowded. The air was cinnamon-scented and warm, and Holly had a momentary craving for mulled wine but thought she'd better stick to hot chocolate. She didn't want the first impression she made on the father of adorable Eliza to be of someone who would dive into the alcohol on a moment's acquaintance. Slade were singing that here it was, Merry Christmas, and Holly experienced her usual cocktail of mixed feelings about this year's festive season.

They settled at a table, shedding their coats, bumping chairs against those of the tables next to them, and Edward Sutton wiped his foggy glasses on his secretary's scarf. It felt oddly comfortable, yet Holly felt worried for a moment. Was it alright to go for hot chocolate with a parent? A single parent. A single parent who was really attractive. Was it alright to *notice* that he was really attractive? In the moment, it had felt very right and natural to accept. He was concerned about Eliza – and she was dying of curiosity about her – it made sense. But could her conduct be seen as unprofessional in any way? She hoped not. She would get right to the point, and stay there.

'So Eliza's doing really well at school,' she said as the waitress brought them huge mugs topped with cones of rippling cream, wobbling on saucers brimming with pink and white marshmallows. 'Wow. This is *serious* hot chocolate. She's as bright as a button, as you already know of course, and there are no problems with her tests or lessons whatsoever.'

'That's great news. Thank you. And what about socially? She seems to have made more friends in her first few weeks at Dean Court Primary than she did all last year in Leeds. Does she seem to have settled in well to you? No problems that she's hiding from me?'

'Absolutely no. To start with, she's really hit it off with Fatima Jefferies. I understand you met her parents.'

'Yes, you heard about that?' He picked up two white marshmallows and embedded them in the whipped cream on his drink.

Holly did the same with two pink ones. 'I heard *all* about that. The girls were so excited. They're a talkative pair once they get going. I'm pleased to see it because Eliza was very withdrawn at first. Understandable, being new. Fatima's a lovely girl, one of the nicest temperaments in the class, I'd say. Eliza's come out of her shell steadily. She's also friendly with Jinny Miller and Indira Khan.' Holly took a slurp of sugary cream and wondered how to broach the questions she wanted to ask. 'She's taken a great interest in the Christmas pageant and she's a great help with it; she's very artistic. But she's not taking part – I suppose you know that? Mr Buckthorn did warn me that there was some sort of issue there – he didn't share any details – so I didn't push her at all. I've never seen how that helps children. I hope you think that was right?'

'Entirely right,' he said, nodding and slicing the peak off the cream pyramid with his spoon. 'All I want is for Eliza to be happy. She thinks the world of you – I think it's helped her a lot to have you be so sympathetic and accepting. I really can't thank you enough. She hated school in Leeds – she was so unhappy there – but after just a few weeks with you... an entirely different story.'

Holly smiled. 'I'm glad. But you don't need to thank me. I love my job and Eliza's a joy.' She dug her spoon into her glass mug to try to reach the hot chocolate beneath the creamy canopy. 'Um, if you don't mind me asking, why *was* she so unhappy in school? She's such a lovely, easy-going child – I can't imagine why she'd have had a problem.'

Edward looked down at his hands. 'Um…' He looked so uncomfortable, so different from just a moment ago, that her antennae prickled.

'Don't tell me if you don't want to. Eliza's doing fine now and that's all that really matters. Only, she did mention there was something that the two of you had agreed not to tell anyone and I was just wondering if keeping a secret was the best thing for her.'

'I've been wondering that too lately. Mr Buckthorn knows but we asked him not to pass it on. It was a problem in Leeds, you see, people knowing.'

'I see,' said Holly, who didn't.

'But even after half a hot chocolate with you I can tell it's a different story here. The children too – they seem different from Eliza's old gang. I'll tell you, shall I?'

'If you want to,' said Holly carefully but encouragingly.

'Eliza's problems in school… they were to do with her mother.'

I knew it, thought Holly. What was she? An alcoholic? Abusive? Surely not – she couldn't bear to think of anyone hurting Eliza.

'She left us, three years or so ago, and Eliza's fear of the stage dates from then. Before that, she loved to perform.'

'A bad break-up?' Holly hazarded gently. Had the mother been unfaithful? Had *Edward*? Had Eliza been traumatised by lots of shouting and bitterness? She couldn't picture Edward Sutton in a nasty row but you never did know with people.

He frowned. 'Not really. An *odd* break-up is more like it. It was very quick, but very complete. Very sudden. We asked Mr Buckthorn not to say anything because we wanted Eliza to stay anonymous. In her old school, everyone knew too much.'

Oh God, were they in *witness protection*?

'Because of who her mother is, you see.'

'I see. Well, I don't. Who is she?'

'Cressida Carr.'

Holly burst out laughing and waited for the real story. But Edward had no quirk of humour in his grey eyes. 'Wait, what? *Really?*'

'Really.'

Holly took a moment to digest this. Only a couple of weeks ago she'd been looking at glossy pictures of the Hollywood megastar in *Hey Up* magazine. And now she was sitting here with the man who'd been *married* to her? Which meant that her new pupil, wonderful Eliza with her big, silvery eyes and crow's-wing hair was her *daughter*? Well, *that* explained why she didn't mind leaving that beautiful, expensive green dress behind! 'Really?' she said again. It was all she could manage.

He smiled sadly. 'Yes. And it became an issue in Leeds. Everyone at school gossiping about Eliza. Gossiping and worse – unkind remarks. Coming here has been the best thing, a fresh start. But she is her mother, after all. Eliza shouldn't have to be *afraid* of people knowing.'

'Of course she shouldn't. Poor Eliza. God, why can people be so horrible? So how…? How…? I'm sorry. I'm still too flummoxed to make any sensible comments at the moment. It's very unexpected. Eliza's so down-to-earth and sweet… And her mother's Cressida Carr.'

CHAPTER NINETEEN

Edward

'Of course, she *wasn't* Cressida Carr when we were married,' Edward tried to explain. 'She was just… my wife. She was always an actress, though, and Eliza inherited her love of the stage. The pair of them lit up any time there was an audience, when there was some make-believe to get stuck into…'

Wham! were singing 'Last Christmas', a song that had tortured him the year that Cressida left. Holly was watching him attentively. He was all over the place and needed to start at the beginning. He hadn't talked about any of this to a woman before. Well, he *had*: his mother, his sister-in-law and Mrs D were all women, obviously. But not a woman that – under other circumstances – he would consider very attractive. Beautiful, even, and intelligent and sparkling. Someone he could imagine taking out to dinner, perhaps. Which was hardly the point here. Edward gathered his thoughts and told Holly the whole story.

He described how young and in love he and Cressida had once been, she just an ordinary but very talented girl, dreaming of stardom, and he happy simply to be in her orbit. The unexpected pregnancy, his joy at the prospect of fatherhood. The part in the British film – Holly knew the film, of course.

'It was a different story after Eliza was born,' he said. 'The film hadn't paid much and it wasn't followed up with any more offers. Because I was the one with the steady job in advertising, whereas Cressida had been getting bit parts here and there for years and barely earned enough to cover bills, it made sense for me to be the bread-winner, we both agreed.

'But that put Cressida in the role of full-time parent, and she struggled. From the very start I could see it; it was as if the light in her had gone out. I hated that things had worked out that way – it so often does for women, doesn't it? But she wasn't the one at home because she was a *woman*, it was because her line of work was so capricious. We talked about it often. If she'd had the chance of a well-paid job, I would've stayed home with Eliza without hesitation. For Cressida's sake, obviously, but also for my own. From the word go, I was never happier than when I was with Eliza. Funny how things turn out, isn't it?

'I used to use my annual leave to look after her so Cressida could audition – a half-day here and there. I took a whole week off when she got a role in a commercial. I prayed some satisfying work would come her way, but not much happened for her, and motherhood became more and more the dominant theme in her life.' He sighed. 'It was the one role she didn't ultimately find that interesting. She *loved* Eliza, and she looked after her well, but she wasn't happy and she wasn't really herself. I kept earning the money because it seemed like it would help no one if I quit at that stage.'

He dared a glance at Holly, who was listening intently. Even now it bothered him, how Cressida, who'd had such a cherished dream, had become trapped in domesticity while he, who would have been perfectly happy at home with Eliza, had enjoyed a rewarding and steady career. It was why, whenever he felt bitter about her, the way his mother did, he'd feel an accompanying twinge of guilt. He had loved Cressida, and he could see her fading as she grew more and more cut off from the life she loved. He'd hate it if Eliza's teacher thought he was some sort of oppressive patriarch, but her brown eyes were understanding.

'Of course,' she murmured. 'Then you'd both have been unemployed. No point in that.'

He nodded in relief and went on.

'We ticked along, still hoping that something would happen for Cressida. We were imagining something small but satisfying. In the UK. But out of the blue, five years later, she was contacted by a US talent scout and invited to audition for a Hollywood blockbuster. There was never any doubt that she would go. The trip was arranged and, between me and the two sets of grandparents, childcare was organised. Eliza was beside herself with excitement about her mother's big adventure – she demanded detailed descriptions and photos when her mum returned.'

Holly smiled. 'I can imagine.'

'A week turned into two, then four. Cressida got the job and was needed for at least six months. We made it work. Her phone calls were full of meetings and parties and photo shoots and it really sounded as if opportunity was blossoming for her at every turn. I was happy for her, but I did wonder where it was all leading. Was it the turning point Cressida had always dreamed of? If so, would we all move out to LA? Was it a good place to raise Eliza? I was open to all of it, but it needed a conversation, obviously. I assumed that at some point Cressida would come home and tell me she wanted us to move out there. But I knew how precarious these things are. I didn't want to bug her about all that while she needed to work and focus.'

'Fair enough,' murmured Holly. They ordered more hot chocolate. The waitress brought a saucerful of complimentary shortbread Christmas trees.

'Seven months later, Cressida came home. She showered Eliza with gifts and kisses, and Lizzie was wild with excitement. It was all a fairy tale to her. Then when she was finally asleep, Cressida sat me down with a glass of wine and said she wanted a divorce. No beating about the bush. She had another part in another film, starting straight away. The press had gone crazy for her British elegance and were calling her the new, more fabulous Elizabeth Hurley. She'd met someone. He didn't want kids.'

'Wow,' said Holly. 'God. Wow.'

'Oh yes. She laid it all out. Cressida was always driven, always dynamic – it was one of the things I'd loved about her, except this time her plans didn't include me. She apologised profusely but she said that her whole perfect life was there. That it suited her exactly in every single detail, as if it had been there all along, waiting for her to slot into it.'

Edward fell silent, back there for a moment. He could still remember his state of shock, the intense expression on her face. 'This life… *doesn't* suit me,' Cressida had said. 'I never imagined this would happen when I went to LA. I thought I wouldn't get the part, or that it would be a one-off thing. I never expected this, but there's no way I'm saying no to it.'

'What about Eliza?' Edward had asked, his head swimming.

'She'll stay here with you. Full custody. You're better at all that than I am anyway, and the life out there is no life for a child.'

He had been dizzy with relief. But at the same time… 'Will you see her at all?'

She'd looked confused for the first time and her forehead had crumpled a little bit. 'I would *want* to, of course, but how would we do it? It's so far away. It's not like I can do every other weekend and have her back in time for school on Monday. I don't want to take her away from you for weeks at a time, and she's too little to travel alone.'

'You could come here?'

'But the film schedules are punishing… and I want *more* work, Edward, if I can get it. Perhaps when she's older we can do lunch; I'd like that.'

Back in Veronica's café, across the table from Holly Hanwell, Edward dunked a shortbread Christmas tree into his hot chocolate and brought Holly up to speed with his memories. 'I could see that she wanted a clean break,' he said, remembering the complexity of emotions that had caused in him. 'A new start, with no backward glances and nothing to hold her back from embracing her perfect life.

'So do you *never* hear from her now?'

'Just a phone call now and then. She's always on her way to some *fabulous party, darling.*' He wiggled his fingers into air quotes. 'I don't mind for myself. I'm not trying to do the bravado thing, making out I never really loved her. I did, very much. But we're two very different people now. I mind for Eliza… y'know?'

'Poor Eliza,' Holly sighed. 'No wonder she went off acting.'

'Sorry,' said Edward, 'to unload all of this onto you. It's hard to get my head around sometimes. Hard to manage too, with Eliza.'

'I can imagine. What does she… say about it? Think about it?'

'It's hard to say. I tried to explain that different people have different destinies, you know? So she doesn't feel that it was about *her*, Cressida's leaving. And so that she doesn't hate her mother, because I don't see how that can help. But she was only five when Cressida went and they're big concepts for someone so little. Sometimes when Cressida phones, I can hear tears in her voice. I imagine her looking stunning at some fancy party, champagne making her nostalgic for her old life… Then she'll get called away by a voice in the background. Eliza's always very quiet for a good while afterwards. They don't really have a relationship at all – from being Eliza's full-time person, Cressida vanished overnight.'

'I cannot imagine. I really, really can't. Has Eliza seen her films?'

He nodded. 'All of them. I cover her eyes in the dodgy bits. It's all she has of her mother.'

'And you mentioned that things got messy in school because of who her mother was?'

'Cressida's fame was all new back then. Local girl made good – *huge* news. The story spread around the school and everyone kept asking her about it. As if a five-year-old had any answers. Then the stage fright started, and she couldn't perform anymore, so they all made fun of her. *Eliza Sutton, greasy mutton* was one of the kinder names she was called.'

'Little bastards,' said Holly hotly. 'Sorry, and that's coming from someone whose whole life is children.'

'One of the kids said to her one day, *Your mum's a harlot!* Who knew kids used words like *harlot* anymore? Turns out his father was a professor of literature. Eliza said she wasn't, didn't even know what it meant, poor love. They got into a fight... How messed up is it when a child's defending her mother's honour? Taking her away was the best thing I ever did.'

'No wonder she seems older and wiser than her years.'

Holly looked so troubled that Edward decided he had to switch up the conversation. She genuinely cared about Eliza – anyone could see. He was touched, but he didn't want to bring her down any more. 'Anyway, I've gone on at you long enough. The thing is, we're here now. It's the happiest she's been since her mother left. She was a bit shaken up by the whole pageant thing, but I know you were kind to her about it and she comes home smiling every day. She chatters on about her day, the lessons, her friends... All of which leads me to believe that you, Miss Hanwell, are a miracle worker. You're truly gifted with children.'

'Thank you. And please call me Holly.'

'Do you have any of your own?' He kicked himself when an unreadable expression that was not a happy one crossed her face. Just because he'd poured everything out didn't mean she wanted to.

'No,' she said. 'Cressida Carr...' She changed the subject neatly. 'Who'd have thought it? She's in the UK now, isn't she?'

'Is she? I have no idea.' His stomach lurched. Cressida? After all this time?

'I'm sorry, I shouldn't have said anything. I read an article just recently. But you can't believe everything you read in the magazines.'

'Never a truer word. That's another thing Eliza's had to come to terms with – celebrity gossip mags writing about Cressida and all the various men she's supposedly dated since moving to Hollywood. If it were all true, she wouldn't have much time to make films, I'll tell you that. I've given Eliza a long lecture about the media and all their distortions, half-truths and outright lies… What did you read? I promise you, I couldn't be more out of touch.'

'Just that she'd be in London filming this December. A period drama. But maybe the schedule's changed – I imagine that happens a lot. Surely she'd let you know if she was so close.'

Edward shrugged. 'I'd *hope* so. But honestly, nothing would surprise me anymore.'

CHAPTER TWENTY

Holly

When Holly got home she realised she'd forgotten to buy the damn chocolates *again*! Meeting Edward and learning the Suttons' story at last had put everything else out of her mind. She made pasta for dinner, purely because she wasn't capable of anything that required any thought, then threw herself on the sofa and chewed her meal, staring into space. Goodness.

She couldn't stop thinking about all Edward had told her – the way his face had creased with pain when he talked about what Eliza had gone through. Holly could relate. She felt such fierce protectiveness towards all her pupils, and Eliza was just special. With her own devastating year still clutching her in its tentacles, Holly couldn't imagine having a daughter like Eliza – and walking away. How was it possible to wake each morning and not wonder how Eliza was? How could Cressida bear to end each day without sending her a good night? Or perhaps she did in her heart. However hard it was for Holly to understand Cressida leaving her little girl, everyone was made differently and it really was hard to imagine Cressida *not* being an actress. She was *Cressida Carr*, for goodness' sake! What she had achieved was next to impossible. But at what cost? At long last, Holly understood why Eliza was so bruised beneath all her joie de vivre and energy.

Edward was great. Such a doting father. And he thought that she was gifted with children. If she had a pound for every time she'd heard that…

When he'd asked if she had children, she'd felt it like heartburn. If Holly were ever to fall for someone again – which was completely hypothetical at this point, of course – Edward would be just the sort of man she would want. The moment was like a pre-run of any promising date that lay ahead of her. What would he think if he knew? She couldn't bring herself to tell him her situation right then; it was too scary. Besides, two unburdenings in one evening would have created an intensity that no amount of marshmallows could dissipate.

And she was the professional in the equation, after all. If anything she had done had helped Eliza and made things easier for that little family, then it made her happy. But oh, it was painful to think that she wouldn't have her own child to nurture, that she would always be there for them in the classroom but never at home…

She felt the familiar rising grief, but it didn't overwhelm her the way it had been doing lately. Perhaps it was the thought of Cressida having a daughter like Eliza and still not being happy… well, it just went to show that life was… strange. Unexpected. Complicated.

She'd always thought that once she knew what Eliza's trouble was, she might be able to help somehow. Now that she knew the story, she couldn't imagine what she could possibly do. In the event, she didn't need to.

The following day, when school finished and the children rushed out, Eliza hung back, waiting in the classroom until it was empty, shifting from foot to foot.

'Eliza? Is anything wrong?'

'I wanted to ask you something,' Eliza said, her eyes a feverish blend of excitement and anxiety.

'Fire away.'

'I changed my mind about the pageant!' she said in a rush.

Holly knew what she meant immediately. What had caused this? Had Edward told her that Holly knew about her mother? Was that sufficient to overcome her fears? 'You did? You want to be in it after all? That's wonderful!'

Eliza nodded. 'Yes please. If that's alright – if it's not too late. It's going to be too brilliant to miss it. I want to be in it. Only... I'm still scared.'

'But that's fine. It's normal to be scared. And of course it's alright. I'm so happy, Eliza. Now, what sort of part would you like? Little? Big? Medium?'

Eliza bit her lip and looked agitated.

'How about medium?' suggested Holly. 'How about being one of the angels that help the children?' It was the part she'd had earmarked for her from the beginning.

'But there are five. We already have five angels.'

'We'll have six. I can rewrite it, easy-peasy.'

'I'd like that. But what if I let you down? You know, because of what I told you...'

'You mean the stage fright? Don't worry, darling. I think when the time comes, you'll be just fine – I really do. I really, really think it'll be different here. But when the time comes, if it is too scary and you feel sick or anything like that, we'll switch it back to five angels again. There's no pressure, Eliza. You really can do anything you want to.'

Eliza smiled, a great happy beam that lifted Holly's heart. 'That sounds... amazing. Thank you.'

'What changed your mind, sweetheart?'

'It's because I love the play so much. And I want to be onstage with the reindeer. But it's also to make Daddy happy.'

'Do you think he's not?'

'He's worried about me. And Granny keeps saying she's going to take me away because he's not being a good enough father. But he is, Miss Hanwell. He's the best father there could ever be. She can't take me away from him, can she, Miss Hanwell? I love Granny but not as much as Daddy, and I'm cross with her now for making him unhappy.'

Oh boy. Holly had thought that on top of juggling single parenthood with a new job and a new house, having an ex-wife who was a world-famous movie star was a pretty big load to bear. Now it turned out that wasn't even the extent of Edward's problems. She had a feeling that he probably didn't realise Eliza knew anything about this. If she saw him again, maybe she should mention it.

'No, darling, she can't take you away. You know what grown-ups are like. Sometimes they want to be right so much they say silly things. I'm sure your granny really cares for you and wants the chance to show it, and she's just taking it a little bit too far. You leave your dad to talk to her. That's his job. OK?' Eliza nodded. 'And you still want to be in the play?'

Eliza nodded again. And smiled. And just for that smile, Holly decided to write her a whole little scene with the reindeer.

CHAPTER TWENTY-ONE

Edward

In the woods to the west of Hopley, winter had settled in. Every morning, the sun fought a half-hearted battle with thin sheets of cloud that lay smooth across the sky like ironed cotton. Even when it did break through for a few minutes, the air stayed cold, with frosts and mists that chilled the bones. But it was beautiful – the stark trees, the roll of frosted field, the occasional wash of pale light. Feeling reassured by Dilip, and understood by Holly, Edward had begun to wake up to a sense of pure well-being that had eluded him for a long time.

On Sunday morning, the sun rose in a frosted sky and directed hollow beams at the stiff and creaking undergrowth. Everything was frozen. But Edward and Eliza had an important mission that they would not put off for another week. They were collecting festive greenery for the house. There was a dell they'd passed once or twice on their walks that was thick with holly and ivy. They were going a-foraging.

They donned jumpers, thick coats and wellies and set off after breakfast. Twigs, leaves and bracken snapped and sparkled under their boots as they entered the woodland kingdom, Eliza keeping a weather eye out for foxes. It was as cold as Narnia and very quiet.

'This is the spot,' said Edward when they arrived at the dell, brandishing his knife. 'All the holly you could possibly want.' It was true. Dark green, glossy leaves prickled and shone all about them, a handsome sprinkling of scarlet berries strung through the trees like jewels. You could almost imagine Father Christmas might emerge from the foliage any minute, perhaps with a tame deer eating from his hand. Instead…

'Oh, look at that,' he went on in disgust. 'Someone's thrown a load of old junk here in this lovely spot. A lawnmower, an old climbing frame. I will never understand the arrogance of people treating our wild places like their own personal dumping ground. Apart from anything else, it's dangerous.'

Eliza gravely stepped over to the junk to take a closer look.

'Careful, Lizzie-Socks.'

'Daddy, there's a fox. It's trapped.'

Edward frowned. Surely not. But when he went to stand beside Eliza, he saw, unhappily, that she was right.

The climbing frame had collapsed and was nothing more than a heap of old metal. The fox, a youngster perhaps, was pinned to the ground by a pole that had toppled across it. Its leg was caught on a metal spike, part of the lawnmower probably. Eliza was bending over the fox, her hands on her knees, her breath puffing out in white plumes. When she turned to look at him, her grey eyes were silver with tears. 'Daddy, he's really hurt. It looks horrible.'

Edward couldn't help it; his heart sank. He hated to see animals suffer, and whoever had dumped that rubbish here should be shot. But did the poor creature have to get stuck just when he and Eliza were passing by? Eliza had been obsessed by those foxes from the minute she'd known they were there. He already knew how this was going to go and it really was the last thing he needed.

'Daddy? We have to help him!'

And of course they did. He would starve or bleed to death if they left him there. That wasn't a lesson you wanted to teach your daughter.

'Perhaps we should call the RSPCA and wait with him till they come.'

'No, Daddy! *We* have to help him.'

'But, Eliza, it's not usually a good idea for regular people to take wild animals in. They need very careful handling and expert care. People might want to help and end up doing untold harm.'

'I know. But we're not regular people. You were a vet.'

'I was *almost* a vet.'

'It still means you know what to do. *Please*, Daddy!' The strain in her voice told him how much it meant to her, as if he didn't already know. 'There must be something you can do.'

'Let me have a look, darling.'

He appraised the situation carefully. The fox was shaking, no doubt from fear and pain, and baring his little white teeth. Edward wasn't going to be able to make a judgement about that leg until he got the creature free, and he wasn't going to do *that* while those teeth were snapping at him. 'It's going to be tricky, Eliza. He doesn't know that we want to help him, you see. He'll try to bite us, just to defend himself. Stay well away, you promise?'

Eliza nodded, her eyes wide.

Edward unwound his scarf, a green and black tartan that Cressida had given him years ago, and crept closer, but the fox only snarled louder and tried to back away, making that spike tear at his leg, producing yelps of pain. Taking things slowly was only going to make it worse. 'Eliza, I need your help. The closer we get, the more he's going to struggle, so I have to move fast. I don't want you anywhere near those teeth, so will you please take hold of that spike in his leg when I tell you?'

She nodded.

'And then, when I say so, will you lift it? Not sideways, not straight up, but at this sort of angle.' He gestured. 'Can you show me?'

Eliza mimed pulling the metal at the angle it had pierced the fox's leg.

'Good. I also want you to be careful not to trip in all that rubbish, or hurt yourself. OK?'

'OK, Daddy.'

'So I'll say *one, two, three, pull*, and you pull it, OK?'

She nodded again. Edward stepped forward and deftly wound the scarf around the fox's muzzle to stop it snapping. 'One, two, three, pull!' he counted at the same time and, just as the fox began to writhe in alarm, Eliza took the spike right out of his leg. Edward immediately reached for the cub and lifted it free, holding it tight and getting blood all over his coat.

'Good girl, Lizzie, well done! Now step away from that rubbish and let's get this little guy home. He's far from happy.'

Eliza crept nearer and he could see that she was dying to reach out. 'Don't touch, darling. He might have fleas and he certainly won't be happy being manhandled by two of us. It's for your own good, little guy,' he added to the cub, who looked almost comical with the scarf tied around his jaws – only the look of distress in his yellow eyes marring the picture. Edward could feel his growls vibrating against his chest.

Eliza led the way. As they marched back to the house, Edward ran over his options. He could ring the RSPCA or the local vet… He didn't want Eliza anthropomorphising wild animals or thinking that life among humans was a solution for them. But the fox did need help, and Edward was trained, and such organisations were all-too-often overstretched… Though the last thing they needed was a flea infestation just when they were getting the house sorted – wouldn't his mother have a field day about *that*? They didn't have a shed or garage. Honestly, all that space and not a single outbuilding! It was too cold to leave it outside; not to mention it was too vulnerable while it was injured. No, the house it would have to be and they'd have to take their chances with the fleas. *And* he'd have to try to keep Eliza away from it – he didn't fancy his chances of succeeding at that. He stifled a groan. Just when he'd started to feel more relaxed.

Back at the house they found a huge cardboard box – they had a plethora of them after the arrival of all kinds of household implements – and some old sheets and blankets that Edward had been using to protect the surfaces when he was painting. They made a den for their unexpected houseguest in the box that had contained their dishwasher and put it in the dining room, which they hadn't used as yet.

'No, darling, *not* the lounge. He's not a pet, and if there are fleas, it's better he's not in our living space.'

Eliza fussed. The den had to be near the radiator so that he wouldn't get cold, but not too near so he wouldn't find it stuffy. Should they leave the window open a crack so he could smell the fresh air? Was he hungry? What did he eat? Edward sent her to fetch his old vet box, since he didn't trust her to stay alone with the fox and not try to stroke it. The good thing about being disorganised was that everything was out – nothing was in the attic – and Eliza was soon back with his kit.

As Edward dressed the wound and inspected their visitor more closely, he told Eliza that the fox was indeed a boy and that he was quite young, had probably been born that summer. They gave him dishes of water and milk, and the chicken breasts Edward had been planning to cook that evening.

'At least you don't have to cook for Blackberry,' observed Eliza, 'so you can't mess it up. And we know he likes chicken.'

'Blackberry?' queried Edward, raising his eyebrows. It was of course too much to hope that she wouldn't name him.

By the time Blackberry was fed and watered, he had stopped shivering. When he moved, he whimpered, his leg obviously causing him pain, and he seemed disturbed by his strange new surroundings. Eventually he lay down in his new bed, growling quietly and regarding them with big amber eyes. Eliza couldn't take her own eyes off him. Edward had been vigilant for any tell-tale bumps from fleas while he was dressing the leg but hadn't seen any, and he couldn't see any jumping from the little animal either; he dared to hope they'd been lucky in that regard. He and Eliza sat on the floor quietly, gazing back at their visitor. His coat was a red-brown ruffle, and his heavy tail, tipped with black and white, was curled around himself.

'He's a handsome fellow,' commented Edward.

'He's the handsomest fox there ever was,' sighed Eliza. 'Welcome to Christmas House, Blackberry. I hope you'll be very happy here.'

'*Until* he's all better and can go back to the wild,' Edward reminded her sternly.

'Well *yes*, Daddy. Of course. But not yet.'

CHAPTER TWENTY-TWO

Eliza

Eliza had mixed feelings about going to school on Monday. She really didn't want to leave her fox; she couldn't help thinking of him that way even though her father had told her not to and even though Blackberry himself clearly didn't. She'd crept down to see him after bedtime last night hoping to stroke him – how could anyone resist that fur? But he had snarled and snapped at her, a wild thing, just as her father had said. Even so, he was beautiful, with his pointed little face and bright, bracken coat.

On the other hand, she was longing to continue work on her patchwork angel – *definitely* a Guinevere, she'd decided – and was planning on using long red ribbons for her hair. She was also, she realised in surprise, looking forward to the next rehearsal of the play. This time, Eliza would be in it! Miss Hanwell had been over the moon when Eliza told her. Her face had lit up with the biggest smile; she really was very pretty. Eliza liked making other people happy. She was going to be one of the angels, so not the biggest part, but not a really tiny one either. She swallowed at the thought of it, her tummy turning over in such a way that she couldn't tell whether it was nervousness or thrill.

She hadn't told her father that she'd decided to be in the play because what if she lost her nerve at the last minute? She would never forget the times that she'd frozen onstage in Leeds. Every time she was on the verge of saying something to him, an image would come into her head: herself, standing onstage, opening her mouth and not a single sound coming out. Of laughter and fingers pointing at her and the news somehow reaching her mother in Hollywood, who would wriggle in embarrassment and disown her daughter. No, she didn't want to get Daddy's hopes up and dash them; that would be worse than never being in it at all.

Shaking her head at the messes she got herself into, Eliza went to say goodbye to Blackberry. There were two sets of paw prints on the lawn this morning but she still hadn't seen the other foxes. They came like shadows in the night and melted away like dreams. She had tried staying up to watch for them but fell asleep long before they made their forays into her little world. Her father had told her that adult foxes often lived together in groups. Eliza wondered if, somehow, they knew Blackberry was here, and if they were coming to check on him.

At the end of the day, Eliza raced out of school. Rehearsal had been brilliant. Everyone had been very excited and giggly and kept falling off their platforms, or making up rude words to the songs instead of the real ones, and Eliza felt fine so far. Fats and Jinny were really pleased that Eliza was taking part. Fatima was an angel too so they had some scenes together and Jinny was Nosy Neighbour #2. It had been a good day but she couldn't wait another second to see Blackberry.

Aunty Pam was waiting, as always, and Eliza flung her arms around her. Aunty Pam had that sort of nice round shape that made you want to hug her.

'Aunty Pam, have you met Blackberry? How is he? I can't wait to see him.'

'Who?'

'My fox!'

'Your what, dear?'

'My fox. Didn't Daddy tell you?'

'He never said anything to me about any fox. What on earth are you talking about, Eliza?'

'Haven't you been into the dining room today?'

'No. I didn't need to.'

Eliza couldn't believe her father had forgotten to tell Aunty Pam there was an injured fox in the house. He was so absent-minded sometimes. At least Eliza had fed him before school, so he wouldn't starve. So Eliza told her all about their adventure of yesterday, but Aunty Pam looked *alarmed*. She didn't seem to be as excited about foxes as Eliza was. She'd feel differently when she met Blackberry, though. Who could resist him?

Blackberry was fine. Perhaps the lonely day had made him miss Eliza, because he didn't growl quite as hard when he saw her, even though he whirled into the farthest corner of the dishwasher box as soon as she approached.

Aunty Pam came in behind her and gave a shriek. 'Oh my eye! It really is a fox. Oh my word, a real live fox. Come away, Eliza – we don't want you catching fleas.'

'He doesn't have any. Daddy made sure.'

'But it can't be safe, standing so close to a vermin like that.'

'Blackberry is *not* a vermin! Blackberry is the handsomest fox ever and he's really nice too. Come and see, Aunty Pam.'

'Not me!' She backed away to the door.

'Aunty Pam. He's just a little animal. He's not a… a *Dementor*.'

'To think he's been in here all day and I had no idea! That gives me the creeps, that does. And the *smell*…!' She took a cautious step forward, craning her neck, and wrinkled her nose at the sight of the box. 'I won't be clearing that lot up, I can tell you now.'

Eliza sighed. There *was* rather a smell now she mentioned it. But it wasn't Blackberry's fault; he didn't have anywhere else to go. 'Daddy says I'm not allowed to clean it up in case I get bitten. He says he'll do it each evening after work. But I *wouldn't* get bitten…' She trailed off, well aware that, actually, she might.

'Quite right too. Well, I suppose now you've got a fox you won't be wanting your after-school treat…'

'Oh I do, Aunty Pam, I do. I'm coming! Bye, Blackberry; see you later.'

Her mouth crammed full of home-made flapjack, Eliza saw there was some post for her on the kitchen table and ripped it open. It was a beautiful Christmas card, one of those expensive *For a Darling Daughter* ones you got in places like John Lewis. It had a picture of a little girl kneeling in front of a roaring fire with stockings hanging from the mantelpiece. It was very pretty. It was from her mother.

Merry Christmas, Eliza! Hope you have some fabulous fun. With lots of love, Mummy.

Underneath, she had scribbled a note: *I wonder what play you're in this year and whether you'll have the starring role. Break a leg, darling.*

She'd obviously forgotten that Eliza had stopped acting, even though Eliza knew that her father had told her so. Eliza frowned. It had been so weird when her mother had left. For one thing, she'd been gone so long anyway, though they always thought it was temporary. Then Daddy told her that it wasn't temporary anymore and, in most ways, it didn't make any difference. Except that it gave Eliza a horrible feeling whenever she thought of it, as though she'd missed something she should have done, and then she felt really guilty. Now, the time when her mother had picked her up from school and bandaged her cut knees and washed her hair seemed a really long time ago. Well, it was. Three years.

Eliza knew what her mother looked like. There were loads of photos of her online and in magazines and sometimes she was on TV. But that wasn't like when she'd really been Eliza's mum.

She'd looked a bit the same, but also quite different then. Prettier, less make-up, more huggable.

Eliza put the card on the mantelpiece in the lounge where there were already two or three others. They never did get around to gathering holly and ivy yesterday.

CHAPTER TWENTY-THREE

Edward

When Cressida's card came, Edward was the only one who noticed it had a British stamp and a London postmark. Eliza didn't, thank goodness. Mrs D wouldn't have recognised the handwriting. So Holly was right. Cressida was in the UK –and hadn't thought to let her ex-husband or daughter know. He scratched his nose and pondered. He didn't know what to do. Perhaps she *was* going to make contact. Perhaps she'd only just arrived and she was waiting until things settled down. Or perhaps she was going to spend weeks filming not a hundred miles away and never bother to try to see her only child.

Did he *want* Cressida to see Eliza? More to the point, would Eliza want to see *her*? He had no idea. He wanted to talk to someone but he couldn't think who. His mother was out of the question. Holly sprang to mind, but that was inappropriate. She was Eliza's teacher, not Edward's counsellor. He'd bent her ear more than enough last week. He had friends, but they were up north and he wasn't as close to them as he used to be. Single parenthood had put paid to weekend football and post-match bonding over a beer. The gang in the office were nice enough, but there was no one he knew well enough to talk to about this.

After a run of late nights and working another Wednesday, he left the office early on Thursday. What a bonus; by the time he was nearing home, it was only 4 p.m. He couldn't wait to see Eliza, as always, but then a thought occurred to him. He slowed down and took a left turn, away from the house. That vicar, Reverend Fairfield, was someone he could talk to. He'd never met Eliza, but he had a daughter – hadn't he said that? Eliza and Mrs D weren't expecting him for ages so no one would worry. Maybe the vicar wouldn't be there this late in the day, but it was worth a try.

Edward wasn't sure how to reach the church from the other side and didn't know if there was parking there, so he left the car in a lay-by near the lych-gate. It was just as he'd remembered it, square and stoic, a grid of scaffolding dark against the gathering dusk, a suggestion of something ancient in a town that was otherwise struggling with an identity crisis in the modern world. This time, gardeners were strimming around the gravestones, giving them their last tidy of the winter. The smell of cut grass filled the air, but it was different from summer grass: not so rich and heady; lighter and more reflective.

Edward went into the church. Once again it had an air of calm and a sense of continuity that had been sadly lacking in his life for a good while. The white flowers of his last visit had vanished and someone appeared to be halfway through dressing the pews with evergreen Christmas garlands tied with red ribbon. Crimson poinsettias were massed in stands at intervals along the aisles and there was a well-worn traditional nativity scene in a wood-and-straw stable in a chapel off to the side. *Lucky Joseph*, thought Edward, looking at his serene face. *His wife didn't go to Hollywood. Though he did have other problems.*

There was no sign of the vicar and Edward was bitterly disappointed. He lit a candle, just to say that he needed help, and sat for a while in one of the gleaming pews at the front of the church.

Time passed but no smiling vicar appeared, though he did hear the door creak open. He turned to see two older woman carrying cardboard boxes that, judging by the trailing greenery escaping from them, must have been the rest of the Christmas decorations.

They smiled at him, dumped the boxes and went back out. Perhaps he would take Eliza to church on Sunday. He could catch the vicar then, and they could meet people and Eliza could see the Christmas display. Actually, that would be a really nice thing to do. If they liked it, maybe they could go often. Not slavishly, but often. It might give them that continuity he was craving.

On his way out, he bumped into the women in the doorway, each carrying a fresh tower of boxes. 'Have you got more to bring in? Can I help you?' he asked.

They had three more boxes in the car, which was parked just in front of his, so he brought them in and was showered with thanks. 'Are you new?' the small, snowy-haired one asked.

'Will we see you on Sunday?' the even smaller, iron-grey-haired one asked.

'I am, yes, and I'm thinking of bringing my little girl on Sunday. Actually, ladies, you're not expecting Reverend Fairfield this afternoon, are you? I'd hoped to see him.'

'No, he's usually long gone by this time. But you could always call at the vicarage. He's always happy to see parishioners.'

'Well, I'm not really a… Where is it? Just out of interest.'

'Take that path out of the churchyard,' said Small and Snowy, pointing. 'Turn left, walk for two minutes. Can't miss it.'

They bustled past him into the church and Edward hesitated. He couldn't quite bring himself to call on a near stranger in his home, just because he felt like a chat. On the other hand, it would be easier to talk about Cressida without Eliza around…

As he stood and dithered, his decision-making process slowed by the soporific drone of the strimmers, he heard the click and creak of the lych-gate. A woman came through it and headed off to her left, through the churchyard. And as he narrowed his eyes to watch her, Edward became convinced that this little church really did have a strange magic, because he was pretty sure it was none other than his first choice of confidante, Holly Hanwell.

CHAPTER TWENTY-FOUR

Holly

Holly had always meant to visit the little Norman church on the road between her house and Hopley. It was one of those things that would pop into her mind at completely inconvenient times, like the middle of the working day, but she never remembered when she had free time. Today she'd been reminded of it by Eliza telling her the story of how they'd found 'Aunty Pam', the woman who looked after her till her dad came home: the vicar had recommended her. Holly decided to go today, while it was fresh in her mind, before it got completely dark. She and Alex had never gone to church, but Holly used to go once in a while in Cornwall with her parents. If she got a good feeling about it, maybe she'd start going here; it would give her something to do on a Sunday.

When she got there, a heavy dusk was already settling about her, sinking into the folds and corners of the place. The atmosphere was still and serene, even though the air buzzed with the sound of strimmers hastening to beat nightfall. It was late in the year for that. Surely the last cut of 2017. She would do a quick circuit of the churchyard while there was still light to see by then pop inside. Hopley was a funny mixture, with its pound stores and tacky pubs mixed with some real treasures of shops, a large library and this beautiful church.

Around the back of the church, she passed a kissing couple. She smiled and hurried by. He was tall and lanky with wild black hair; she was curvy with long chestnut hair and steamed-up glasses. A fairly new relationship, Holly reckoned, if that kiss was anything to go by. And suddenly, the impossible happened: Holly wished that *she* could feel like that again. How amazing! Holly hadn't once been tempted to date or daydream since she and Alex had broken up. Given the complexities of her situation, she'd wondered if she ever would. It had been a long time since she'd experienced that first heady rush of love. She had loved the stability and continuity that she and Alex had shared, but seeing as she *had* been cast aside, she may as well look forward to the return of passion. There had to be *something* good about her situation.

Unexpectedly, Edward Sutton jumped into her head. But that was surely only because she'd been talking with Eliza about him earlier. The poor man. He'd obviously been at his wits' end to pour his heart out to her last week. He must be lonely – he was new here after all. And not just lonely but overwhelmed as well: she'd also learned from Eliza this week that on top of everything else, he'd rescued a fox!

Eliza's eyes had been brighter than ever on Monday.

'The weekend was brilliant! We found a fox!'

'You found a…'

'A fox. It was injured in the woods. We took it home and we're looking after it, because Daddy used to be almost a vet. He says I'm not to start thinking of it as a pet because it's a wild creature and belongs in the woods, but I've given him a name because I can't just call him Fox, can I, while he's staying with us? I've called him Blackberry, because he's got this lovely purply-black on his nose and his tail.'

So now, on top of a new job, a demanding mother, Christmas and a new house, Edward Sutton was nursing a wounded fox too. Not to mention cleaning up after it. The man had his work cut out.

'Hello,' said a voice behind her. She turned round and who should be hurrying over the grassy tussocks towards her? Edward

Sutton, dressed more appropriately for the weather this time, in a smart winter coat and a sensible navy scarf.

'*How* weird,' she said. 'I was just thinking about you.' Oh God, like *that* couldn't be misconstrued. 'I mean,' she added, recovering from the uncanniness of it, 'I was talking to Eliza earlier. She told me about the fox. I was just thinking how much you've got on your plate at the moment.'

'Tell me about it,' he said with feeling. 'And how are you?'

'I'm good,' said Holly, and for once she didn't feel she was putting on a brave face. 'Work is amazing, as always, and the rest of it's getting better too.' His questioning expression reminded her that he didn't know the first thing about her. 'I've been trying to get my head around Christmas alone,' she explained, because that was the thinnest end of the wedge. 'Everyone's away this December. But honestly, I'm too old to be a baby about it.' She scuffed her toe against the base of a lichen-spattered gravestone and looked up at Edward with a wry smile.

'Well, no one really wants to spend Christmas alone,' he said, 'unless they hate everyone they know, of course, and then they've got bigger problems than Christmas. But I'm glad you're feeling OK about it.'

'I am. Oh, I hope you don't mind me saying this to you – I don't want to overstep – but Eliza said something to me the other day and I thought maybe I should mention it to you if I saw you again.'

'Oh God. What?'

A parade of jackdaws flew overhead, straight and serious, making for home as dusk drew in and the evening grew colder. 'Nothing awful. But something about your mother wanting Eliza to go and live with her?'

'How on earth does she know about that?'

'No idea. But you know kids. They seem to pick up everything you don't want them to. Osmosis, I believe.'

Edward sighed. 'She must have overheard something. There've been a few rather fraught phone calls lately. My parents seem to think Eliza would be better off with them because I'm single and I've bitten off more than I can chew with the house. It's nonsense, of course; my mother's just getting carried away. She means well, but it still infuriates me. It's hard not to feel insulted.'

'I understand. It's a stress you don't need. You want your loved ones to support you when you go through tough times, not pull the rug from under you. Of course, it doesn't always work out that way,' she concluded.

The strimmers grew louder as the gardeners worked their way nearer and the dusky air was filled with flying bits of grass.

'Look, am I holding you up?' asked Edward. 'I commandeered your time last week and I don't want to do it again. You look as if you're on your way to visit a gravestone, perhaps.'

'Oh no, nothing like that. I just finally got around to having a look at this place after living in Hopley for nine months. It has a wonderful atmosphere, doesn't it? If you want to talk, I've plenty of time.'

'Actually, I finished work early today so no one's expecting me. I don't suppose you fancy a hot chocolate rematch? I think I definitely won last time.'

Holly arched her eyebrows. 'I wasn't aware it was a competition. But I rarely say no to hot chocolate.'

They drove in tandem the mile into town and met up again at Veronica's. Garlands of plastic holly were now festooning the ceiling. There was only an hour till the café closed but even so, all Holly could think was how nice it was to have something sociable to do of an evening. By the time she got home, instead of just working in her empty classroom, she would have done something fun and had some conversation. She would invite Phyllis over one evening, she decided. Cook dinner, say thank you.

A young man in a Santa hat came to take their order. Holly threw caution to the wind and ordered a mulled wine.

'Good choice,' said Edward when it arrived in a sizeable china mug.

'It's my favourite,' she admitted, wrapping her hands around it and taking a deep inhalation of the sweet-spicy steam. 'Christmas in a mug.'

'So how come everyone's out of town this Christmas?' Edward asked. 'You listened to me for hours last week so it's your turn today.'

Quickly Holly filled him in on her parents' holiday, Carla's Paris trip and Izzy's new love. 'And my partner of ten years broke up with me last January,' she added, aiming to sound matter-of-fact about it. 'So there isn't that anymore.'

'I'm sorry,' he said. 'That's hard, and crap timing for the others to be away. But I understand reflection is good for the soul… that or it'll drive you completely mad.'

Holly laughed. 'Weirdly enough, I'm finding it *is* good for the soul. Alex disappearing like that has made me think about a lot of things.' Then she changed the subject because she didn't want to have a conversation about her uterus with the father of one of her pupils. 'How's the new job going?'

He told her about a client bid he was in the middle of. A big break for him, if it came off. Maybe a promotion, already. The chance to work on a really glamorous campaign. He deserved it, after everything.

'I hope you get it,' she said. 'I'm certain you will. You sound so busy. I'm really sorry the school's landed you with *another* job to do with the costume for the play. We don't like prevailing on the parents, but we just don't have the resources to make sixty-odd costumes as well as sorting out everything else. If I can help at all, I'd be glad to.'

'What play?' asked Edward.

'The Christmas play. For the pageant? *A Christmas Wish*,' she prompted, waiting for him to slap his forehead and say *Oh of course, silly me*, or something similar.

Instead, his expression remained blank. 'Eliza's not in the play.'

'Er, yes she is.'

He looked at her quizzically. '*No*. She's too scared, remember? We talked about it last time.'

'Of course. But she's changed her mind. I assumed you knew? The day after you and I spoke last week, she came to me and said she wanted to take part. I thought you'd told her about our conversation and maybe that's what made the difference.'

'No! I mean, I did tell her I'd seen you and she was glad that you know about her mum now. But she hasn't said a word about being in the play.'

'She's an angel. In the play, I mean.'

'Seriously? But why hasn't she told me?'

Holly shrugged. 'Maybe she wants it to be a surprise. She did say she wanted to prove to you that she's all better now. That's when she told me about her grandparents wanting to take her in.'

'Oh God, the things she carries on those tiny little shoulders. Typical Eliza, wanting to make everything right.' He smiled. 'She must be feeling so much better. That's a testament to you, you know. You're amazing.' Then his face clouded again. 'I hope you're right that she wants to surprise me. What if it's because she's afraid she might lose her nerve and back out?'

'Surely not.'

Holly's heart sank. It wasn't that it would inconvenience *her* – working with large numbers of small children, she was used to things going wrong at the last minute on a regular basis. Stage fright, sudden vomiting, tears and tantrums… she was a genius at pulling together a cast to cover holes. It was just that Eliza was so good in the play, and seemed so happy to be part of it.

'She lights up when we rehearse. She seems to have forgotten all her fears. You should see her, Edward – she's absolutely radiant… What? What's wrong?'

Edward paled. Just at that moment a plastic garland fell from the ceiling and landed across their table. He didn't even flinch. 'Wait,' he said. 'Did you say something about a *costume*?'

CHAPTER TWENTY-FIVE

Edward

'I can help you,' said Holly, searching through her bag, looking very flustered, while Edward sat silently, feeling slightly stunned. 'I feel awful. So much on your plate and now this. You've had so little notice. Ah here it is, here's the letter. You should have had it, well, last week.' She held out a sheet of paper.

'No, no,' said Edward, taking it, feeling as if he were moving through thick soup. 'I absolutely won't be that dad who's afraid of a bit of sewing. I'd hate for someone else to make Lizzie's costume. It can't be that hard, surely?'

Holly looked at him doubtfully. 'Lots of mums freak out about costume making too, you know. I'd be happy to help.'

He shook his head absently as he scanned the letter. *A Christmas Wish… Eliza Sutton… Angel of Starlight… long white dress…*

Then he saw the date of the pageant. 'Oh shit.' Forgetting for a minute that he wasn't alone, he banged his head among the crockery on the table. Several heads turned in his direction – he saw them in the periphery of his vision. Then he remembered Holly and sat up, noticing her alarmed expression. The end of his scarf was trailing through a spill of chocolate. Even now he felt glad that it wasn't Lindy's hot pink one today but a manly navy one.

'Mr Sutton? Edward?' Holly murmured, fishing the scarf out of the puddle and squeezing it back into his empty mug. 'Are you alright? What's the matter?'

'It's on the twentieth.'

'Yes.'

'The presentation at work is on the twentieth. Normally I'd be off, as it's a Wednesday, but that was the only day the clients could do.'

'Oh,' said Holly. 'Bugger.'

There didn't seem to be much else to say. Edward's head was spinning. On the one hand was the presentation – his big opportunity, his defining moment at his new job – which he needed, of course, to pay the mortgage and the bills and everything that held his and Eliza's lovely life together. On the other, there was his emotionally scarred daughter finally, three years after her mother walked out, deciding to try once again, a seminal moment in her young life.

'OK, keep calm,' Edward muttered. 'What time is the play?'

'Six.'

'The presentation's at four. No way I can make it back in time. OK. Think… think… I'll change it. I'll get them to change it.'

'Can you do that?'

Edward looked at her desperately. He was the new guy. He was supposed to be proving himself, doing whatever it took, not making waves. To change the time of the presentation would mean the whole team would be affected and the whole of the client's team too. Could that many people reschedule, just for him? But it wasn't for him, it was for Eliza. And it was his job to move heaven and earth for her. 'I'll have to.'

He glanced at his watch. 'I'd better go, Holly. I need to get home and start figuring out what to say, how to sell a change of timing to everyone. I'll get right on it in the morning.'

'Sure thing. Good luck. Look, about the costume…'

'No. Thank you so much, it's amazing of you to offer, but I want to do it. Her mother used to make all her costumes… I have to try.'

'OK. Well, let me know how you get on. I'll be wondering. Will you tell Eliza that you know?'

He thought about it then shook his head. 'No. I don't want to put pressure on her. If she doesn't want to tell me for *whatever* reason, I'd rather let her handle it her way, I think…'

Holly nodded. 'OK. I know not to say anything. Well, good luck. Again.'

'Thank you. I'll need it. And thanks for the company – again.'

'You too. Oh no, it's my turn this time.' She stopped him as he reached for his wallet and put some money on the table. She looked very determined so he thanked her, then they hurried out to their respective cars, their respective evenings.

As he drove home, his phone rang. His parents' number. He groaned. He thought about not answering but noticed a convenient lay-by just ahead so he pulled in and picked up.

'Hello, Mum.' He could hear the weariness in his voice.

'Edward? It's your father.'

'Dad? What's up? Everything OK?' His father was not fond of the phone. His mother was always the frontman of their duo.

'Not so great, Edward. Your mother's in hospital. Now you mustn't worry, but she had a little fall…'

For the second time that day, Edward's head spun. He gripped the steering wheel with his spare hand and leaned his head back against the headrest to ground himself.

'A fall, Dad? Where? How bad?'

'Down the stairs, son. At home. It was a nasty tumble. Scared the life out of me if I'm honest. But you know your mother – tough as nails. No serious damage done, thank God, but her leg is broken or sprained, we're not sure yet. She'll be less than able-bodied for a while – you can imagine how she's taking that. I'm at the hospital now. I'll ring again when I know more.'

'Which hospital, Dad? I'm coming now.'

Feeling sick to his stomach, Edward set off again, turning the car and heading out of Hopley the way he'd just come. That note in his father's voice, of plaintive fear, was hard to hear. It didn't matter how old or tough you were, having a fright about someone you loved made you feel like a small child again. And for a son, even a grown-up one with a child of his own, to hear his father sound that way shook the foundations of everything. His mother in hospital. For God's sake, what next? His mother was usually the biggest pain in his neck in any given moment. But she was his *mother* – as eternal and fundamental as the sun.

As he drove, it occurred to him that he hadn't thought to ask *why* she fell. Was it simply mechanical – a trip or stumble? Or had she had a dizzy spell, which would be far more worrying? He inhaled deeply and blew out a long breath to try to steady himself. His parents were too young to start deteriorating. As much as they drove him nuts, he couldn't imagine life without them there in the background, too nosy for their own good and trying – unsuccessfully – to pull all the strings.

At the hospital, he trekked along miles of corridor until he found the ward that his father had named. It was a large, open ward, the glare of hospital lighting and the blare of television not softened by the rats' tails of tinsel that hung in loops from the ceiling. And that hospital smell… A mix of meaty food, antiseptic and fear. Bracing himself, he hurried in and spotted his father at once, wearing his pale blue golfing sweater with lemon diamonds on it, sitting beside a bed. And in the bed, that small figure, was that his *mother*?

'Edward?' she said, appearing equally astonished by his appearance. 'You came!'

'How are you, Mum?' Edward bent to kiss her cheek then clapped his dad on the shoulder. 'OK, Dad?'

'Yes, lad, I'm alright.'

'I'm fine, darling, just fine,' said his mother. 'Except that I've broken this silly ankle, so they say I'll be in a cast for weeks. I'll have *crutches*, for heaven's sake. And no contact sports, they were careful to tell me.' She laughed scornfully and Edward felt relieved that she hadn't lost her acerbic view of everyone else's stupidity.

'You'll have to skip that basketball tournament then,' he said with a smile. 'Well thank goodness that's all. You've been lucky, Mum.'

'Oh yes, best thing that's happened to me all year.'

Edward rolled his eyes. 'No concussion, I mean. I'm assuming that's right? No broken ribs, or spine?'

'No, none of that. Some nasty bruising. Nothing else. You're right, of course – it could have been worse. But it's still the most terrible *inconvenience*. Right before Christmas! And they won't even let me out of here. They say a fall like that is a trauma and they want to keep me in for a couple of days for observation.'

'Well, I should hope so! Of course it's a trauma. Was it the whole flight of stairs, top to bottom?'

His mother nodded and actually looked proud. His father looked slightly sick.

'But *how* did it happen?' demanded Edward.

His mother looked shifty.

'She was up a bloody ladder, wasn't she?' his father burst out.

Edward frowned. 'A ladder? At the top of the stairs? *Why?*'

'I was dusting the pelmets, if you must know.'

Edward looked at her. 'You were dusting the pelmets.'

'Yes! Christmas is coming and I'm going to have a houseful. Not *you*, obviously. There was dust inside the pelmets. Thick dust.'

'You're nearly seventy and you climbed a ladder at the top of a flight of stairs to clear some dust that no one will ever, ever see?'

'Don't say it like that, Edward. I have standards, you know.'

'Yeah, and you have a broken ankle.'

His mother tutted.

'He has a point, Sarah,' said Edward's father.

'Oh not you too, Derek. Go and get me a cup of tea, would you?'

His father stood and stretched. 'Want anything, son?'

'Apart from a sane mother? No thanks, Dad.'

His father ambled out, muttering something that sounded like, 'Can't help you there.'

'Don't start,' warned his mother when they were alone. 'I won't do it again, alright? I must admit it was… quite a tumble. A nasty shock.'

'OK,' said Edward. A big admission for Sarah Sutton. She subsided in the bed and he wondered how she could look so different from the last time he'd seen her. She hadn't shrunk or lost weight – she wasn't ill, thank goodness – yet she looked vulnerable somehow, a completely new look for her. It was the papery hospital gown and the look of fear in her eyes – the same fear that he'd heard in his father's voice on the phone.

'Dad seems better than he sounded on the phone. He sounded really scared.'

'He was. I've never seen him like that. I felt bad.'

'I bet. But it'll be OK, Mum. A couple of days here, then home and you'll have to take it easy for a bit. Nothing wrong with that.'

'Nothing wrong…? Edward, I can't be laid up for Christmas! Who'll cook the dinner? I've got Adam and Julie coming to stay for four nights with the children. I've got all the neighbours in for drinks on Christmas Eve and Boxing Day. I still haven't dusted the landing lights.'

'It's true that everyone will inspect the lights very closely. And write a report for the local council.'

'Sarcasm isn't becoming, Edward.'

He raised his eyebrows but said nothing. 'Mum, those things don't really matter, you know. Especially not in comparison with your health. Adam can cook the dinner – you know he's a dab hand at a roast. And the neighbours can spoil *you* for a change. Or you can cancel the whole lot and you and Dad can come to me and Eliza instead. Mrs Dixon's sorting us out with a dinner – you wouldn't starve.'

She gave a wan smile and shook her head. 'No thanks, darling. Not this year anyway. I think I'll be better off at home with everything familiar around me. You know… if Eliza was living with us…'

'Oh, Mum! Not this again.'

'No, hear me out. I was going to say, if you'd listened to me and she was living with us, I wouldn't be able to look after her the way I kept saying I would, would I? We'd be stuck. Your father has the domestic skills of a rhino. I mean, the man can't boil an egg. What would happen to Eliza then? They say pride goes before a fall – well, I had quite the fall. I'm not invincible after all, it turns out.'

Edward took her hand. 'No one is, Mum. But thanks for saying that. If you need anything when you get home, let me know. And whether you're on crutches or in a whole-body cast, I need you to be well rested and hobbling about by the twentieth.'

'That's the date of your presentation, isn't it? Do you need me to babysit?'

'No, I want you to come to the school play. It's on the same day and guess what? Eliza's taking part. She's going to be the Angel of Starlight. And we really want you to be there.'

CHAPTER TWENTY-SIX

Holly

There was another maths test on Friday and Evie Greavey cheated again. It was one of the many things that Holly pondered throughout that weekend. She'd made a tradition of a Monday morning discussion slot – a chance to debate or process anything the children might need to, whether difficult or just interesting. The subjects ranged from current affairs to school news to family concerns to the big themes of life (equality, self-esteem, chewing gum). The children would all get comfortable, curling up on their chairs like cats, chin in hand, or leaning their whole arms on the big white tables they sat around, some of them even sitting sensibly the usual way. Holly liked to think the classroom, with its creaking pipes and high Victorian ceiling and dust motes circling in sunbeams, provided a safe space for them to talk about anything and everything.

On Monday, Holly asked the children to come up with the first three words that came to mind when they thought of school and learning. (Jason Tillwell: *Boring. Torture. But Miss Hanwell rocks.* Holly laughed and gave him a special exemption for his extra words seeing as they were so patently true.)

Then she asked them each to come up with the *one* word they most closely associated with their three main subjects – maths, English and creative studies (which encompassed art, music and drama). She went round the whole class, making it casual and fun. When it came to maths, there were a lot of 'borings' and 'hards'. Indira's word was 'beautiful' and Eliza's was 'rewarding'. Matt Simmons described it as 'eye-stabby'.

'Remember and use that gift with words the next time you write a story!' said Holly at once.

And poor Evie, quite forgetting that they were only doing one word for maths, said, 'Success. Clever. Key.'

Of course. Evie's father was a city banker and her mother was the finance manager of a care home. Evie's older brother had achieved ten As in his GCSEs. Her sister was trying for Oxford. Hers was a very driven family. Very *rich*. Holly's guess was that money was the Great Oz in that household, and if Evie was struggling, it could well be an issue. But she couldn't just assume...

At lunchtime she asked Evie to stay behind and asked her straight out about the cheating. Evie looked mortified and scared and tried to deny it, but Holly had seen her twice with her own eyes and said so. 'I'm not angry, Evie; I just need to know why you did it.'

And sure enough, Evie felt like the dunce of a very bright family. She couldn't understand maths and didn't really enjoy it but, because her parents and siblings adored numbers, she pretended to fit in. She was worried that if she didn't do as well in school as her brother and sister, her parents would be angry and disappointed.

'Have they specifically said to you that you must follow in the others' footsteps?' asked Holly.

Evie shook her head. 'But only because I've never told them I don't want to. Because it's all they talk about all the time – what their friends at work are earning, what jobs Jeff and Callie will get with their grades and how much money they're going to make... but I don't think I can do that.' Her little face looked utterly woebegone.

Ghastly people, thought Holly. 'I can understand why all that would make you worry,' she said. 'But you should try really hard to stop, Evie. For one thing, you're a *lot* younger than your brother and sister so you've got a long time before you need to worry about grades and university and jobs. Years. For another thing, secondary school is really different from primary school, and you might find that you're better at some things than you thought and worse at others. You really can't tell yet. Even if maths *isn't* your best subject, there are plenty of ways to be successful and happy. But you don't need to think about any of that yet – you're only eight! You just need to enjoy school as much as you can, and if you don't understand something, you ask me and I'll help you, alright?'

Already she knew what next Monday's discussion topic would be. Success. She would get them all to talk about different successful people they knew or admired and what different kinds of success there were… That way, even if Evie's parents *were* demanding, Evie would know that other people, outside the family, thought differently. It might help, a little.

'What do *you* like, Evie? What do you think you're really good at?' she asked. It was the sort of thing she could have told you about ninety per cent of her pupils, but Evie was one of those quiet kids who didn't seem to have much colour about them, or put herself forward. Easy to overlook, if truth be told.

Evie flushed. 'Oh, nothing, it's stupid.'

'Please tell me. Nothing's stupid if it makes you happy.'

'But you can't make a living out of it, my dad says.'

'Maybe that's true. But you're still allowed to like it. That's why people have hobbies. Like, I'm a teacher, but my hobbies are writing plays and going for walks and cookery. I'll never make money out of those things, but I love them, and I think doing them makes me better at my job.'

Evie frowned, ruminating. Holly loved the moments when she helped one of the children see life just a little bit differently. 'Do you like music?' Evie asked after a long pause.

'Music? I love it! I have music playing all the time when I'm cooking. Do you?'

Evie nodded. Her hair, mousy-brown and wavy, fell over her face, which was turning slowly red. 'The thing I'm good at? It's singing. But you can't make a living from it.'

Holly laughed. 'I bet Beyoncé would beg to differ. But that's wonderful, Evie. I can't believe I didn't know that about you. What do you like to sing?'

Evie's little face flamed acer-leaf bright. 'Pop,' she said in a small voice.

'Amazing. What's your favourite song to sing?'

'I like Camila Cabello and Taylor Swift. And Luis Fonsi.'

'"Despacito"?'

Evie nodded eagerly. Holly had never seen this child so animated. She began to sing – badly – the chorus of 'Despacito' and when Evie joined in, Holly stopped. 'Oh please sing more,' she said, when Evie reached the end of the chorus. 'Do you know the rest?'

Evie looked at her with an expression that seemed to say, 'Duh!' She took a step back, drew in a deep breath and sang the whole song right through – Spanish pronunciation *perfecto*. Her voice was as sweet and clear as a bell. It had some power too.

'Oh my God,' said Holly when she'd finished, clapping madly. 'Evie, you're amazing! Your voice is just beautiful. You're right, that's definitely something you're good at.' The poor kid was beaming – she looked like a different child. You couldn't overlook her now. 'How do you feel about singing in public?' asked Holly. 'Would you enjoy it or do you think you'd be scared?'

'I'd enjoy it,' said Evie without hesitation. 'I mean, I've never done it, so I don't know, but I think so.'

'Want to sing a solo in the Christmas pageant?'

'Really? You'd let me?'

'Are you *kidding*? Everyone would go crazy for it. No pressure, though.'

'No, I'd like to, I would. But how will you put another song in our story? Isn't it already full?'

'Oh that's easy.' Holly's mind was already whizzing. Her greatest genius, if she did say so herself, was adapting her plays as the weeks went by to highlight little things that were tailor-made for the individual children. For instance, when Griff Heaton had demonstrated why they should have an alien space monster in the play, his performance had been so cryingly hilarious that she'd written in a cameo for him that very evening. It might even be the best bit of the play. Squeezing in a song for Evie would be a piece of cake. Or maybe she could be an entr'acte between parts; then they wouldn't be limited to Christmas songs. She was sure Mr Buckthorn would agree. 'Leave that to me, Evie. Are you willing to sing something this afternoon in the rehearsal to practise singing in front of the others?'

Evie's eyes shone. 'Absolutely!'

So there we have it, thought Holly. *Evie Greavey is a star. She's just been waiting and waiting for her chance to shine. If she sings like that in the pageant and her parents see it, that should give them a clue that she might be cut from a different cloth than the rest of them.*

The class had its first start-to-finish run-through of the play that afternoon. Six children forgot their lines, blanking completely, and several more got mixed up and said everything in the wrong order. The Simmons boys insisted on singing the rude versions of the song words, and despite everyone else's best efforts to drown them out, they *were* audible. Because they had no reindeer, when the time came for Fatima to lead Bob/Skydancer onstage, Vicky stood in and tied Fatima's scarf around her own neck to act as a lead rope. Vicky's performance as Skydancer involved a lot of theatrical mooing, which Holly sincerely hoped wouldn't feature in Bob's performance. Then, when Vicky tried to take the scarf off to revert to her usual character of Nosy Neighbour #1, she couldn't undo the knot. Neither could anyone else, and for a while it seemed that Vicky would have to spend the rest of her life in a lead rope, or that Fatima's lovely scarf would have to be hacked off with scissors. But eventually Holly managed to work the knot free and the crisis was averted.

Despite all this, she could see the pattern of it taking shape. It was only very roughly staged – she'd have to talk to the other teachers and draw up a schedule to practise on the stage in the assembly hall – but it was joyful and it was obvious the children loved it. The story worked well – just the right length and the right amount of sweet and funny. And now that Eliza was in it, and Evie was going to be singing, it had a real sprinkle of star magic too. Evie's talent was beyond belief, Holly thought as she listened to her sing for a second time, her classmates' faces all agog and disbelieving. And Eliza, well, you could see that acting ran through her veins. It was there in the way she carried herself, the way she moved. It shone through her expressive face, which conveyed everything that she, as the Angel of Starlight, was thinking and feeling. The children were all fantastic, but Eliza made you believe the whole thing.

Once again Holly felt a pang of something deeper than teacherly affection for Eliza, accompanied by a random, wistful thought about Eliza's kind, stressed, good-looking father. Once again Holly remembered with a jolt that Eliza's mum was Cressida Carr, and wondered how she could ever have borne to leave Eliza and miss out on all this. Holly had gone to drama school herself. It was inevitable, since it was the only subject she'd had any interest in back then. She'd found the theatre thrilling and did amazingly well at college, since there was no module that didn't fascinate her. While some students shone in particular roles – comedy, musical theatre, Shakespeare – Holly aced everything, even stage management and writing. She'd had some great reviews in student productions, and won several parts afterwards. Everyone thought she would be an actress.

When a school friend had gone into teacher training, Holly had found herself intrigued by her anecdotes. Because acting was so unpredictable, she'd done the same training to have a back-up and quickly learned that she loved working with children even more than she loved the world of drama. This bringing together of both worlds, her two great loves, was perfection. Teaching primary-age children might not be as glamorous as a Hollywood career, but for Holly it was the heart and soul of things.

A whole little person, each and every child. With histories, already, and futures, please God, and potential as vast as outer space. More sparks than a Catherine wheel. And Holly would never have her own. Even amidst the mirth and excitement, she felt it as a kick to the gut. Her hand drifted involuntarily to her stomach. If she adopted or anything else, she still wouldn't feel her body change and swell, share her own self with her own little baby and go through that most extraordinary journey with him or her.

There were fourteen leaves left on her acer tree. She'd counted them on Saturday morning, hands wrapped around a mug of coffee while the house warmed up around her. And she was still clinging to this dream of carrying a child. But if it *couldn't* come true, she could still keep bringing this much happiness to twenty-five children every year. And that wasn't such a bad life, was it?

CHAPTER TWENTY-SEVEN

Edward

Edward had been thinking a lot about Cressida lately. He hadn't heard from her and he'd decided it was probably for the best. Eliza wouldn't be disturbed just when she was regaining her equilibrium. There wouldn't be yet another situation to manage and he wouldn't have to go to prison for murder. He usually kept his anger towards his ex firmly under wraps, but it was still there, he realised now. With bells on. It was because of her actions – albeit indirectly – that Eliza had suffered in Leeds and, much as he tried to respect Cressida's choices, that imperative was *nothing* compared with his protective instinct as a father.

And, he'd realised lately, he spent so much time thinking of her as Eliza's mother that he sometimes forgot that she had once been *his* wife – and he felt pretty wronged himself, come to that. He'd done everything in his power to support her and make sure she could grab opportunity when it came her way. He'd managed a really unconventional living arrangement for seven long months and he'd done it cheerfully. He'd been open to moving to America, if that had been what she wanted. And what had his thanks been? A quick 'Well hey, I've met someone else and I don't want you anymore'! And that was only the thin end of the wedge.

Their divorce had been handled entirely by paperwork and solicitors – not a single conversation had taken place between the two of them. He wouldn't have expected her to stay and hold his hand if she'd fallen out of love with him – no way – but he'd found himself wifeless overnight. Not only that but he'd been bombarded with images of her looking irresistible at every turn, just when he was at his most raw. Not to mention the pictures of her with a succession of handsome A-listers. Worst of all, she'd left him completely unsupported as a parent.

He knew divorced couples who kept a frosty distance. He knew divorced couples who hated each other and argued regularly. He even knew divorced couples who stayed friends and went on holiday together – *weird* – but if the chips were down, they all managed to find time to talk about their children, to iron out any problems that arose. They all knew that whatever murky water had gone under the bridge, the kids' interests came first and they would enter a neutral space to discuss it.

When Eliza was bullied, when Edward's heart had been breaking because he couldn't help her, Cressida's input had been exactly zero. Her role had stopped when she created the situation. Edward's sister-in-law, Julie, had always been a conscientious listening ear and there was his mother too, of course. But only Cressida was Eliza's mother. She was the one who had known Eliza moment to moment, the way he did. Then she was gone as surely as if she were dead.

Yes, it was a good thing Cressida hadn't been in touch, he decided as he swiped his card across the ticket barrier at Greenwich and headed to the office, because neither he nor Eliza needed that hassle in their lives right now.

Lindy greeted him with a huge smile. 'Good news, Edward! We've changed the time of the presentation – confirmation came through first thing this morning.'

He sagged against the coat stand for a minute, pulling himself together when it rocked and nearly fell over. 'Seriously? They've gone for it? No hassles?'

'None. It's at ten in the morning now. I've forwarded you the email. It's fine.'

'Thank God for that. One less thing to worry about.'

He went into his office to look at his emails. After nearly having a heart attack when Holly had told him that Eliza was taking part in the play – *for him* – and realising that the presentation was the same day, Edward had emailed his counterpart at WRM directly. He didn't want to go to his own boss with the problem; he wanted to offer a solution. He'd come up with some sort of professional-sounding reason for needing to make the change and the two secretaries had been bashing it out ever since to find another time that suited everyone. And they'd done it, with an administrative wizardry that was beyond him but for which he was profoundly grateful.

He worked hard, all day, putting in a couple of hours' graft on the budget – always the sticky part of any campaign – then treating himself to a good long session of brainstorming and working on mood boards. When he had six or seven he really liked, he called an impromptu team meeting to get the others' input, and when that was all done, he took the latest ideas to his boss, Bill. Last thing, he jumped onto the internet and ordered another present for Eliza. A label-maker. Apparently, this was now essential to her life as she knew it.

It had been a good day, he thought as he ran down the stairs to the main lobby, an echoingly large space with a shining ice rink of marble floor and a vast reception desk with a granite top. The cramped office cubicles once you were inside did *not* live up to the building's first impression. The presentation time was sorted, a lot of progress made, and Bill was pleased with the direction he was taking. His mother was home and mending, apparently, and appeared to be mellowing. Eliza was happy and they joked that Mrs D's official job title should be House Elf because the changes at home were so rapid and miraculous. Even the fox was healing. It really did seem as if he was getting on an even keel at last. He could do with a break, he reflected. He really, really could.

There was a funny atmosphere in the lobby, a sort of expectant hush. Edward glanced at the twelve-foot Christmas tree by the glass revolving doors, wondering if carol singers were gathering, or if Santa had appeared. But there was no Christmas magic beyond the glowing tree lights and the giant white star. Even so, people who had obviously been on their way out were standing about in little knots of two or three, looking over their shoulders towards the waiting area with its dark leather seats, whispering together urgently. A disproportionate number of them seemed to be clutching their phones. Edward followed their gaze and saw a woman sitting alone.

She was wrapped in a long grey coat with the collar turned up – her hair was tucked inside – and an oversized cream woolly hat was pulled down low over her ears. Between the edge of the hat and the collar of her coat, only an inch of hair could be glimpsed. She wore large, mirrored shades even though it was December and she was indoors, and her chin was hidden by coils of cashmere scarf. Baby Jesus himself had not been more thoroughly swaddled. There was so little of her showing that Edward marvelled anyone could see any reason to get excited at all. She could have been anyone. Yet somehow they recognised her – or suspected. *He* knew who she was at once, but then he had been married to her. It was Cressida.

CHAPTER TWENTY-EIGHT

Holly

When Holly got home that evening she found a package the size of a shoebox sitting on her doorstep. It was wrapped in matt red paper and tied with a white satiny bow. She looked all around, once again, to see a quiet street then picked it up; it was weightless. And of course, there was no label. Another anonymous Christmas donation. She was over the hanging about, dithering phase now. Apparently, someone wanted to keep giving her stuff. It was hard to feel threatened when it was all festive cheer. So she unlocked the door and took it inside.

In the hall she paused: was this wise? It could be a bomb. Then again, it was light as a feather; wouldn't you expect a bomb to have a bit more heft? She gave it a little shake and heard a faint rustle, like tissue paper shifting.

She closed the door behind her, sat on the sofa and opened the box. Inside, nestled among sheets of white tissue paper with silver stars on it, was the most beautiful Christmas angel she had ever seen, with a spangly dress and feathery wings and a halo studded with tiny crystals. Holly sighed. It was so irregular. But what could she do? It seemed so *rude* to put all this stuff out in the rubbish. And the angel was possibly the most beautiful gift yet.

She sat on the sofa a long time, holding the angel and gazing into space. She hadn't even put the decorations on the tree yet. *Oh well*, she thought at last. *I may as well accept what I can't change, even if I don't understand it.*

She hung the beautiful paper ornaments on her tree, then added the tinsel, then placed the angel carefully on top. The decorations were attractive and unusual, and the perfect number for the tree; it looked neither overloaded nor sparse. Her stalker had impeccable taste. Now, the tree only needed fairy lights. *I would buy some*, Holly thought, *except they're bound to appear at some point.*

Her tummy was rumbling, but before starting dinner, she dug out her torch and went into the garden. She didn't want to wait another week to look at her little acer, so she picked her way across the lawn in the fall of light from the kitchen window – the tree stood just outside its yellow rectangle – flicked on the torch and moved the beam carefully across the branches. Another two leaves had fallen. Devoid of most of its fiery plumage, it looked small and bare. But ever so pretty. There was a simplicity to its lines that was graceful, minimalistic. It was just as much tree as it had ever been.

But then trees were designed to flourish and shed, flourish and shed, Holly reflected. Were humans designed to lose all their dreams? Of course they were, she answered her own question immediately. Look at all the people who'd gone to war. Look at the people who had suffered devastating losses in their families. Look at the people who'd lost their careers through ill health or injury. Some of them, yes, withered and died. But many, many of them were reborn, finding new purpose, new meaning, a new life to fit them. It could be done. It didn't mean Holly's sadness wasn't legitimate, but it did mean there was hope. Without motherhood, without Alex, she was still just as much Holly as she had ever been. And she was prepared to think that might be something to be proud of.

It was freezing. She'd thrown on a coat and wellies but the cold cut through the lot and made Holly shiver. She stepped closer to the little tree and rested a hand on its slender trunk. 'You're very beautiful wherever you are on your journey,' she told it. Then she pulled herself together and went inside. She was cooking dinner for Phyllis tonight and it was time to get started.

She prepped the ingredients for a hearty chicken soup – it was definitely the season for soups and stews. Then she went to change; she wouldn't start cooking till Phyllis arrived – it wouldn't take long. When she was ready, she poured two glasses of wine; she happened to know that Phyllis was partial to a nice drop of Sauvignon Blanc. Well, who wasn't?

She took a sip of hers then went to sit in the quiet lounge. She'd put some music on in a minute, but first she wanted to sit with the silence, as Penny put it. Since her conversations with Phyllis, she'd begun to enjoy living alone. Now the quiet didn't feel like a void where a loved one used to talk and laugh; it felt soothing and sensual, like the softest pashmina wrapping about her. As for the absence of Alex's running shoes and cycle helmets in the hall, the plugs and cables scattered about everywhere else, well, she spent every working day in the midst of chaos. It was rather nice to come home and have everything around her neat and ordered and beautiful.

A tap at the door. She switched on the music – Ludovico Einaudi playing quietly in the background made every dinner more beautiful – and let Phyllis in. 'A new addition,' she observed at once, looking at the angel on the tree.

'Yes, it just appeared today. It encouraged me to put the decorations up. I wasn't sure if I should but they're so very lovely.'

'I'm sure no harm can come from it,' said Phyllis encouragingly. 'Though it is very peculiar, I grant you.'

They spent the evening talking about all sorts. Holly was careful to ask Phyllis about herself and her family, conscious that previous conversations had been dominated by Holly's heartache; she didn't want their friendship to be a lopsided thing.

Phyllis had been widowed six years earlier – that was her heartbreak. Holly learned all about her husband Stan and their two sons, Matthew and Paul. Matthew was married to a wonderful woman, the most perfect daughter-in-law anyone could wish for. They visited all the time with their three noisy, good-hearted children and had boisterous family dinners with games and laughter on a regular basis. Matthew and Serena made sure that she never felt alone.

Paul was married to Spiteful Samantha, as Phyllis shamefacedly admitted she called her, a woman who ruled her only daughter with a rod of iron, who ruled her home with a rod of iron and, come to that, ruled Paul the same way. Phyllis never saw him anymore.

'That's bad,' Phyllis admitted. 'I miss him; he was a sweet boy and grew into a good man, but what's worse is that he's not happy. If he was, I could take it. I've only seen him once this year – June it was – and he's thin and pale. He hasn't said one word to me about his marriage – that's like him; he's loyal – but my guess is that he can't even think about divorce in case she takes Lilah and never lets him see her. I don't know if she could, but she's the sort to try, and just the thought of it would put him off putting his foot down. But how are things coming along with you, dear? How is school? Are you any happier? How many leaves are left on the tree?'

Holly smiled. She'd forgotten that she'd mentioned the tree to Phyllis. 'There are twelve. And I'm at about the same level. Clinging to a few things but so much better, Phyllis, honestly.' She described her newly shifting feelings and told Phyllis about the pageant and the progress with Evie and Eliza.

'Can I buy a ticket?' asked Phyllis. 'I'd love to see it.'

Holly promised her a free seat and, while she stirred the soup and served it up, she told her a little bit about Eliza and Edward. Nothing about the famous mother, of course, just her affection for the new girl and her admiration for the father.

'He sounds like a good man,' Phyllis observed, buttering a second piece of bread. 'Is he handsome?'

'Is he…? What?'

'Handsome, dear? Is he eye candy?'

Holly laughed. 'Actually, yes. He is. Tall, dark, curly hair, kind eyes. Kind of dishevelled but in a hasty, doting-dad sort of a way, not a can't-be-bothered sort of a way. But that's not really relevant, is it?'

'In my day a handsome man was always relevant.' Phyllis pressed her lips together as if there was no further point to make.

'In my day too. But you know, it's early days for me after…'

'After Loser left you? Quite long enough, I should say.'

'And he's the parent of one of my pupils, so you know, professionally it's not a good idea…'

'Mmm-hmmm.'

'And anyway, he's never given me the remotest idea that he thinks anything… *you* know. I'm just his daughter's teacher, and he likes me.'

'And isn't that a good start?' said Phyllis.

Holly shook her head and smiled. It was far too soon to start tying herself in knots about whether or not some guy liked her. Although… now she came to think of it, Alex didn't feel like much of a loss anymore. And she did like Edward. As in *like* him. She admired him too, and it wasn't often you met a guy you could say that about…

Holly switched the topic to Christmas.

CHAPTER TWENTY-NINE

Edward

'What,' asked Edward in a voice that sounded, even to his own ears, strangely menacing, 'are you doing here?'

'Hi,' said Cressida, standing up gracefully and removing her shades. Out of the corner of his eye, Edward noticed the security guard watching them with curiosity. 'I wanted to see you, of course.' Was that a hint of an American accent? *I wanned to see you...*

'Of course,' said Edward. 'What could be more obvious, given that I haven't seen you for over three years and I never hear from you. Come on, Edward, keep up!'

'You're mad,' she observed. 'Don't be mad.' Her eyes were very blue and imploring.

'What do you want?' he hissed. 'I'm on my way home.'

'I wanned to talk.'

'So you show up at my office without a word of warning? You couldn't pick up a phone and give me a little notice? Find a time that was convenient to me too?' He noticed that his voice was rising and that the guard was still watching, as was the little knot of people by the door. He stopped abruptly and tried to breathe deeply.

'It's the schedule, Edward, the movie. It's crazy, very demanding. I had an afternoon off and I realised I wasn't too far from you. I wanned to seize the chance...' Cressida's slouchy cream hat slid forward a little into her eyes and she pushed it back. A lock of dark silky hair fell over her face. She was undeniably as beautiful as ever but Edward was too irritated to care.

'You know what else is very demanding? A child's schedule. If I don't get home, I won't see Eliza before she goes to bed. I know that won't seem much to you, seeing as you can happily go three years without seeing her, but me, I'm old-fashioned – I like to see her every day. I think she probably gets something out of it too. You know, like security, safety, a sense that she's loved…'

'Edward, really? You're going to punish me and just go home when I'm finally here after all this time?'

Exasperation washed through him, taking his breath away. 'I'm not punishing you; I'm going about my daily life. Cressida, I'm not closed to the idea of talking to you. But everything can't always be on your terms. If we're going to have a conversation, it has to work for both of us. I may not be an international film star, but I do have a full-time job and a young daughter.'

Her big blue eyes gazed at him steadily. 'Just half an hour, Edward, please. I'd love to make an arrangement for three days from now or whatever works for you, but the truth is I don't know when I'll next be free. It could be tomorrow morning or Wednesday night or I don't *know* when the hell. I want to talk to you about seeing Eliza.'

His heart sank. 'Oh God.'

'Don't sound like that. I'm not the wicked witch. I'm not planning on eating her in a gingerbread sandwich.'

'I'm thankful for small mercies. When you say *seeing Eliza*, do you mean just once or twice, while you're over here, or do you mean regularly, on an ongoing basis?'

'That one. The second one.'

Edward felt suddenly physically sick. With all the mad things that had befallen him since Cressida had made it big, with all the injustices heaped upon him and Eliza, the one thing that kept him going, the one big comfort he'd had, was that Eliza was with *him*. What this could mean for him… what this could mean for her… Suddenly he no longer wanted to put Cressida off just to make a point. He wanted to get this conversation over with, know the worst. 'Half an hour,' he growled. '*If* the housekeeper can help me out.'

He pulled his phone out of his pocket and swung away from her then called Mrs D, saying something had come up. He couldn't bring himself to voice the words *ex-wife* or *Cressida*. She could stay an extra hour, she promised him. More if needs be. All her programmes were being recorded, and Mr Dixon could get his own tea for once. He thanked her effusively and asked to speak to Eliza. He told her something had come up at work. 'I'll be there before you go to sleep, though, Lizzicles.'

They both sounded cheerful but he hated doing this again. He'd been late home often enough lately because of work – which at least was part of their actual life. He resented Cressida for imposing another late night on him, another evening where he didn't get to talk to Eliza for long before bed, more than he could say. Now, where the hell could he take her? The last thing he wanted was for them to get delayed by star-struck fans. Or for them to get papped and Eliza to find out the wrong way that her mother was in town.

In the end, they walked briskly out of the office without looking left or right, and the nosy people by the door stood back reverently as Cressida passed. Edward led the way to a dimly lit bar around the corner. It was small and off the beaten track and shaped like an L inside. Cressida waited at a table at the far end of the L's short side while he went to get the drinks – still water for both of them. The selection was suitably cold and lacking in festive cheer.

'So how are you, Edward?' she asked, wrapping her slender hands with their beautifully manicured nails around her glass. 'How have you been?'

'It's been tough. Eliza had the guts bullied out of her in Leeds – that's why we moved. It's better now. I'm fine. We're both fine. Recovering. Making a new life in Kent. A really good one, Cressida. Please don't mess it up.'

'That's not what I want to do. I do… think about Eliza, you know. And you. I made some tough choices, Edward.'

Suddenly he felt unspeakably weary. 'OK, right, it's been really tough *for you*. Poor you, I'm sorry to hear that. How you must have suffered. Is that what you want to hear?'

Cressida looked uncertain and Edward felt a red heat of impatience seethe within him. She looked confused, as if she couldn't understand what he was driving at.

'Cressida, for God's sake. I'm sure your decisions *were* tough. Most adult decisions are. But you are actually an adult. You're not a small child, dealing with the fallout without the support of a mother, wondering what the hell happened when your world turned upside down. That's Eliza. And you're not the guy who kept the home fires burning for seven months only to be told, after all that, that he was surplus to requirements and that he wasn't going to see his wife again. That's me. So whatever difficulties you've encountered – and I'm sure there've been plenty – at least you could comfort yourself with the knowledge that those choices were yours to make. Eliza and I didn't have any of that. I'm not trying to say we're victims here, because we've handled it and we're happy now. But for the love of God don't string this out or expect sympathy from me. Get to the point, tell me what you want and then we'll deal with that too. But please think of Eliza. Try to imagine, if you're remotely capable, what it's been like for her, and put her first.'

'That's what I'm trying to do. That's why I came to you here and not to your house. That was my first thought, to show up and surprise her. But I thought this was probably better.'

Edward laughed. 'Thank God for that! *Surprise* her? You'd probably have given her a heart attack. You're a stranger to her now, Cressida, don't you see?'

'Don't say that.'

'But it's *true*. I'm not trying to be cruel. Do you know *anything* about children? Do you *know* any children, out in LA? No? Cress, when you went, she was five. She was traumatised. Now she's eight. She's growing up, she's smart, she has her own ideas. You're a distant figure to her now and that's your doing. I've taken her to see all your films. I've shown her some of the magazine articles. You could have phoned more, visited, written... but you gave her no more than any other child has of you. Pictures and dreams. I'm worried, Cressida, about whatever it is you want. I'm worried that you're going to hurt her again, disrupt our life. You say you don't want to mess things up for us but you've turned up out of the blue and you say you want to start seeing her. How is that not the same thing?'

Edward was dimly aware that behind them a group of people had taken a table a little way away. They were young and rowdy – liberated office workers probably – and he was glad because their din would drown out the conversation he was finally having with his ex-wife. He hadn't been in this bar before. It was one of those glossy, chrome-trimmed ones, with framed posters of European beers on the walls.

Cressida was silent a long time and Edward was conscious of the pounding of his heart. It was good to say his piece, good to lay it out as he'd wanted to so many times, but he still didn't know what she was thinking and he thought maybe he was going to explode. A huge instinctive part of him wanted to run home, snatch Eliza up and run far, far away. Deep into a forest to keep her safe. But he knew that wasn't the adult thing to do. He also knew it would break her heart to leave Christmas House and Dean Court Primary and Fatima and Miss Hanwell... He had to stand his ground and fight for the life they were building.

It wasn't only Eliza who didn't know Cressida anymore, he realised. He didn't either. She sat beside him – they were both angled away from the rest of the bar – and looked impeccably glossy. With the hat and coat finally removed, he could see her face and figure. She was glossy and gorgeous and glamorous in a way that real women just *weren't*. And yet she looked somehow fragile and baffled. How long was it since she'd had a real conversation about real things that happened in the real world?

'All I was thinking,' she began in a low voice, 'is that when I left, I thought I was doing the right thing. I mean, definitely the right thing for *me* – I deserved that break and I thought you and Eliza would hold me back. Not in the sense that you were a millstone round my neck or anything like that. But because they were two different lives – the old one with you and the new one I wanted. If I tried to live them both at the same time, I would have cracked down the middle. It *had* to be one thing or the other. But that doesn't mean I never thought about Eliza. Now time's moved on. I'm properly established. I can start making some room in my life for her. And she's a little bit older so she's, you know… more interesting.'

Edward nearly choked on his water. 'More *interesting*?'

'No, I don't mean that. She's more, you know?'

'No, I really don't. What?'

'Well, she can fit in with me better.'

'What do you *mean*? She's still too young to go to cocktail parties, Cressida.'

'I just mean, she doesn't need care round the clock. She can entertain herself. She has more… resources.'

'I don't get it. So you want to start seeing her because you figure she doesn't need much attention and what? You can have her around, but just get on with your life while she reads a book or something?'

'No. No, I want to spend time with her – I do. But it might not be so… tiring.'

He rubbed his hands over his face and groaned. 'Oh my God, Cressida, you're doing my head in. She's an eight-year-old child. A sensitive, somewhat damaged, very affectionate eight-year-old child. So yes, she does need attention and caring and entertaining *all* the time. And yes, it's still tiring. Parenting is, in general, I'm told. What did you have in mind? Are you going back to LA? Or are you moving home?'

'I'm still in LA. I'm here till mid-January, I think, then I fly back. I'm still seeing Reuben. Things are good between us.' Edward had no idea who Reuben was. 'But I thought I could see her before I go. Reconnect. And then maybe she could come visit.'

It was all feeling more and more surreal. He could feel his face crumple into incredulity and he thought maybe it would stay that way forever now. 'How? Alone? You want her to hop on a plane? Jot the flight numbers down on her iPad? Pack herself a little Gucci bag with a couple of pairs of heels? Check out of school for a week or two? Take a sabbatical?'

'Well, *no*, obviously not miss school. But maybe in the holidays...'

'So I'm supposed to look after her every single day of the school year but you're supposed to enjoy all her school holidays?'

'Not all of them. I don't know, Edward. I haven't thought this through.'

'Well, might I suggest you do that before you turn up in her life? She might want her mother to have a clue.'

'God, Edward. Why are you making this so hard?'

'I'm not, Cressida. It just *is* this hard. And we have to deal with it. Us, her parents.'

'OK. Well, thank you for that. For acknowledging that I am... anyway. Look, I know you want to go. If I give you my new number, will you think about it and call me? I won't turn up without warning again, I promise. I won't give Eliza a fright. I just want... I don't know. Something.'

'Right.' Edward found that she was right. He wanted to go. He badly wanted to get away from her. 'Give me the number.'

She drew a card from a white leather card case and handed it over. 'This is the number you need.'

'Right,' he said again and stood up, discovering that his legs were shaking. He walked out, passing the busy table of revellers, then another small group of young people clutching wine bottles on their way in. They rounded the corner to the short leg of the L. As he neared the door, he heard a shriek.

'Oh my God! It's Cressida Carr!' The flicker of a camera flash lit up the air behind him and he sighed. Even in this out-of-the-way corner she was instantly recognisable. How on earth would Eliza cope with any of it?

CHAPTER THIRTY

Eliza

Eliza was on the horns of a dilemma. (She liked that phrase; she'd heard it on a TV programme and asked her dad what it meant.) To tell her dad or not to tell her dad about the play. That was a sort of quote from Shakespeare's play *Hamlet*. They'd been talking about it in school. She really *needed* to tell him. There was a letter from Miss Hanwell burning a hole in her school bag; it described what Eliza needed for her costume, thanking him for his help in providing it. All the children had one. If she didn't hand it over soon, he wouldn't have any time to sort it out and she would have nothing to wear for the pageant!

But she was afraid to tell him because then she would *have* to be in the play. At the moment, she still woke up from bad dreams about it and comforted herself with the thought that she could just run away on the day if it got too bad. Even so, she couldn't help picturing his face when he saw the big Christmas tree and his little Lizzie dressed as one of the angels on it. He'd be so happy to see her onstage again. But she had to have a costume to wear!

There was only one week left before the pageant and it wasn't just Daddy coming but Granny and Grandad… *and* Aunty Pam. That was a lot of people who'd love to see her up there. The rehearsals were brilliant. Last week they'd even had a class trip to the wildlife centre where Bob the reindeer lived. (Honestly, who had called him Bob? Eliza didn't think people with so little imagination had any business naming animals.) All the children who had scenes with Bob during the play had run through those bits so they would all feel comfortable and to check that Bob was happy too. The others had watched, and afterwards they went all round the centre and saw sheep and chickens and a barn owl and two Shetland ponies.

Eliza knew all her lines, the other children were throwing themselves into practice, often with more gusto than talent, and somehow it all came together into a great happy, magical, Christmassy *marvel*. Exuberant was another word she'd learned lately and she thought it meant just the way they were together. She didn't want to drop out and miss all the fun – she didn't. She was sure she could do it, this time, without getting stage fright. Maybe she'd just give it to the end of the week and if she still felt fine on the weekend, she would tell him.

CHAPTER THIRTY-ONE

Holly

'How's your costume coming along, Eliza?' asked Holly after school on Wednesday.

'Good thanks!' called Eliza over her shoulder as she ran from the classroom. 'Bye, Miss Hanwell.' Eliza, who always, always stopped to chat. Holly smelled a rat. She'd bet Eliza hadn't told her father about the play yet. But had Edward started sewing?

Usually she stayed in her classroom until the school pickup throng had died down; otherwise she could feel a bit like Madonna backstage after a concert, so many people wanted a piece of her when she made an appearance in the yard. But Wednesday was Edward Sutton's day to collect Eliza and there were a couple of reasons she wouldn't mind seeing him, of which checking how Eliza's costume was going was only one, so she ventured forth.

Emerging into the concrete yard surrounded by low red-brick walls, she spotted him at once, near the wrought-iron gates, talking to Jinny's mother. He was taller than all the other dads and Eliza, in her bright red coat, was speeding towards him like a comet. She reached him with a hug that sent him staggering and laughing. Then he looked up and saw Holly. She waved and he smiled back, then lifted a hand in a sort of 'Hang on a sec' kind of a way, as if he wanted to talk to her. Or was that just wishful thinking? *Oh noooo*, groaned Holly in the privacy of her head. *Don't start all that.*

She started her way over but got waylaid by Lily Orton's mother. Mrs Orton was halfway through making Lily's costume. Could Miss Hanwell take a quick look at the pictures she'd taken of Lily wearing it, and let her know if she was on the right track. *Halfway through, my foot,* thought Holly. The pictures showed an angelic-looking Lily modelling the most sophisticated school play costume Holly had ever seen, with brocade and lurex and ostrich feathers… it was the court of Louis XIV meets 1980s Duran Duran video. The other children would be eclipsed. Holly tried to tread the right balance between fulsome admiration and a tactful suggestion that she pull it back, 'just a tad'. Holly only ever used words like tad when she was talking to Hermione Orton.

She was relieved when Edward came over and hovered, giving her a chance to excuse herself. 'Can we talk?' he said, as soon as he had her attention. 'Sorry to be so abrupt – I don't want Eliza to hear. It's Cressida. She showed up at my office out of the blue and she wants to see Lizzie and I don't know what to do.'

'Of course,' said Holly more calmly than she felt. Cressida. Well, if ever there was a reason to stamp down on her barely burgeoning feelings for Edward, Cressida was it. The ex-wife to end all ex-wives. 'When?'

He spread his hands helplessly. 'I don't know. Obviously, I don't want Eliza to be around. And I need to get back to Cressida soon… I'm really, really sorry to ask but would you be willing to come over tonight? I can't leave her asleep in the house…'

Eliza, who'd been giggling with some of the other children, spotted them talking and looked aghast, probably afraid Holly would give the game away about the play. Little did she know that ship had sailed. 'I'll come,' Holly said. 'Give me your number so I can text and check Eliza's asleep. She's coming over so make it quick.'

Edward whipped out a business card from his wallet and handed it over. 'Thank you so much. You're a lifesaver,' he muttered and walked away.

Holly drove home and went straight to see Phyllis. 'Cressida's back,' she announced on the doorstep and Phyllis pulled her inside. Phyllis's house was laid out exactly like her own. It was odd to be somewhere in one way so familiar, yet utterly different. Where Holly had chosen strong Farrow & Ball colours and smooth, classic furniture, Phyllis was all neutrals – magnolia, beige and sage – and old-fashioned mahogany and teak. Where everything in Holly's was brand new and carefully chosen to her own taste, Phyllis's was more of a mish-mash; even though she was alone now, there were family photographs and ornaments and souvenirs of a long, full life. Holly had left most of her bits and pieces behind with Alex. He could do as he pleased with them; she hadn't wanted to surround herself with memories of happy times that had come to an end.

'Of course, if there's one consolation in this whole nasty mess,' said Phyllis when Holly had told her what little she knew, 'it's that I don't think he'll have any residual feelings for her after this. She sounds like a complete nightmare, as my grandson would say.'

'How do you work that out?' demanded Holly, texting Edward her number while Phyllis made a cup of tea. 'I was thinking the opposite. Have you seen her? The woman's Aphrodite. Turning up after all this time… it must make him wish… *something.*'

'Most men are stupid, I grant you,' said Phyllis, giving the National Trust mugs a stir and handing one to Holly. 'Ruled by their appetites, a sucker for a pretty face. But once in a while, you get one that's sensible and I think your Edward must be one of them from everything you've told me. His first priority is that little girl. He's not going to get involved with any woman who's not good for her. And he can't *think* she's good for her or he wouldn't be getting his knickers in a twist and looking for advice, would he? She's the mother, for heaven's sake. If she was any good, he'd just bring the two of them together, wouldn't he? Turning up at his office unannounced? That's not respectful. He won't like that.'

Holly took a comforting slurp of tea, following Phyllis into the round lounge, trying not to be distracted by an alarming collection of shiny Toby jugs.

'They were Stan's,' said Phyllis, following the line of her gaze. 'Hideous, aren't they? I gave him hell about them when he was alive and now I can't bring myself to throw them out!'

Holly smiled and gave her hand a squeeze. 'I suppose you're right about Edward. And now he wants to talk to *me* about it. Personally, after working with Eliza for five weeks, I think it's the worst possible timing and it could set her back by miles. But she's her mother. How can he say no?'

It was a question that troubled her all evening, as she went home and made fajitas, as she waited for Edward's call, as she heard her letter box flap and something solid being pushed through. She darted to the door to see a flat, narrow box stuck halfway. She wrenched the door open and ran outside in her socks, intent on spotting its deliverer, but once again, the street was empty. Whoever it was could move very fast. She sighed and went inside again, her feet instantly chilled, and opened the box to discover a string of delicate white fairy lights. Then Edward called and she drove the twenty minutes to Christmas House. He'd started to give her directions but she'd stopped him. 'I know where you live, and I mean that in the least sinister possible way. Eliza talks about the house so much I feel as if *I* live there.'

It was true. Whatever demons had troubled Eliza in the past, they were dormant now. She bubbled with enthusiasm whenever she spoke, and Holly had rarely seen a child so straightforwardly happy with life. It would be more than a shame if that all got ruined now by one selfish woman's whim. It would be a tragedy.

Christmas House – what a name – loomed out of the night – a large, square mass. Holly couldn't make out much in the darkness, only gateposts and gravel and stone columns either side of a central front door with a carriage lamp glowing above it. It looked gracious and inviting. The door opened without her knocking; Edward had been looking out for her. He was wearing faded jeans and a navy sweater. Holly resisted the urge to put her arms around him.

'Thank you, thank you,' he murmured as she stepped inside. 'I'm at my wits' end. But I shouldn't have asked. I feel terrible. You must think I'm such a disaster area.'

'Not at all,' she whispered. 'I don't suppose I can help but I'm happy to listen. God, this house is *fantastic!*' She looked around at the generous proportions of the hall, the wide staircase, the glimpse of a large kitchen through one of the open doors. True, the paintwork was tired and scuffed, the hall was lit by only a light bulb and the floor underfoot was shabby old lino. But oh, the potential.

Edward's weary face was relieved by a grin for the first time. 'Thanks. This place is Marmite. People either love it or hate it. It's how we sieve for kindred spirits. Now what can I get you? I opened a bottle of red but of course you're driving. Do you want a glass? Or just tea, coffee, hot chocolate? We have quite a good selection thanks to Mrs D.'

'I'll have one small glass. Then something herbal if you have it.'

'Brilliant. Let's go into the lounge. Eliza and I had to detain visitors in here until a couple of weeks ago,' he said, leading her into the kitchen and pouring wine. 'It was the only room that had something to sit on. But then Mrs D came and magic happened and now…' He flicked the light off and went down the hall to another room. 'Now we have this. Ta-dah!'

The lounge walls were a tired magnolia, dingy and dull, but the furniture was brand new and inviting. A log burner roared and crackled, and lamps softened the dark corners. 'Oh *very* nice,' said Holly admiringly. 'Just as well it's not mine – I'd spend a fortune.'

'I already have, and that's without paint and all that. But to be honest I don't have much of a clue about that sort of thing so it's just as well the finances are forcing me to press pause. I'd probably go with Eliza's judgement and paint the whole place purple and banana yellow or something.'

'No, that wouldn't do. But a nice soft, hazy plum on that wall around the bookcase, and in the alcove there, and the rest a deep buttery cream perhaps. That's what I'd do.'

'You know about interior design?'

'Only as an enthusiastic amateur. Very enthusiastic.' Holly grinned and threw herself into a big soft armchair. 'Oh my God, heaven. What a fantastic room. Oh, and a couple of sheepskin rugs and a couple of tapestry rugs to pick out the plum – it's big enough that you could have the variety. And accents of orange, a nice dark amber colour… Don't ever let me loose with your credit card.'

'But that sounds really classy. Can I write it down? I'm genuinely clueless, you see.'

'I'll text you. We shouldn't get sidetracked – I'm terrified Eliza will wake up and I'll have to leg it out of a window.'

He smiled. 'All the windows stick. If she comes down, we'll have to say we're talking about the pageant. It's the lesser of two evils.'

Phyllis might have a point, thought Holly. If Cressida could be described as the greater of two evils, he probably wasn't too enamoured with her. Quickly Edward ran through what had happened with Cressida and the conversation they'd had. Holly couldn't quite believe it – or at least, she wouldn't be able to if Edward weren't so clearly honest and bewildered.

'But hasn't she got a clue how Eliza must feel?' Holly queried. 'Actors are supposed to have empathy. Imagination. And she was a kid herself once.'

'That's the worst of it – she's so disconnected from the whole situation. I don't really understand. She looked genuinely perplexed as to why her turning up now could be problematic in any way for Eliza. Is it just an act, to get her own way? Or does she really not get it? And which would be worse? She never used to be like that – at least, I don't think she did. But I'm questioning everything now. *Was* she the warm, vivacious, genuine person I thought I'd married and she's changed, or was she like this all along? It didn't feel like talking to the Cressida I used to know. Is she basically an OK person who's a bit selfish and spoiled because, y'know, she's world-famous? Or does she have some sort of… personality disorder that stops her empathising? Sorry, that sounds harsh. But I have wondered.'

'I can see why. And obviously I don't know any of the answers. But I can see why it's driving you nuts. If she truly wants to make amends and go about things differently from now on, that would be… one thing.'

Holly couldn't quite bring herself to say it would be brilliant because from where she was sitting, Cressida was nothing but bad news. Selfishly, she'd rather Eliza got by with her dad and Aunty Pam, and Holly herself at school. But kids needed their mothers – didn't they? 'But if it's a *whim*, if she's just going to disrupt things then vanish… that's not good. And as for Eliza flying out to LA for goodness' sake…'

'I don't want to lose her,' said Edward.

'Neither do I,' said Holly, without thinking. Then she felt embarrassed; that was wholly inappropriate. But Edward was looking at her warmly, as if he knew what she meant.

'But she *is* her mother,' she added quickly. 'She has a right to see her and, all other things being equal, it *should* be a good thing for Eliza. I guess if you tell Cressida no, she can't see her, she'll fight it. So all you can really do is make sure it *is* a good thing for Eliza, control it.'

Edward nodded. 'That's what I was thinking. Like tell her she can see her but not until after the pageant. I know it's still days away but Cressida said she's here till the middle of January, so there's ample opportunity.'

'Oh I'm relieved you said that,' Holly admitted. 'The courage of Eliza, getting back onstage after all she's been through, the trust she's showing in me and the other children… She's loving it so much, Edward. You should see her up there – she shines. I'd hate for all that to be taken away from her.'

'Exactly. If Cressida were to be there… or even if she turns up beforehand, Eliza's bound to be rattled, isn't she? Right, I'll tell Cressida that I'll tell Eliza she's here – but not until after the twentieth. And as for LA, well there's no way Eliza's travelling out there as a regular thing. If Cressida wants her daughter to see what her new life is all about, I'll take her myself. It's not the holiday I would've chosen for us but it's better than the alternative. Thank you, Holly.'

Holly drained her small glass of wine then leaned her head against the cushiony armchair. Despite the difficult topic, she felt relaxed and mellow thanks to the firelight, the wine, the comfy seat and especially Edward's company. 'I haven't done anything.'

'But having someone to talk it through with really helps. Especially because you know and love Eliza. There's a guy at work who used to work in family law so I'll talk to him too, about the LA thing and Cressida suddenly turning up like this, just so I know the rights and wrongs of it, but that's different from the emotional impact, you know?'

'I do.'

He rested his head back too and sighed. 'It's a relief to have a course of action. Do you need to rush off or will you stay for a herbal tea? I'm horribly aware that since we met, I've done nothing but tell you all my problems and I'm not usually that guy. I promise I'll stop.'

Holly laughed. 'I'll take chamomile if you have it. Please don't worry – I haven't felt imposed upon. It was bound to be a fraught time moving to a new place. And it's just bad timing that Cressida should come back now. But I'll tell you all my problems if it'll make you feel better.'

She was only joking, but once he returned from the kitchen with two large mugs and a plate of Hobnobs, he asked her what had gone wrong with Alex, and when she had moved to Hopley, and she found herself talking for over an hour. She told him everything; they even had the dreaded uterus conversation. First Penny, then Phyllis and now Edward. Saying it was becoming easier.

'I'm really sorry,' said Edward quietly after a reflective pause. 'I know it's not my place to badmouth your ex but he's…'

'Driven? Determined? Focused on his goals?'

'I was going to say he's a tool.'

Holly laughed – she couldn't help it. 'He wants what he wants,' she sputtered, wiping chamomile tea off her chin.

'Yes but… for God's sake. Please don't take this the wrong way but anyone would be *lucky* to have you. Kids are a bonus, sure, but whatever. I just don't understand how he could walk away after so long together because of something like that. I mean, I know it's no small thing – I get why you'd be devastated – but isn't that the *point* of a partner? To be with you through thick and thin?'

A little shiver of emotion ran through Holly and for a horrible moment she thought she might cry, but it passed. His words felt so warming and solid. 'So I thought. And I *have* thought that a lot over the months, and felt really hurt and angry. But you know what conclusion I've come to? It can't have been right, can it, the relationship? There was a lot of good stuff along the way, but he obviously didn't feel the way about me that… well, that I'd want someone to. And I'm starting to feel OK with that. I want better than that.' Holly felt reassured by his indignation on her behalf.

'I'm glad you're coming to feel that way. I heartily concur, by the way. I can see why everyone said you were born to be a mother and I'm really sorry that's proving difficult, but the way I see it, you were born to teach, and you're doing it with panache. I'm so, so thankful that Eliza's come to you.'

'Thank you,' said Holly, wrinkling her nose in embarrassment, but basking at the same time in his good opinion. 'That's a lovely thing to say. It means a lot.'

'You're amazing,' said Edward simply. 'The way you have with those kids, the way you see them, I think it's possibly the best gift anyone can give another person. That complete, unwavering belief in their potential, and acceptance of their flaws. And from what Eliza tells me, you have plenty of flaws to accept. I hear there are some... how shall I put it? Some spirited young men in the class?'

'Oh you can say that again.' Holly started telling him tales of Jason Tillwell's obsession with zombies and blood and Griff's passion for alien space monsters. She told him about Javai's complete inability to colour between the lines, both literally and figuratively, and David Kanumba's addiction to ice cream.

They were both in stitches when she checked her watch and her eyes widened in alarm. 'Oh my God, it's midnight. I cannot believe I've been sitting here talking your ear off for so long. I think we're even now, Edward, on the problem-sharing scale.'

'I'm glad,' he said, getting to his feet. 'I've really enjoyed our conversation. Thank you again for coming over. I'm starting to feel that you're a friend. I don't know if that's frowned upon or anything because you're Eliza's teacher, but I do really appreciate your support and company.'

'I feel the same. I've wondered, too, about the teacher-friend thing. But then, teachers *are* allowed to *have* friends. And in a small place like Hopley, if I avoided all my pupils' parents, there wouldn't be many people left. All the same, I might just have a word with Mr Buckthorn and check he doesn't have any issues with it. The last thing I want is to compromise my job – it's the most important thing I have at the moment.'

'Absolutely. You check – I'd hate to put you in any sort of awkward position. But if it is all OK, and if you'd like to, maybe we could do something again, with Eliza. She adores you, as you probably know. Maybe a woodland walk one weekend? Or Christmas drinks one evening? I could invite Fatima's parents too, and you could meet Mrs D…'

'They're both wonderful ideas. I'll talk to him tomorrow and let you know. And please text me about how things go with Cressida. I care so much about Eliza.'

As they stole out into the quiet hallway, they heard a clunk and shuffle and Holly jumped guiltily. Had they woken Eliza with their laughter? But Edward put a reassuring hand on her shoulder. 'It's our fox,' he whispered. 'Do you want to see?'

'Oh my word, I'd forgotten about the fox. Yes please.'

Quietly, Edward opened the door next to the sitting room and switched on a lamp so the flood of light wasn't too harsh. The shuffling came from a large box near the window and Holly crept nearer. 'Blackberry,' she murmured. 'Hello, Blackberry. I've heard a lot about you.'

The fox got to its feet and tried to stand on his hind legs with paws on the edge of his box, but it seemed to be too uncomfortable and he sank back onto his haunches. He regarded Holly through bright inquisitive eyes, growling softly, and she grinned. 'He is lovely. I wish I could stroke him. Oh I know I mustn't, I know he's wild, but *look* at him!' That thick, russet fur was irresistible.

Edward rolled his eyes. 'You're as bad as Eliza.'

'Says the man who trained as a vet and rescued a fox and keeps him in his house,' teased Holly, crouching down in front of the box and gazing into Blackberry's yellow eyes.

'We'll have to let him go soon. His leg's much better. And he has a group to return to, I'm pretty sure. There are two or three that keep coming through the garden – I'd be surprised if he wasn't part of the same gang. Admittedly, he's a fetching little fellow. Aren't you, Blackberry?'

'A fox in a box,' murmured Holly, quite enchanted by the magic of the moment of communion with a wild creature.

'At least we don't feed him lox,' said Edward.

CHAPTER THIRTY-TWO

Edward

The next day, Edward rang Cressida on his way to work. He got her voicemail but she called back an hour later. He was between meetings so he closed his office door and took the call. His small office had a massive desk and a view of the Thames (beyond a mass of grey buildings). The walls were decorated with corkboards, all pinned with dozens of images relating to various projects he was working on. He was glad he was talking to Cressida here, surrounded by the visible evidence of his success and autonomy. He didn't sit down.

'I'm happy for you to see Eliza, of course,' he said. 'Look, you're her mother and you have every right. I'm just concerned about the handling of it. I want to tell her you're here and give her a bit of warning but, Cressida, I'm not going to do it until after her school play on the twentieth.'

'Oh!' Cressida sounded joyful. 'She's going to be in a play?'

'Yes, but I'm so sorry, I don't think it will be good for Eliza if you're there.' Edward felt awful saying it. He picked up the framed photo of his daughter that sat on his desk and put it down again. 'I've told you about the trouble she's had – she's been terribly unhappy. I feel it's really important that she doesn't have anything extra to contend with, that she isn't disturbed or upset in any way before then. Can you understand?'

'I think so. Can you tell me more, Edward, or are you busy just now? It's just that we have to redo a bunch of scenes today so I might not be able to talk again later.'

'I have a little time.' He went through it all again, the things he had told her in bits and pieces over the years. Eliza's stage fright in Leeds, her terror and sickness every time she tried to act. The bullying. Her decision not to go onstage in her new school. And then her change of heart. He kept it brief, because he needed to get back to work, but he was very clear. 'It's all so fragile,' he concluded. 'She still hasn't told me she's taking part – I only know because her teacher told me – so I'm pretty sure she's still afraid she might need to bolt on the night. Add one more thing into the mix and her big night could be ruined. Especially you, I hate to say, because you're all bound up in it for her.'

Cressida sighed. 'Oh God, Edward. I feel awful that I've made it all so hard for her. I know you've told me before but I guess I wasn't listening properly. I guess I didn't *want* to listen. You're right, of course. I'd give anything to see her big night but it could really rattle her, so we'll wait till after, like you said.'

'Thank you, Cressida, for understanding.'

'Better late than never, right?' she answered wryly.

Flooded with relief and reassured that she finally got it, Edward wanted to be conciliatory. 'So the play's on the twentieth, as I said, and I'll tell Eliza about you the very next day. Assuming she's fine with it, you can come over that evening. Or the following day. Whenever you're able. We'll work it out.'

'That sounds fine, Edward. Very fair. I'll keep my schedule as clear as possible for after the twentieth. I appreciate it, really.'

'Well OK,' said Edward. 'I'd better get back to work but if you have any questions, just call me again.'

It wasn't until he'd hung up that he realised he hadn't men-tioned LA. He'd wanted to say up front that Eliza wouldn't be going alone, not for many years. But perhaps one battle at a time was enough. At least Cressida had agreed to stay away until after the pageant. She'd been more agreeable than he'd expected, actually. And he was profoundly grateful for it. It gave him a sense of cautious optimism that they might be able to negotiate a gentle way forward after all. Because he really, really didn't want the lovely life that he and Eliza had just started to build turned upside down. If Cressida could be a thread woven lightly through it, that wouldn't be so bad. What frightened him was the thought of having to share Eliza significantly. Of there being times when she would be with Cressida and not with him and he would be… empty.

But he didn't need to worry about that now. He'd won that time for Eliza so that she wouldn't be disturbed before the pageant. It was Eliza who needed to be protected at all costs.

He cracked the window open a centimetre, letting in a trickle of cool city air. Of course, the twentieth was an important day for him too, but at least all the drama didn't seem to be affecting his work. He had the ability to compartmentalise, and right now he was profoundly grateful for it.

CHAPTER THIRTY-THREE

Holly

To Holly's relief, Mr Buckthorn had nothing disapproving to say about friendships between teachers at Dean Court Primary and their pupils' families. 'It would be unreasonable and unpoliceable,' he pronounced. 'Many teachers have friends with children, and those children grow up to be primary age and come to school here. Those friendships do not have to be disbanded. And new ones are bound to arise in a small community like ours.'

Holly had deliberately not mentioned that the parent in question was the single dad of the new girl. If Mr Buckthorn wanted to imagine she was bonding with one of the mums over tea and cake, so be it. The principle was the same. She was glad Edward wanted to be friends, because she really did like him, and there was no need to tear away to thoughts of romance, as Phyllis had done, because a friendship was a valuable thing. So she told herself, feeling very proud of her wisdom and maturity – until she found herself daydreaming about his kind grey eyes smiling into hers as he bent down to kiss her... and then she kicked herself and went and did something useful.

After school on Thursday, she found a text from him: *C OK about waiting to see E. Says after pageant is fine. Thanks again and hope you've had a good day.*

Great news, she replied. *I'm so pleased. I spoke to Mr B today and no rules against teachers and parents being friends.*

Then there was a long wait and she started to wonder if he'd forgotten that part of their conversation, or if he'd decided that it was a bad idea after all, or if he was put off by her following through with such alacrity... Wow, so this was what it was like to be single again. She was thirty-six but feeling sixteen. *Not* enjoyable.

Then a reply came through. *Just out of meeting. Good to know. Are you free for a walk in the woods Sat? We're letting fox go – Think would cheer E up to have you there.*

Lovely, she answered. *What time?*

At midday on Saturday she arrived at Christmas House for the second time. It was even lovelier by daylight, built with stone that was a soft, restful grey, not dark and forbidding, and had tons of character – a pitched roof with plenty of eaves, a laburnum tree shivering to its left, stone gateposts that had once been magnificent, now blobby. It was a pale, cold day, with fragments of luminous gold shot through a woolly white sky. She wore several layers and her powder-blue bobble hat. The door flew open as she got out of the car and Eliza shot out to hug her.

'Miss Hanwell, I told Daddy! I told him I'm in the pageant. He's ever so pleased. Even though he has to make me a costume now. I'm glad you're coming with us to say goodbye to Blackberry. Will you stay for lunch? Aunty Pam made something last night, so you needn't be afraid. Daddy can't cook. You should know that now if you're going to be friends. I can't either, but Aunty Pam is going to teach me to make peppermint creams on Monday. Can you cook?'

'I'm not bad...' Holly began, then Edward came out, carrying the fox in his arms. It lay there quite content, as if being carried around like a queen in a litter was just what he expected from life. 'Do you need anything before we go?' he asked Holly. 'Loo? Biscuit?'

'I'm fine.'

'Great.' He gave the key to Eliza to lock the front door and they set off. Eliza told Holly that when she'd heard Holly was joining them on their weekend expedition, she'd come clean about the pageant at once. 'I couldn't keep it secret anymore. And now that he knows, we can talk about it! I knew I wouldn't be able to spend all afternoon with you without talking about the pageant.'

'Good thinking, Eliza. And maybe when we get back to your place, we can give him a little preview. What do you think? Just one of your scenes?'

'Not the one with Bob…' Eliza frowned. 'Maybe the first one, where I talk to the children for the first time. You could read Sophie's part, Miss Hanwell.'

They tramped down a hard earthen path. It hadn't rained for a few days and it was very cold, so the going was firm and uneven underfoot. The trees were bare and the colours muted. 'I don't think we need to go too far,' said Edward. 'We probably could have just let him go in the garden because the foxes definitely swing by on a regular basis. But not every day, and we don't want to confuse him, so we thought a little way into the woods might help.'

'Daddy's checked the dell where we found him,' Eliza explained. 'He called the council and they've been and cleared it. So Blackberry should be safe in the woods now.'

'How about here?' asked Edward, sinking down to a crouch when they reached a certain bend in the path. The woods were quiet and the foliage dense. A few stray sunbeams played tag in the wind.

Eliza shrugged. 'Good as anywhere,' she said, sad but resigned. They all said solemn farewells to Blackberry then Eliza, chancing it, reached out a hand to stroke his silky head. Blackberry instantly snapped, lips curling, and Eliza snatched her hand back, frowning in frustration. Edward set him on the ground and opened his arms. Blackberry hopped down and for an anxious, marvellous moment, he stood there looking at them.

'It's alright, Blackberry. We'll always be your friends but you can go back to the other foxes,' said Eliza. 'You're a wild animal and the woods are your home. You remember, don't you?'

Blackberry stared at her with unblinking yellow eyes. Edward rose to his feet and Blackberry waited a moment more. Then he sniffed the air and shot off into the dense tangle of undergrowth, vanishing into the knotted brambles as if he were made of air.

'And then he was gone,' said Edward, putting his arm round Eliza. 'Well done, Lizzie-Loops. I'm very, very proud of you today.'

'Well done, both of you,' said Holly. 'I really admire what you've done. Saving the little guy, and then letting him go back to his wild life. I think it's really… beautiful.'

It was hard to say who looked more gratified, Eliza or Edward. They continued their walk, meandering through the woods, showing her all their favourite spots. A couple of yelling magpies swooped alongside them for a while, flashing across their path in an exuberance of shiny black and white. 'What a racket they make,' Holly observed, laughing.

'I like magpies,' conceded Eliza, 'but they are ordinary. I wanted you to see an owl, Miss Hanwell, or a badger. Something exciting.'

'Well, I happen to love magpies, so I'm pleased, Eliza, and don't forget I've already seen a fox today so that was pretty special. I love this walk. Thank you for showing me around.'

When they emerged from the woods an hour later, Eliza was mollified by the appearance of a pheasant, burnished and nervy, with a dragging tail and a nodding head. It leaped into the air with a whir of wings when it saw them and flew back to the naked fields.

Then followed lunch, a huge risotto left by Mrs D, and asparagus that Edward over-boiled. Still, if you cut it into the risotto you could barely notice. Holly, used to doing all her own cooking, felt nurtured and happy.

After lunch, Eliza and Holly acted out the scene from the play where Eliza first appears, a divine vision in front of two lonely children. Edward clapped and whistled and they took their bows, laughing. Then they played Monopoly, which took forever, and which Holly won decisively several hours later. By the time they'd indulged in nachos and hot chocolate, it was somehow 9 p.m. and past Eliza's bedtime.

'Good grief!' cried Edward when he saw the time. 'I literally had no idea.'

'Me neither.' Holly shook her head. How was it possible to lose track of time that spectacularly when there was no alcohol involved? She was filled with a sense of well-being that was understated yet profound.

'*I* knew!' Eliza hugged herself, grinning. 'I was watching the clock the whole time. I couldn't believe my luck – this is the best day *ever*!'

Edward laughed. 'You monkey. You *know* bedtime is eight. Say good night to Miss Hanwell and go and brush your teeth. I'll come and tuck you in in ten minutes. You don't have to go yet,' he added to Holly. 'Don't feel that we're booting you out.'

'No, no, I must go,' said Holly, scrambling up from the excessively comfy armchair where she was lolling. The sense of being at home, of belonging, was too dangerous. Because it wasn't her home and she was a very new visitor. She had to keep a grip on reality. 'I really never meant to stay so late. Good night, Eliza darling – thank you for a wonderful day. Sweet dreams.'

'Good night, Miss Hanwell. Daddy and I are going to try church tomorrow. That one on the way into Hopley. Do you want to come with us?'

Holly glanced reflexively at Edward, who nodded. 'Yes, do. The service is at ten. I told you I spoke to the vicar? He's a good bloke.'

Holly was sorely tempted. Too tempted. 'I'd love to but I can't. I'm seeing my friend Penny tomorrow. Another time maybe. But I'll see you at school on Monday, Eliza, and I'll see you at the pageant, Edward.'

'I'll be there with bells on. Propping up my injured mother and cheering you both on. Good night, Holly; thanks for joining us today.'

'I had a lovely time,' she answered simply and disappeared into the cold night.

CHAPTER THIRTY-FOUR

Edward

Sunday afternoon saw Edward staring glumly at Holly's letter, printed on the school's headed paper. He didn't know where to start. He should have done this much sooner but the weekend had been so busy. First, they'd gone to the woods to let Blackberry go. The little fox's leg had healed beautifully and not even Eliza could pretend he needed them anymore. The afternoon and evening had slipped away so swiftly with Holly's company. After she'd gone, and Eliza was in bed, he'd thought about starting the costume – he knew he really needed every moment he could get – but he wasn't in the right frame of mind to start such an alien endeavour. He'd felt relaxed after their day of laughter, and decided to have an early night; with so little time left before the presentation, he knew he needed it.

He'd slept like a log, better than he had in ages. Probably it was the fresh air and then spending the rest of the day doing something fun, instead of rushing around like a loon ticking things off a never-ending to-do list. And maybe the feeling of support. Another adult with him who knew and loved Eliza. Eliza had come clean about the pageant, and seeing her rehearsing with Holly had been balm to the soul; they'd laughed and joked, and you could tell that Eliza was completely at ease. It was a relief the likes of which Edward had wondered if he'd ever feel.

He'd slept late on Sunday – unheard of – and they'd rushed off to church without breakfast. They'd had a moment's hesitation about whether to skip it and stay warm and eat bacon sandwiches, but they liked to stick to a plan, did Edward and Eliza, so they dressed in a flurry, ran to the car and made it to the service. Eliza had been enraptured by the beautiful old church, the romantic stained glass, the nativity scene and Reverend Fairfield's warm welcome afterwards. They'd stood talking for ages, Eliza chattering nineteen to the dozen, and the vicar had introduced them to a few people – a couple of old ladies, who seemed to make up the biggest percentage of the conversation, and a family whose children went to a different school. They seemed friendly and suggested getting together after Christmas. Edward thanked them. It would be good to have friends not connected with the school and broaden their circle of acquaintance.

By the time they left St Domneva's, it was nearly noon and tummies were rumbling. They decided they couldn't wait another minute for food and went to the pub just down the road from the church, which looked cosy and family oriented. The bar was thick with gold tinsel, and shiny 3D bells dangled from rafters. Christmas music played at a bold volume – the ubiquitous Slade yet again. There they piled into a hearty brunch. After they got home, Edward's mother phoned for a long in-depth conversation about the pageant, and Christmas week, and when would Edward and Eliza visit them? Edward consented to the day after Boxing Day, but only if his parents returned the visit the day after that.

'Really?' asked his mother. 'Will we be quite comfortable?'

Edward rolled his eyes. 'I think you'll be pleasantly surprised, Mum, I really do.'

There was a long pause and then – perhaps Edward's father gave her a little nudge – she said graciously, 'That will do very well, darling. Thank you for the invitation.'

'You're welcome. We'll look forward to having you.' Edward smiled and for a moment contemplated telling his mother about Cressida's return. But Eliza was around, in and out of the garden, up and down the stairs, and now wasn't the time. Besides, he still had a few days' reprieve. Until then, it wasn't a problem. He couldn't let it be.

By the time he dug out Holly's *Dear Parent* letter it was well into the afternoon. He tried to brainstorm but it turned out a child's dress was a completely different proposition from an advertising campaign. *And* he was distracted, fretting about Holly. He'd been wandering about all day feeling quite contented after their enjoyable time yesterday. But now he found himself second-guessing all that. He couldn't help wondering about the fact that they'd invited her to join them today and she'd said no. Obviously she had other friends so a prior arrangement was no big surprise – that wasn't what troubled him – but was it his imagination or had there been a look on her face when she'd said no? A sort of awkward, determined look. And had she said it quite hastily? They'd got to know each other very quickly and yesterday they'd spent a long time together. Perhaps the prospect of seeing the Suttons again so soon was a bit much for her. And it was fine if that was the case, but he'd hate for her to feel uncomfortable, like there was any expectation. Had he been a bit needy during their short acquaintance?

Yesterday had been… well, if he was honest with himself, the word that came to mind was *blissful*. It had been fun, warm, relaxing… like hanging out with a really good friend, not a brand-new one. And the weirdest thing was that it had felt a little bit like a date and yet Eliza had been with them, so it had also felt a little bit like family time… yet it had been neither. If any of those feelings had transmitted themselves to Holly, perhaps she would want to retreat a bit. She'd been through hell this year. Family, romance, those were red-raw areas to her right now. He really hoped that she knew that he knew that, and respected it.

He toyed with his phone, wondering whether to text her. But what to say? He couldn't very well say, *By the way, in case you were worrying, I'm not trying to get in your knickers and I'm not trying to slot you into my daughter's life as her new mum. I just think you're a really spectacular person.* Because that was the long and short of it. He could just send a *Hey, how you doing?* sort of text, to test the waters, but if she *was* feeling a bit overwhelmed, it would be better to leave her alone for a bit. And she was with her friend today so it might seem a bit intrusive. They'd said all their thank yous last night and there was nothing else to say. He would see her on Wednesday, which wasn't long to wait, although it would be a professional occasion for her. There would be crowds of people around and it might be hard to gauge how things stood between them.

Another thing – she hadn't asked Eliza to call her Holly yesterday. Several times Eliza had addressed her as Miss Hanwell and it had sounded a bit... odd, out there in the woods when Holly's blue hat had been slipping down over her eyes, her face flushed with the cold, when she was doubled over with laughter or watching the swoop of the magpies with spellbound eyes. She hadn't *looked* like a Miss Hanwell; she'd looked like Holly. Each time, he'd expected her to say, 'You don't need to call me that when we're not at school, Eliza. Call me Holly.' But she hadn't. He knew she was fond of Eliza, but she was basically super-teacher. She would always treat each pupil fairly and equally. Perhaps she was protecting Eliza, not letting her get too used to Holly being around out of school, in case she had reservations about the situation. It made sense, and he was grateful for any safeguarding of Eliza, but still it felt oddly disappointing.

Then Edward caught himself. These were silly worries. She hadn't come to church because she was busy. She hadn't texted him for the same reason. She was probably so used to children calling her Miss Hanwell that she hadn't even noticed. If he was going to stress about anything, it should be the damn costume. Time was running out.

But then Eliza appeared, brandishing her DVD of *The Emperor's New Groove*. She wanted to watch it for the four hundredth time. Edward knew that he needed to start the costume, but weekends were for together-time after all… and who on earth could resist a story about an emperor who got turned into a llama? Not Edward Sutton. Well, there were still two more evenings to go. He'd always been one of those kids who did his homework at the last minute. He responded well to pressure. Somewhere between now and Wednesday morning, the magic had to happen.

CHAPTER THIRTY-FIVE

Holly

'You're distracted,' said Penny when Holly arrived at the community on Sunday afternoon. They'd arranged to meet at four. Holly would have had plenty of time to go to church with Edward and Eliza and still keep her date with Penny. It wasn't as if she hadn't loved every minute with the Suttons yesterday, and it certainly wasn't as if she didn't relish having plenty of company. But something had warned her away, something that had kept her awake most of last night, despite all the fresh air and the wonderful relaxing day. Perhaps it had been a little bit *too* wonderful.

She liked Edward more all the time. Seeing him with that little fox, for instance. Enjoying his exaggerated applause when she and Eliza took their bows. He was a kind man, and that was a rare thing. He was also clever, practical (aside from cooking), humorous and easy-going. And *so* good-looking. As for Eliza, Holly had been besotted with her from the word go. If she could have had a daughter, she'd want her to be exactly like Eliza. Holly wanted to be friends with them both, no shadow of a doubt, but she needed to be a tiny bit careful. She didn't want Edward to think she was pushing herself forward as some sort of mother figure for Eliza, that she was trying to turn some innocently intentioned company into some sort of *date*. It had felt so nice, so comfortable, playing games and chatting and munching on nibbles, the three of them together. The prospect of going home had felt positively jarring.

How could she feel so at home at Christmas House, with people she'd known only a few weeks?

'Holly? Earth to Holly? Are you alright, mate?' Penny was looking at her with a baffled expression. They were in the ecolodge that was the heart of the community. It was a wooden hall with huge beams supporting the woven, wooden roof. There were great metal urns of hot water on a table at one end; members of the community took turns to tend them so that, when it wasn't being used for workshops or meditation, the hall functioned as a sort of free drop-in café and social hub for the collective. The air was fragrant with incense.

'I'm fine, sorry. Just… preoccupied. I've got a bit of a situation. Nothing bad. Just… preoccupying.'

'So I gather. Tell me. Hang on a sec.' Penny poured two mugs of herbal tea and grabbed a handful of home-baked granola bars. Then she towed Holly to a wooden picnic table with benches at the far end of the hall. By its unusual ashy colour and knobbly, wonky structure, Holly knew it had been made here, like all the furniture. There were wicker chairs and little round tables, velvet cushions around tiny little Turkish-style mosaic tables and beanbags sewn from what was clearly old clothing. Penny knew that Holly liked the Turkish tables and cushions best, but the hall was busy today and they'd have more privacy down here. 'Tell me,' she repeated.

'There've been some developments since I saw you last…' Holly glanced up into the wooden rafters, where little dust motes danced a merry jig in the winter sunlight.

'Good. Developments are good. Flux is the nature of life,' Penny said, nodding. 'We cannot stop still or we petrify, we stagnate. We must flow.'

'Yeah. Exactly. Well, I guess I'm flowing. Coming to terms with everything. My neighbour Phyllis is helping me a lot – I told you about her, right? But it's not that. It's… well, I've sort of fallen in love with someone. And I think I might be really attracted to someone else.'

Penny's eyebrows hitched up. 'OK,' she said, drawing the word out. 'Well, hey, polyamorous relationships are a thing these days. There are a couple here at Soul Pastures. I wouldn't have seen you as the sort, though.'

Holly laughed and took a sip of tea from her chunky blue china mug. 'No, it's not like that. The person I'm definitely in love with is one of my pupils. An eight-year-old girl called Eliza. Oh, Penny, she's heaven – even you'd adore her. She's an old soul, you know? Really quirky and funny but serious and sensitive and pretty…'

'Sounds like the daughter you always should have had,' observed Penny, poking at her teabag with a spoon.

'That's how I feel. Like we belong together. But anyway, she's *not* mine, she's my pupil, and I do my best for her, as her teacher, and I've been helping her with some stuff, and that's that.' A couple in matching red-and-purple tasselled hats came and sat at the next table. They smiled and raised their hands in greeting before settling down to their own conversation.

Penny waved back then turned her attention back to Holly. 'Right. So much for the kid. So who's the person you *might* be falling for?'

'Her dad.'

'Woah.'

'Yes.' Holly told Penny all about the previous day. She didn't mention the Cressida situation. She doubted anyone at Soul Pastures would have the slightest interest in the Hollywood glamazon, but it was Edward's business and it really wasn't relevant to this part of the story. 'I could have gone to church with them,' she concluded. 'It was at ten this morning so I had loads of time. But…'

'But you didn't want to attend an institution rooted in the patriarchy that expects everyone to believe the same thing and where entry to heaven depends on being a card-carrying member?'

'*No*, it's not that sort of a church. Edward told me about the vicar and he sounds like seriously good people. It's such a pretty place, I've been wanting to go anyway, to get to know people, to feel less like the new girl in Hopley. It was the thought that… well, for one thing, it was actually *Eliza* who invited me, and Edward just nodded and agreed. He wouldn't say, "Actually no, don't come," would he? It would be rude and awkward and he's a nice guy, you know?'

Penny frowned and nodded thoughtfully. 'Yeah, that's a problem. You don't want to get mixed up with a *nice* guy.'

'Oh, shut up. You know what I mean. I didn't want him to be saddled with me because he was too polite to take back Eliza's invitation. And… the thought of the three of us walking into church together was a bit much. We'd have looked like a proper family. Everyone would have *thought* we were a family, and we'd have been explaining the whole time: "No, we're not together. We're just friends. And I'm not Eliza's mother, I'm her teacher…" Too weird.'

Penny nodded and started pushing some spilled brown sugar into a tiny mandala pattern on the table. 'Bit intense, I guess. You probably made a good call. I mean, there's time for all that if the friendship continues. Which I don't see why it wouldn't – they obviously both really like you. And if you've got a little crush on Sexy Dad, well, that's not illegal. He might well feel the same about you – you're so pretty and, like, the nicest person *ever*. And even if he doesn't, well, you'll survive. At least this shows you're getting over Alex and all that bollocks. I think this is a very good thing.'

'You're right,' declared Holly. 'Good for me.' But as she bit into her granola bar, she couldn't help thinking that Eliza would only be in her class for this one year. If the friendship didn't work out, if her feelings for Edward didn't go away, Eliza would be moving up to Viv Conroy's class next September and Holly wouldn't see her every day anymore. She wouldn't be responsible for her during the daytime. That was why being a teacher was different from being a parent. At some point, as a parent, you had to let them go, but you got a good eighteen years or so first. As a teacher, you only ever had nine months and then they passed through your hands, out of reach.

CHAPTER THIRTY-SIX

Edward

Tuesday night. Once again, Holly's letter about the costume was spread out in front of Edward. This was the moment of reckoning. If it didn't get done tonight, his daughter would be playing the part of an angel dressed in leggings and a Spider-Man T-shirt. The pressure was officially on.

The letter stipulated that the Angel of Starlight costume should consist of a plain, ankle-length white dress with short sleeves. It should have wings, shoes and a halo. A minimum of decoration was allowed. He'd hunted through all her old clothes – he really had to take some things to a charity shop – but Eliza wasn't a party-dress kind of girl; the only thing he could find that was even remotely suitable was an old nightie of hers – white with pink rosebuds scattered over it. He told himself that loose and shapeless would work – it would look *flowing*. It was too long – it always had been and she hadn't stopped wearing it because she grew out of it, just because she went off it. But he could shorten it to ankle-length. The rosebuds were very delicate and small. It was as good as plain white.

The wings might have presented a problem had he not had the presence of mind to stop off at an art shop near the office and buy some huge sheets of white card – enough to allow for mistakes and starting again. He congratulated himself on his forethought and set to work at last. It worked every time, leaving things till the last minute; his creative juices were flowing at last. Tea was over and cleared, and Edward was working at the kitchen table where the moonlight streamed through the window, augmenting the electric light inside. It was rather magical. He wouldn't let Eliza or Mrs D see what he was doing, partly because he was self-conscious about it and partly because, as he worked, a vision of Eliza's finished angel costume rose up before his eyes and he became utterly engrossed.

He could clearly imagine Eliza as the trumpet-blowing, dramatic kind of angel, with long feathered wings and a circlet in her hair. He sketched the wings on the card and cut them out quickly, then shredded bits of tissue and stuck them all over with glue to look like feathers. He turned up the hem a couple of inches, using big crooked stitches, which he assured himself wouldn't show from the stage, then sliced enthusiastically at the sleeves and hemmed those too. He frowned when he saw how ragged they were; he didn't know how to make them any neater. Undaunted, he had the bright idea of trimming the sleeves with tinsel. Tinsel might be a bit random on an angel costume, but Lizzie loved the stuff and it would cleverly hide the wavy edges. Why shouldn't she be a completely original angel? A minimum of decoration was allowed, after all. He raced to find some silver tinsel, and while he was at it, he grabbed Eliza's pots of glitter.

He was quite pleased with the effect of the tinsel. Mrs D left. Eliza came to say good night and he rushed to hug her at the kitchen door so that she wouldn't see the costume before it was finished. She went to bed and he kept working. He decided to put some glitter on the wings and daubed them with streaks of glue. Unfortunately, the tissues stuck to his brush instead of the wings and started to look a big mangy. He found more tissues and did battle for a while, then emptied a whole pot of silver glitter over them so they would be shimmering and splendid, before tiptoeing up to Eliza's room. She was already asleep. He stole one of her Alice bands and took it downstairs, where he carefully wound tinsel all the way around it so that none of the tortoiseshell showed through.

Then he poured himself a glass of wine and sat down to assess his progress. He wasn't sure. It all looked a bit amateurish, and he wasn't sure the effect was quite what he'd been aiming for. Worst of all, surrounded by all the white and silver, the pink rosebuds really stood out. He sipped the wine and crossed the kitchen to survey the dress from a distance. The rosebuds still showed. Then he switched the light off to simulate the effect of sitting in a dark hall where hopefully he would be dazzled by the stage lights, but he could still see the rosebuds. Clearly. Edward swore under his breath. He hadn't thought it would take quite this long. Were there really people who enjoyed this home crafting business?

He'd expected to be up all night working on the eve of the presentation but this wasn't quite what he'd had in mind. He needed to get this done so that he could spend an hour at least going over his notes for the presentation tomorrow – he wanted it all fresh in his mind when the clients arrived – and he wanted an early night. But this felt like a never-ending project! What to do about the dress?

He considered it over another glass of wine, though it was rare that he ever had a second, and came up with a solution. Methodically starting at the top of the dress and working his way down from left to right, he dabbed glue onto the rosebuds and covered them with glitter. Silver spots, he decided, might be very effective. She was the Angel of Starlight after all. It might look as if she actually carried the stars with her as she walked. Eliza would love that. He dared to hope that Holly might too.

It seemed to take hours. Soon, it appeared to Edward that the whole world was made of white cotton and silver glitter. The pattern danced before his tired eyes, and no matter how organised his approach, more rosebuds kept breaking out like a rash. At this point he put the wine bottle firmly back in the fridge. He grew so tired that at last he fell asleep, hunched over the table, his head cushioned by folds of soft material and a spill of glitter covering his hands.

He was woken by his phone ringing. It was Lindy. 'Edward, I'm sorry to ring you so early,' she said.

Edward missed the next bit in a wave of confusion. Didn't she mean *late*? It wasn't early, it was *late* for her to be calling. But just as well she had, so he could get to bed. He cast his eyes about for a clock then realised he was wearing his watch and squinted through sore eyes. It was 6.30 a.m. Horrified, he slapped his head to dislodge the sponge that seemed to be lodged there. An avalanche of glitter showered onto the table. He gave a strangled groan.

'Edward? Are you OK?' asked Lindy.

'I'm fine, fine,' he said hastily. He couldn't face explaining a night spent among the glue pots to Lindy, and besides, it was the day of the presentation. He had to be professional. 'Sorry, Lindy, I was a bit distracted for a moment by something here. Tell me again what you need.'

She needed him to bring an extra laptop to the office. Fine. That, at least, he could do. Not like making angel costumes. He couldn't even bring himself to look at it. He ended the call and staggered to the bathroom where he was confronted with a shocking reflection. He was covered in glitter; it was in his hair, in his stubble, in his eyelashes. He had a bright red mark on his forehead where it had rested on the table all night. Having fallen asleep after a glass and a half of wine, without brushing his teeth, his mouth was as rank as a bear pit. He looked and felt like someone who'd spent a night getting completely planked at some bizarre party, instead of someone who'd spent the night at home sewing children's clothing.

'Oh, this isn't good, this isn't good, this isn't good,' he muttered as he gripped the bathroom sink and panicked. Then he pulled himself together. It wasn't too late to salvage things. Alright, so he hadn't had the organised preparatory evening he'd planned. But he knew that presentation inside out. He was passionate about the concepts. He was a master of the art of winging it. He'd be fine; he just needed to get a move on.

At top speed he shaved, bits of black stubble mixing in the sink with the inevitable silver glitter, then showered under a steaming jet of water, which jolted him into consciousness and self-recrimination. 'What an idiot,' he sputtered through the water. 'Total loser, what a time to choose to do your *Blue Peter* act. Know your limitations!'

Whatever had made him think he could do it? He should have been working, resting, preparing. Every single word of the presentation was utterly absent from his brain. So much for knowing it inside out. 'Why should we choose your organisation, Mr Sutton, over the very impressive competitors who have also approached us?' asked Craig Daniels, the suave chairman of WRM, in Edward's imagination as Edward threw on shirt, tie and underpants.

'I have absolutely no idea,' responded imaginary Edward. 'I, for one, am a complete disaster; perhaps you should try someone else.'

The panic eased as he realised that he'd made good time getting dressed. He polished his shoes thoroughly, something he always found calming, taking deep breaths as he watched them begin to gleam, then found the laptop and put it beside his briefcase. His stomach was too knotted for breakfast so he would just have a coffee. Eliza was still asleep. Because he was leaving so early this morning, Mrs D was taking her to school; she'd be here any minute.

He'd caught up with himself; it was all in hand. Edward went into the kitchen to make his coffee and confront last night's handwork. It looked like something from a nightmare. Suddenly he felt very, very old and tired. Never mind staying up all night on the eve of the presentation and getting himself in a state, he hadn't even succeeded in making a costume for Eliza.

In the cold light of morning, his moonlit flight of enthusiasm well and truly scarpered, the dress looked terrible. The blobs of glitter all over it looked like a ravaged, pewter-coloured pox. The stitching holding the tinsel onto the sleeves had come loose and the tinsel dangled tiredly. The hem was so wavy it made him feel seasick. The wings were less reminiscent of angels than of a chicken with mange – great tufts of tissue had come away despite his best efforts and bald patches exposed the dull card below. Altogether, Edward decided, it was the sorriest thing he had ever seen; Eliza couldn't wear it.

He heard Mrs D's Mini come crunching into the drive and glanced at his watch. Time to leave. Hastily, he swept the whole mess into a black bin bag, tied it and tossed it next to the kitchen bin before brushing all the glitter from the table into the palm of his hand and emptying it into the sink. Then he scrawled a quick note for Eliza.

> *Darling Lizzie-Tops, I'm sorry but I don't think sewing is my thing. Horrid disaster with your costume; you can't use it. Sorry, sorry, sorry! But never fear, I have another plan. There'll be a brilliant one here by lunchtime. Mrs D will bring it to you at school. See you later and break a leg, love Daddy xxxxx*

He hastened out, exchanging quick hellos with Mrs D in the cold, blue-black outdoors. In the end, he salvaged the situation the only way he could think of. On the train, instead of going over his notes for the presentation, he trawled the internet for fancy-dress shops and found a children's angel costume that was everything he'd had in his mind's eye. He paid extra to have them courier it to his house by midday. Then he forced himself to shake off his feelings of failure and devote all his concentration, for the next few hours, to work.

Later on, he felt that his great achievement that morning was calming down the rest of the team before the presentation, giving advice and a few last words of inspiration. He couldn't imagine how this was possible when he himself was in turmoil and uncomfortably underprepared, nevertheless he did it. All too soon, it was 10 a.m. and the troupe from WRM arrived. Even as he stood at the window, watching them walk across the car park, he found himself checking his emails to make sure there was no problem with the order for the angel costume. The WRM team came walking up the corridor towards the boardroom; five people, including their inscrutable chair, Craig Daniels, and their MD, Emma Buchannan, whom Edward hadn't met before.

'Good to meet you, Mr Sutton.' She had a fierce handshake and a direct gaze. She was the sort of person you found yourself wanting to impress. 'I'm looking forward to seeing what you've got for us.' Then she squinted up at his hairline. 'Is that *glitter*?'

CHAPTER THIRTY-SEVEN

Holly

Darkness had melted into palest blue and gold. The trees were a dark filigree against the sky and a gauze of icy air wreathed the park and houses visible from Holly's classroom window. A light frost still shimmered; winter was so beautiful. She felt dreamy and reflective for a moment, standing pressed against the radiator's warmth, taking in the view. She'd come in early, of course. It was the day of the pageant and there was so much to do. These few quiet moments would be the last she'd have all day.

Then Sam, the caretaker, crashed through her door and the crazy began. He'd offered to help her carry all the things they would need for *A Christmas Wish* to the assembly hall before the day got properly started. Between the endless boughs of evergreen, the precious patchwork angels, the decorations and the painted platforms for the Christmas tree scene, there was far too much for Holly to lug over there alone. When the children started to arrive, they helped too, Javai's diminutive figure staggering under a teetering pile of boxes, Lily and Vicky each carrying two evergreen boughs at a time, twirling and wafting them like chorus girls with ostrich-feather fans.

Each time Holly returned to the class, more children had turned up, not remotely fazed to find a teacherless room – everyone knew that Christmas pageant day was a day like no other. Sometimes she found already overexcited kids fighting duels with rulers or engaged in elaborate parkour circuits of the classroom. These she quickly pressed into service until she felt like the Pied Piper with a trail of small figures following behind her, each with their arms full.

Because their play was the last of the pageant, they couldn't set it all up in advance. There was to be a ten-minute interval before *A Christmas Wish* and they had to get the stage all set during that break. They did a couple of run-throughs, practising getting everything set up in the short time; Eliza, Fatima, David, Griff and Kyle were her roadies. Then they had one last full rehearsal, before vacating the hall for the other classes to do their prep.

They all had lunch together in the classroom. Each child had brought in something to eat or drink, and Holly had brought an enormous supply of American-style Christmas cookies and gingerbread men, chicken legs and coleslaw, flatbread and hummus. She pushed the tables together to lay out the spread on a primary-coloured Christmas tablecloth and they all crowded round, dropping crumbs, getting fingers dirty and, most of all, laughing. Holly quashed any budding food fights but otherwise let them relax. It was a special day; self-containment was too much to expect – the cleaners were forewarned and expecting a massive tip. It was pure joy, thought Holly. She was comfortable with barely contained chaos; nothing made her heart sing like the sound of children laughing, and she knew, with some pride, that she was creating magic: memories they would remember for many, many years.

In the afternoon Bob and his owner, Andrew, turned up and the children made a huge fuss of them both, proffering carrot sticks (to Bob) and cookies (to Andrew). Since it was dry, they waited in the small garden behind the hall. Bob would enter through the fire doors to the rear of the stage and hopefully wouldn't be spotted until he made his grand entrance during the play; like his character in the story, he was to be a great surprise.

Through it all, Holly found her thoughts occasionally straying to Edward. During the rehearsal, she glanced at her watch and thought, *He'll be in his presentation right now. I wonder how it's going.* Over lunch she found herself wondering where he was on his journey home and whether he was victorious or disappointed. And as they all trooped out to see Bob, she found an opportunity to ask Eliza the question she'd been wanting to ask all morning: 'Is your costume all sorted?'

'Oh yes,' replied Eliza, with shining eyes. 'And it's *wonderful*!'

'Did your dad have time to make it?' asked Holly, but Fatima ran past calling Eliza's name and dragged her off before she had a chance to answer.

Finally, it was time. The hall was quiet, rows of waiting chairs (with suitable fire-safety spacing) ready to be filled. The children were all backstage, boys on the left, girls on the right, climbing into their costumes. Holly was running back and forth, helping where needed, applying artful stage make-up. And then the audience started arriving. Jimmy Claybourne from the *Hopley Post* came nice and early and tucked into the mulled wine laid out on the tables that lined one side of the hall. Holly's guests were Phyllis and Penny – she was touched that they'd both wanted to come; it was hardly Penny's sort of thing – and she gestured madly to the two of them with an angel wing in one hand and a Santa cap in the other, so they could each realise who the other was. She just had time to see them hug and take seats together near the front before a detached fox-tail – costume crisis, not animal cruelty – called her away.

Parents and grandparents started to trickle in. Evie Greavey's family were early, and while her siblings went to sit down (with large paper cups of mulled wine), Mr and Mrs Greavey came over to the stage, waved at Evie, then asked Holly if they could have a word.

'*Now?*' Holly couldn't help but ask. She was struggling with Neil Burrows' snowman suit, which was an overhaul of his

Easter Bunny costume from April. Despite his mum's attempts to pin the ears down, they kept popping up. Holly was seriously considering hacking them off, but she had a feeling that come Easter, she'd be seeing this costume again and that Mrs Burrows wouldn't thank her.

'If you could,' said Mr Greavey in a tone that meant, *Yes now, whether you can or not.* That didn't bode well, thought Holly, stepping down from the stage.

'I'll get back to this, Neil,' she promised, leaving him looking like a tearful snow bunny. 'Mr and Mrs Greavey, hello,' she said briskly. 'What can I do for you?'

'Is it true that you have Evie *singing* tonight?' Mr Greavey wasn't beating around the bush, for which Holly was grateful.

'Evie is singing a solo, yes.'

'But what on earth possessed you?'

'Me? I don't understand.'

'Why would you suggest such a thing? It's so… unexpected, so out of nowhere. It's preposterous, actually.' Mr Greavey's brows were drawing together like thunderclouds. Holly's heart sank. She didn't need this. More to the point, Evie didn't need this. She glanced around. Various small scenes of chaos were unfolding in the wings. The hall was a quarter full now, and an excited buzz could be heard.

'Preposterous? I'm afraid I don't understand. Evie loves singing – she has a beautiful voice – so it seemed obvious. I asked her if she'd like to and she said yes. I assure you it was quite her decision.'

'No she doesn't,' said Mrs Greavey with some angst.

'She doesn't…?'

'Like singing. *Or* have a good voice. You've set her up to fail, Miss Hanwell. She's a sensitive child. I'm afraid we can't allow it.'

Holly bit back impatience. What on earth had Evie said to them? 'May I ask when you learned about the solo? Has Evie only just told you?'

'She didn't tell us at all!' Mr Greavey looked outraged. 'We overheard her on the phone to a classmate this morning, saying she was so nervous about her solo that she could die. This isn't healthy, Miss Hanwell. She needs to concentrate on her lessons. A solid academic background will give her certainty, security. That's what we want for her. She said you've been giving her maths tutoring. We were pleased about that; we thought you had the right idea.'

Holly took a deep breath. 'I see. I can understand that must have given you quite a surprise. Let me explain. Yes, I've been helping her with maths. She was struggling, just a little, and she's a conscientious girl. We've seen some real improvement, which is wonderful. But she's only eight, Mr and Mrs Greavey. As well as studying, she deserves to have a bit of fun and do the things she loves – which, in Evie's case, is singing. As for what you overheard, all performers get nervous before a big night. They all say things like that. I spoke to Evie five minutes ago and yes, she's nervous, but she's far more excited.'

'But Evie's not a performer,' insisted Mrs Greavey, almost tearfully. 'She's a… a… Well, what is she, Albert?'

'She's a mouse.' Albert Greavey was decisive. 'Of our three children she's the one who… well, she has nothing about her. I know that sounds a harsh thing to say about your own child. Don't get me wrong, I love her to bits. But she's not sparky like the others, not strong. She'll crash and burn up there, to put it frankly, Miss Hanwell. She hasn't got what it takes.'

Holly smiled. 'Evie's no mouse. Didn't you ask her about the solo when you overheard her?'

'We weren't eavesdropping,' her mother put in at once. 'We just *happened* to hear. But no, we didn't ask her about it. We were running late at the time and completely taken aback. It was only this afternoon when we talked about it that we decided we really must put a stop to it.'

'So Evie doesn't know that you know anything,' said Holly. 'That's good, because she wants to surprise you. I promise, she's very excited about this. If you're seriously worried and insist on talking to her before the show, I'll call her for you, of course. But if you're able to trust me, I'd advise you take your seats and settle in to enjoy your daughter's big moment.'

'Big moment?' Albert Greavey looked at his wife with bewilderment and she shrugged.

'Is she really alright, Miss Hanwell?' she asked, biting her lip.

'Perfectly. I assure you.'

'But… it's *Evie*,' she whispered.

'Yes. Exactly. Now if you'll excuse me, I still have lots to do.'

Holly clambered back onto the stage, fuming on Evie's behalf. She quite understood that the Greaveys were driven by concern and wanted to protect their daughter. Even so. A *mouse*? *Nothing about her*? Had they paid *any* attention to her at all? Simmering, Holly went in search of Neil. She'd skewer the damn ears to his skull if necessary. She glanced back once and saw the Greaveys still hovering by the stage, their body language a portrait of anxiety. She glanced again a moment later and they were gone. The hall was almost full.

Mr Buckthorn appeared in an unnecessarily vivid chequered sports coat. 'It's time, boys and girls, teachers. Everyone except for Mr Brown's class away from the stage, please, and complete hush. Break a leg, everyone.'

Holly and her class gathered together in their allocated part of the backstage area. It was dusty and shadowy and absolutely deliciously exciting. The children giggled and whispered, but Holly put a finger to her lips and they simmered down. She'd given them a pep talk on all the work the other classes had put into their performances and how they absolutely mustn't be silly on the night and spoil it all.

That done, she reached out a hand and grabbed Neil by his fluffy arm and pulled him to her side. She'd found a giant safety pin in the sewing room. If that didn't do it, nothing would. While Mr Brown's class, the 'little kids' as Dean dismissively referred to them, stumbled through their ten-minute nativity play, getting the pageant off to a traditional start, Holly jabbed at the thick fabric of the libertine ear until the pin went through.

Then she sat back to listen and enjoy, wondering if Edward was here yet, wondering if he'd won the fragrance campaign, wondering if he'd enjoy the play she'd written...

CHAPTER THIRTY-EIGHT

Edward

Four hours after WRM arrived at his office, Edward left to go home again. On the train, he sat and simmered with suppressed glee but once inside his car, he whacked the radio up to full volume and whooped with abandon. They'd got the deal. All the ins and outs and implications had quite faded away, and he'd left the office popping champagne and celebrating, full of conversations like 'I nearly died when…' and 'Could you believe it when…?' Everyone was disappointed when he gathered up his things to leave, but there was no conflict in his mind. He had done his job and it was time for Eliza now.

He got home with a sensible amount of time to change and make it to the school. He hoped the costume was OK; he wondered if Lizzie might have left him a note about it.

He let himself in, relishing the smell of bolognese in the air, the residual warmth in the hallway and he blessed Mrs D a thousand times over for the changes she had wrought in their lives. Then he went into the kitchen to see if there was a note but there wasn't. Instead, on the scarred pine table, was the costume, in its glossy fancy-dress-shop box; he recognised the purple and white branding at once. Mrs D must have forgotten to take it to school. But *twice*? She was the most organised of women. If she'd forgotten to take it to Lizzie at lunchtime, well, that wasn't beyond the realms of possibility; anyone could have an absent-minded moment. But she wasn't here. The house was empty, no Mini on the drive. She'd gone to see the play and left the costume behind again.

Oddly, the box had been opened. The lid was off and a mass of white tissue paper foamed out. He picked up the costume: dress, wings and halo, all just as he'd ordered. It was a really great costume. He looked around for an explanation but saw nothing to give him a clue. A worrying thought occurred to him. Had Eliza been so upset over his failure to provide a home-made costume that it had thrown her off? Had she decided to drop out at the last minute? If he'd ruined the pageant for her, he'd never forgive himself.

Then he spotted the black plastic bag from this morning, on the floor by the bin; it was torn open and empty. A tell-tale trail of glitter ran from bag to front door.

'Oh, Eliza,' he murmured, feeling his eyes prickling. He couldn't believe she'd chosen to wear his diseased-looking creation instead of a proper outfit. She didn't need any stupid costume to be an angel – she was already one. He changed quickly into a smart sweater and jeans, grabbed his coat and ran to the car, seizing the fancy-dress box on his way out. If he got there in time, he could give Eliza the chance to change her mind.

Just minutes before the pageant was due to start, he bounded into the wings of the assembly hall, passing outraged teachers who tried to stop him, but he was on a mission. The tiny children were already onstage in their starting positions, behind the curtain. He spotted a cute little Joseph, an adorable Mary and a couple of clockwork sheep.

Backstage, the rest of the school sat in class groups and he spotted Eliza's at once, with Holly bright in a red jumper and skirt, at their centre. There was Fatima and there was Jinny and there was that young reprobate Jason Tillwell. And there was his daughter, tinsel and long threads trailing, pox-like glitter splotches shining feverishly. A few tissues had dropped off her wings and lay scattered around her as if she had the flu. He felt deeply ashamed.

'Psst! Lizzie-Boots. Eliza!' he hissed. She turned and beamed at him and waved. Holly also turned and looked delighted, shocked, curious. He waved, but now was hardly the time to chat. Eliza climbed to her feet and ran silently to him, bits of tissue drifting off her as she came.

'What are you doing here, Daddy? You should be in your seat.'

He held up the shiny box and shook it at her. 'It's not too late!'

She frowned. 'Don't be silly, Daddy – I like this one.'

'Darling, you *can't*.'

'I do.'

'But think how it reflects on me. Sewing isn't my best skill, darling.'

'Get over it,' she reprimanded him. 'Go and sit down.'

'*Seriously?*' He couldn't believe she was quite that devoid of vanity, but it seemed she'd inherited his own genes on that score, rather than Cressida's.

'Seriously. It's the one I want, Daddy, I love it. You should have known.'

He sighed, defeated. 'Alright. Break a leg, Lizzie-Tops. I love you.' He began to tiptoe out of the wings.

'Daddy!' she hissed and he turned. 'Thank you for my lovely dress.'

He saluted her ironically and went to find a seat.

CHAPTER THIRTY-NINE

Eliza

Soon, Eliza was standing on her green-painted bench, ready to stand in her opening attitude (arms raised, wings proudly displayed) when the curtain rose. Her grey eyes were shining with excitement and her cheeks were burning. Miss Hanwell had helped them put some stage make-up on earlier and she knew that the face that looked out at the audience would not be her own, but an altogether rarer and more magical Eliza, who could float on feathered wings and do marvellous things. It was strange, but she wasn't nervous at all.

When she'd woken that morning, she'd thought she couldn't go through with it. She'd climbed out of bed to discover that her stomach was in snakes and went downstairs to reread her mother's Christmas card. Her mother was a stranger now, she realised, and she was a stranger to her mother. It was horrible. She stared at the message and remembered all those other plays, the ones her parents had watched together, taking it in turns to hug her afterwards, and then the ones that came after, when she'd frozen onstage and it had all gone horribly wrong. Eliza just didn't want to go through that again. She'd gone back upstairs to her window seat, always her favourite place to gaze through the window and think, but the panes were misted by squares of condensation and she couldn't see a thing.

Then she'd dragged on her dressing gown and slouched to the kitchen, sure she was going to let Miss Hanwell down at the last minute and disappoint her dad, certain that she was going to hate herself for it. But Aunty Pam had been waiting in the kitchen with Eliza's favourite breakfast cooking: pancakes. And Eliza had realised that although her mother might be a stranger now, she had plenty of other people. Aunty Pam was a new friend really, but she felt as if she'd known her all her life. The same went for Fats and Jinny. Miss Hanwell was the loveliest teacher on the planet. And of course, there was always her dad.

'Your father's sending a fancy costume,' Aunty Pam had told her, flipping a pancake deftly. Eliza still hadn't mastered that art. 'He texted me. His went a bit wrong, he says, so he's having one couriered over. There's a note there.'

Eliza had read the note and frowned, then looked around and spotted the bin bag by the door. She'd pulled it open and gently lifted out the things her father had made. 'But I like this one,' she'd said and Aunty Pam had come to see. She'd helped Eliza to stick the moulting tissues back on and had hastily reattached the tinsel with safety pins. They'd both agreed that nothing could be lovelier. Proud and happy, Eliza had packed the dress into her bag and Aunty Pam had carefully laid the long wings across the back seat of her car. Eliza hadn't needed to see the lunchtime costume to know which she'd prefer.

Now her early morning melancholy had vanished and she felt wildly fizzy, like a Coke bottle after a good shaking. She had the longest wings of all the children and the sparkliest dress. Thick tufts of tinsel framed her face and made her head itch. It was the very best discomfort there was.

Now, Miss Hanwell was chivvying everyone into place and whispering encouragement to the children. 'Everything alright?' she asked as she passed Eliza.

Eliza nodded, grinning.

'Good,' whispered Miss Hanwell. 'That's good.' And she stepped out through the curtains to welcome the audience.

CHAPTER FORTY

Edward

Edward had found a seat in the third row. He smiled through the toddlers' nativity and enjoyed the offerings from the other classes, particularly the Christmas song-dance medley and a tuneless but spirited extract from *Les Mis*. Then there was a ten-minute break to stock up on mulled wine and scoff a couple of mince pies. Meanwhile the curtain was drawn to hide the stage and from behind it came a great deal of thumping and scraping, as well as a burst, at one point, of Eliza's unmistakeable silvery laughter.

He found his parents, who were thoroughly enjoying themselves. His mother had cause to criticise him (for cutting it so fine timewise) so that meant *she* was happy, and his father was so pleased to be out and about with her after seeing her tumble the length of the stairs that he was in unusually jovial humour.

'That song about the donkey,' he kept saying fondly. 'Wonderful. Just wonderful. And when Mary dropped Jesus – priceless!'

He also found Mrs D and introduced her to his parents. His mother did the thing she always did when she met new people and tried to act superior and condescending, but Mrs D wasn't one to stand for any nonsense and quickly squashed all of that. She entertained them with stories of Eliza's after-school antics, and Edward's parents listened avidly, lapping them up. He really must arrange for them to see more of Eliza, he thought; maybe in the new year, when the house would be more acceptable to them…

When people started to take their seats again, Edward's mother hobbled here and there on her crutches saying, 'Excuse me,' and, 'I'm ever so sorry to ask but I wonder if...' waving her right crutch about like a conductor directing a complicated game of musical chairs, and within minutes eight people had moved to different seats, leaving a line of four vacant seats so they could all watch Eliza together.

When Holly came out to welcome everyone, Edward thought how stunning she looked with her golden hair shining, her red, Christmassy outfit and long glossy black boots. She introduced the play then stepped off to one side before the curtains swung back.

A collective gasp rose from all the families, nannies and neighbours in the audience. The scuffed school stage was unrecognisable. The floor and backdrop were lavishly strewn with green boughs that released their pine scent into the hall. It was like looking into the heart of a giant Christmas tree. Hung all over the background were the cardboard decorations the children had been making in class, and the patchwork angels that they'd made at home. In addition, twelve motionless children looked as if they too were hanging there, from the branches of this magical tree. Edward knew the secret from Eliza and Holly, that they were standing on almost invisible platforms. Anyone who knew Eliza, Fats, Lily, David, Javai and the rest couldn't help but marvel that they were staying still for so long. The effect was breathtaking.

Murmurs went round the hall.

'This teacher's very good.'

'Terribly talented.'

'So creative.'

For a moment the spectacle was frozen, the way they'd rehearsed, to give the audience time to react and then settle down. Edward feasted his eyes; there was his little girl, luminous and part of the magic. There could be no mistaking her streaming wings, the glitter on her dress bobbing like water in the stage lights. He'd been afraid that her dress would make her look silly, that she'd stand out as the only one with tissues on her wings or spots on her dress. He'd imagined sitting in a row of smug parents all muttering at each other about the state of Eliza Sutton's dress and sniggering that what could you expect, after all, from a single dad? But it was nothing like that at all. All around him, he could hear whispers but all they said was, 'Look, Ma, there's Jai. Is his waistcoat on backward?' 'Where's Claire? Oh, there on the end.' 'Oh no, Indira's hat's got squashed!' and so on.

One of the children was Neil Burrows dressed as a snowman in a white suit that looked suspiciously furry. In fact, he had a distinctly fawn-coloured tummy, Edward noticed; he suspected a bunny costume had been hastily pressed into service. As everyone watched, spellbound, a long rabbit ear slithered down his cheek from underneath his hat. He looked horrified and stared into the wings, presumably at Holly, then he nodded and resumed his impressive stillness.

Edward suddenly understood that close up they all had sagging seams and precariously attached wings, that maybe a few people in the whole audience were really good at this sort of thing but that the rest of them had just done their best, pulling together odds and ends as best they could. The acid test, of course, would be his mother's reaction. As subtly as he could, he turned his head to watch her, beside him, staring with laser-eyes at Eliza. Did she look critical? Scornful? Embarrassed? No, she looked enraptured – and very proud. The children were all patchwork angels, he thought, pieced together, and a little odd, but very beautiful. And he settled back to watch the show and relax.

As the story unfolded, he saw the significance of the different bits Eliza had told him about. The two children, played by Sophie Lewis and Kyle Mortimer, and their bitter, joyless uncle, played by Matt Simmons, who hammed it up to the max. The magical Christmas tree where the decorations came alive and started walking and talking. The six angels sent to make all the children's Christmas wishes come true. The big reveal when Eliza led Bob, a real live reindeer, onto the stage, sending a Mexican wave of disbelieving smiles around the audience. And Evie's solo, which was so beautiful and moving, Edward actually felt tears in his eyes. That kid was *talented!* Griff Heaton's brief but passionately felt appearance as Space Monster #1 had everyone howling with laughter. And Eliza, delivering every single one of her speeches with all of her old aplomb and then some, never faltering or forgetting a word; Edward was stewing in pride like a pudding in brandy.

As the children gathered onstage to take their bows, applause rang out and a sense of well-being hung in the air like woodsmoke. Edward clapped till his hands hurt and so did Mrs D and his parents, not even stopping when his mother's crutch slipped down and whacked his father on the ankle.

Edward gazed all around the hall, taking it in: so much happiness, so many different families all brought together by the magic Holly Hanwell had wrought, magic that had been brought to life by his Eliza and her friends. Everywhere he looked he saw smiling faces, and he laughed out loud as he applauded… until, at the back, in the corner, he saw a figure that struck a chill in his heart. Unmistakeably a woman, standing on the edge of things instead of sitting down with everyone else. She wore a headscarf hijab-style to cover her hair and the lower part of her face and big specs with tinted lenses and a long shapeless coat. A strange way to dress for a school pageant. A strange way to behave too, almost as if she didn't want to be noticed. Or rather, thought Edward, looking away and then instantly looking back again, the figure looked like someone who *wanted* to be noticed but was *acting* as though she didn't want to be noticed. His stomach clenched, his happy vibes draining away. Surely it wasn't… *Cressida?*

CHAPTER FORTY-ONE

Holly

The play was a huge success. Even after all their hard work, Holly could hardly believe it had come together so well. Not one of the children had made a mistake or fluffed their lines. Bob had behaved like the pro he was, and Eliza had rather stolen the show in her own quiet way – to Holly, it was clear that her talent was something special, something apart. As for Evie, well, Evie had blown them all away. When the moment came for her solo, she had frozen for just an instant in the spotlight; from the wings Holly could see the ice-cold fear on her face. She was just about to hiss something motivational when Evie gave herself a visible shake, shifted on her feet so she was standing nice and square, as Holly had taught her, and began. And her voice was *unbelievable*! Even stronger than the day she had sung to Holly in the classroom and just as sweet. Since they'd started rehearsing Evie's song in class, Holly had seen her grow in confidence, just a little at a time, day by day. This evening, she was like a different child: poised, happy, radiant. If her parents didn't see her for what she was after this, well, there was no hope for them.

Mulled wine and mince pies were still being served, and members of the audience were chatting in a haze of festive well-being. Jimmy the journo was scribbling away in a corner, hunched over a notepad in one of the small children's seats. Holly, circulating through the throng to congratulate proud parents, could hardly believe how kind everyone was being. They seemed to think she was some kind of miracle worker and looked at her with perplexity when she told them how clever and special their children were. She picked her way from group to group, keeping an eye out for Eliza and her father.

There they were! She hurried over, noting that they were with Pam Dixon and two people who must be Edward's parents. Edward and Eliza both waved and grinned when they saw her, and Edward broke away from the little group to hurry towards her.

'Holly, that was phenomenal. *You're* phenomenal. Well done.'

She smiled. 'Thank you, Edward, that's kind. And how did the presentation go? I've been wondering about it all day.'

His grin told her all she needed to know. 'We nailed it. We got the deal. It hasn't sunk in yet really…'

'Of *course* you nailed it. Congratulations. I'm so happy for you.' She found herself reaching for him. Oh God, involuntary touching in public wasn't the best way to keep her feelings for him to herself. But he grinned again and returned her hug. Well, a friendly hug was alright, wasn't it? It was just that he was so warm and tall. And then he was looking at her in a way that turned her knees to water. 'Edward…'

'Holly, I hope this isn't horribly inappropriate but I wanted to say…'

'Edward? Are you going to introduce us?' Edward's father.

Holly shook herself – what on earth had he been going to say? – and Edward turned to the little group that had crept up on them. 'Mother, Dad, this is Holly Hanwell, Eliza's teacher and a good friend.'

Was she? That was nice to hear. *Only* a good friend? Oh, never mind that now. They all shook hands and his parents congratulated her warmly. Pam Dixon was beaming, and Edward's dad fetched Holly a glass of mulled wine.

Eliza tugged her arm. 'Miss Hanwell, will you come back to our place afterwards? I'll be too excited to go to bed yet and we could all drink hot chocolate and talk about the play.'

Holly couldn't think of a single thing she'd rather do. It would be terribly deflating going home to a silent house after this. Phyllis and Penny had already hugged her and left, Phyllis tired and Penny with a substantial drive through the winter dark ahead of her to get back to Soul Pastures. But the invitation had come from Eliza again, not Edward. She *badly* wanted it to come from Edward. But he was nodding and adding his own invitation. 'Please do. Unless you're heartily sick of the play after all these weeks and never want to think of it again. We'd understand. But we'd really love to have you. You'd be our guest of honour. Mum, Dad, Pam – why don't you come too? We can have a little after-party.'

'Oh no,' said his mother quickly. 'We're looking forward to our Christmas visit on the twenty-eighth. We'll wait till then. It'll get too late for us old folks otherwise and you'll enjoy having Holly all to yourselves.'

'*If* she's coming…?' said Edward. Even Holly could see that his expression was genuinely hopeful and she allowed herself to trust it.

'That would be absolutely—'

At that moment, Mr Buckthorn climbed onto a chair, swaying precariously – he wasn't generally considered nimble-footed – and shouted for her to make a speech. 'Our very own Miss Holly Hanwell!' he cried. 'Writer and producer, set designer, discoverer of talent and the best and most supportive of teachers. Please come up here and say a few words.'

Holly was mortified. After all, she wasn't the only teacher who'd put on a show tonight. But around the hall, everyone was clapping and cheering, and several hands reached out to push her in Buckthorn's direction; she could hardly run away.

She went towards him reluctantly. Mr Buckthorn jumped from the chair in a flat-footed flump that shook the floor and must have wrecked his knees. 'Up! Up!' he cried expansively.

Eliza rushed over and threw her arms around her. Holly clasped her arms around Eliza in turn and staggered slightly, not because Eliza was any great weight but because she was rocked by the rush of love and joy that coursed through her.

'You must say something,' Eliza whispered. 'I had the best night, and I couldn't have done it without you. Everyone's saying the same, all of the class. Evie's so happy she's crying. There's never been a play like it.'

'Thank you, darling,' said Holly, untangling herself and climbing up onto the chair with the aid of Mr Buckthorn's outstretched, flamboyantly checked arm. From the seat of the chair, she saw a sea of faces, large and small, upturned towards her.

Before she could begin, she heard a slow clapping and saw an unfamiliar figure walk from the back of the hall through the crowd, shedding clothing as it went – a mac, a scarf, some sunglasses… For a moment she wondered if she was watching some sort of bizarre striptease, whether the stranger was drunk, but as the glasses came off, she realised she was looking at a face that was familiar after all. Instantly recognisable, in fact. It was Cressida Carr, the film star. Eliza's mother. Edward's ex-wife. The three realisations dropped from her brain to her stomach: thud, thud, thud.

'Brava!' cried Cressida, her stage voice ringing around the hall. All heads turned in her direction. Happy, excited faces slackened into dropped jaws and astonished eyes. 'Brava! What a splendid little play, and how proud I am of my talented daughter!'

She neared Eliza, reached out an arm and pulled her into an embrace. Now everyone in the entire place was staring at Cressida, mesmerised, and Holly was just a woman standing on a chair.

Like everyone else, she couldn't help looking. Cressida wore a stunning, sexy, electric-blue dress that made her blue eyes look neon in their intensity. Her black hair was Hollywood glossy, long and waved and snaky. Her heart-shaped face scintillated with emotion, and her entire demeanour was that of someone who expected to command attention. Holly tore her eyes away and searched for Edward in the crowd.

His face was blazing, just as intense as Cressida's, in fact, except that no one was looking at him and his expression was very different: a complex mixture of horror, fear and absolute fury. As Holly watched, he took three very determined steps forward, his entire body coiled like a cat, but his mother caught his arm. He stopped and she whispered something in his ear. His shoulders sagged for a moment then he nodded and carried on, but with the deadly determination gone from his stride. Holly understood. He couldn't make a scene, not with Eliza here, but she needed to know her dad was nearby. Holly couldn't see Eliza's face from here and she was quite glad.

Edward said something to Mr Buckthorn and went to stand beside Cressida and his daughter. Mr Buckthorn, like a man emerging from a spell, also approached Cressida and said a few words. Holly caught, '… very welcome… very honoured,' and then, 'If you could please just wait a moment.'

Then he addressed the hall again. 'As you can see, we're honoured to have a celebrity guest with us tonight. I'm sure you all will recognise her at a glance and I very much hope she'll agree to say a few words later on, but now we'll hear from Miss Hanwell. Holly, would you, please?'

Holly had been on the verge of clambering down from the chair. She could hardly think. All she wanted to know was whether Eliza was alright.

Cressida stood back, looking royally ticked off, and loosened her arm from around Eliza's shoulders. Eliza immediately ran to Edward, who bent down and spoke to her urgently. Eliza's small face was whiter than paper and her silver-grey eyes were completely bewildered. Unhappy. But she was nodding as she listened. Holly had to say something. At least half the room now was looking at her again. And she had been an actress too. She knew how to make a speech, how to push aside the things that were troubling her long enough to say what needed to be said. She couldn't reveal the depth of her feelings for Edward and Eliza from the top of a chair.

So she said how happy tonight had made her, how proud she was of the children. She praised the other classes and the hard work of their teachers, and said how grateful she was to their principal for supporting the dramatic arts so whole-heartedly in their school. She explained that although Mr Buckthorn had been kind enough to give her all the credit for her own play, the children were actually *her* inspiration, her motivation and her raison d'être. 'So when I get off this chair,' she concluded, 'I will be raising a glass to each and every one of my wonderful pupils. Their happiness is all that matters. They always should and they always will come first.' Then she jumped down, landing gracefully, and made a little curtsey.

There was applause, and a few people crowded round to pat her on the shoulder, though the majority were still gawping and training their phones on Cressida, who had sidled over to Jimmy the journo. He was listening to her closely, like a hare in a headlight. She was a show-stealer. She was, in theatre parlance, pulling focus from the people that mattered. Not her – she didn't care about that – but from the children. From Evie and Eliza and Fatima and Lily and Griff… inwardly Holly was growling.

She made her way back to Edward and Eliza. 'Edward,' she said, 'is everything alright? Eliza, are *you* alright?'

Edward was apparently so stunned he couldn't speak. He looked at Holly imploringly but couldn't seem to articulate his thoughts. His parents and Mrs Dixon appeared behind him, supportive and silent. And then Cressida returned to her one-time family, with Jimmy trailing in her wake.

CHAPTER FORTY-TWO

Edward

He should have known. That was the thought that kept drumming in his head, that he should have known she would break her promise. But when the mother of your child agrees to a plan of action in the child's best interests, you *should* be able to trust that, shouldn't you? To assume otherwise would mean to think very badly of her indeed. And Edward hadn't seen her for years; he had no reason to think that badly of her. No reason, although shouldn't his intuition have kicked in? But she'd been so charming and understanding. Even if he *had* suspected, what could he have done? Posted security at the school gates? Taken out a restraining order? Hardly.

His hand rested on Eliza's shoulder as she leaned into his legs like a much younger child. He could feel her quivering. Perhaps some of it was the adrenaline from the pageant, but in an instant, she had gone from exuberant and shimmering to silent and watchful, and he actually wanted to cry. He was aware of his parents and Mrs D behind him, like backing singers, and Holly at his side, radiating staunch support. Now here was Cressida, dragging the reporter over and beaming that scintillating smile. She was more beautiful than ever in one way: flawless, glamorous, perfect, the visual equivalent of making your mouth water. Yet she was less beautiful in another. She was no longer the Cressida he'd known and adored. That young woman with her wild tangle of hair, her bare feet, her ready laughter had been more vital, more enticing somehow. This Cressida looked a lot like her but that was as far as it went.

'Darling, well done, so very well done,' she squealed, grabbing an unresponsive Eliza and hugging her tightly. 'You were absolutely marvellous. Quite the best thing in the whole shebang. I'm so proud.'

'Thank you,' said Eliza in a small voice.

'And congratulations to you,' Cressida went on, turning to Holly. 'A very nice effort indeed.'

'Thank you,' said Holly, sounding unimpressed.

'And Edward, darling. It's so lovely to see you. Heavens, you look like you've seen a ghost. Please don't say you're mad that I came tonight. You said not until after the show. And it's after the show. I was very good, I took ever such care not to be recognised on my way in. I thought about what you said, that Eliza shouldn't be disrupted before the play, and you were right. But it's done now, and I couldn't bear to stay away from my little angel a moment longer.'

'I *said*,' he corrected through clenched teeth, 'that I wanted Eliza to have this night. This whole night. And that I would speak to her tomorrow about you and check that she was happy to see you – so she could *choose*. You've somewhat robbed her of that liberty, Cressida.' There was so much more he wanted to say but he was aware that a newspaper reporter was standing right next to them. 'Still, you're here now and it is what it is. You've seen the play. Shall we make an arrangement for another day?'

'Another day? But there's no time like the present, darling. I want to celebrate with Eliza. Shall we all go home together? I'd love to see your little house.'

'Cressida, she's eight. It'll be her bedtime soon.'

'I know she's eight. I *am* her mother. What do you say, Eliza, would you like Mummy to come home with you and we can have a hot drink together before bed and you can tell me all about your new school and everything?'

'If you like.' Eliza's tone was flat but she was always polite.

Edward hunkered down to talk to her. Above them, he was aware of his mother engaging Cressida in conversation to give them some sort of privacy and he felt grateful. 'What do you want to do? If you're tired you can just say no – your mum will understand. But if you'd like to talk to her, she can come home with us for a little bit. Whatever you like, sweetheart.'

Eliza shrugged. 'She can come. We need to see her sometime. And she did come all this way to see me.'

And to steal the show, he thought, but he only said, 'OK.' He stood up and looked at Cressida. 'Just for an hour, Cressida. You've taken us by surprise and it's late for Eliza.'

'An hour's fine, Edward. Thank you. And it was a good surprise I hope!'

No one answered. In the flat silence Cressida looked at Holly again and said, 'You're still here. How lovely. But don't you have lots of parents you need to talk to? Shouldn't you be doing the rounds?'

'I'll get to it,' said Holly, not budging, and Edward felt a shoot of something like joy in his heart that she was still beside him, that she wasn't taking any crap.

'Well, I'm sure you know what you're doing.' Cressida let her double meaning hang for a minute then beamed at Jimmy. 'I'm about to leave with my family. I expect you want to get some shots before we take off. It's such a wonderful reunion. I couldn't be happier.'

Dutifully, Jimmy moved them into position, Edward, Cressida and Eliza. She threw an arm around each, tilted her chin and smiled, as if posing for a selfie with fans. Jimmy took a couple of shots.

'Is that all?' Cressida sounded disappointed. 'Didn't you want one of me with just Eliza? Or if you like, I'll get up on the stage for you. All sorts of photo ops – it'll be the scoop of the year for you.'

Finally Jimmy spoke. 'These will be fine, thank you, Miss Carr. It's already the scoop of the year, trust me. But what I was sent here to do was cover the pageant. Could I have a photo of you please, Holly? And any chance I could get one of you with your class before they all start to head home? Would that be very fiddly? And is Bob still here? I'd love a shot of you with our animal celebrity.'

Holly roused herself and smiled. 'Of course, Jimmy – it's no trouble. I'll go and sort it all out for you.' Edward watched her walk away, glad of an extra few minutes before he would have to go home; he felt a tremendous reluctance at the thought of Cressida entering the magical space that he and Eliza had created for themselves.

'*We* don't have to wait, do we?' Cressida sounded bored. 'Eliza needs to get to bed – you just said it. Let's go and leave them to it.'

'Eliza's needed for the photograph,' said Edward in outrage. 'She's part of that class.'

'But there'll already be a photo of Eliza in the paper – with me. She won't miss out.'

'She'll miss out on being in her *class* photo,' Edward explained wearily. 'With her *friends*. Just wait, Cressida – it won't take long.'

Sure enough, in a couple of minutes, Holly had all the children gathered around her, and Jimmy asked them all to get up onto the stage. Eliza hurried after them and Cressida laughed. 'My goodness, I must admit, I didn't expect to be upstaged by some sort of modern-day Maria von Trapp and a *deer*!'

Her voice carried, quite clearly. Perhaps she hadn't intended it to, or perhaps she had, in a moment of bravado, but when several faces turned in her direction with shocked or disbelieving expressions, it was clear that she regretted saying it. Holly looked over from the stage and gave her a hard stare; Cressida was the first to look away. But Edward had had enough. Now that Eliza and Jimmy were out of earshot, he could speak his mind.

'Cressida, enough. What the hell were you thinking coming here tonight? Don't give me that shit about the play being over and you being so noble because you waited until it was finished to make your grand entrance. Because you have stolen Eliza's thunder *and* Holly's. You've turned Eliza's happy night, which should have been nothing but celebrations, into an emotional minefield. Have you seen how she's shrunk since you announced yourself? She doesn't know how to be around you anymore. And now you've invited yourself into our home without giving me any chance to prepare her. It's shabby of you, you know that?'

The busy hall, the crowds of people, had all faded around him, pushed to the very edge of awareness by his anger. Just now he felt that he and Cressida were the only two people in the world, as if they were floating in an ocean on a raft. And he was desperate to push her off it.

'Edward, look, now that I'm here, I can see I misjudged. I've been longing to see Eliza so much I thought she'd be just as happy to see me. But I was wrong, I can see that. And I thought that by making an appearance I'd get some coverage for your little school, and the play, and that it might be a good thing for them. But perhaps I was wrong about that too. But I wasn't wrong about one thing, Edward: I'm Eliza's mother and it's beyond time we got to know each other again. So please don't send me away.'

Edward groaned. 'We've already established that you're coming back with us for a hot drink. Then Eliza's going to bed and you and I are going to have a serious talk, lay down some ground rules. Which I could do without, by the way, since it's been a pretty big day for me too as it happens. But this can't happen again, so we're sorting it. Tonight.'

Behind him, Mrs D mmm-hmmed in agreement. He could practically hear her biting her tongue.

Cressida nodded and they watched as Jimmy took his photos. The smile had crept back onto Eliza's face. After a couple of minutes snapping away, Jimmy had a word with them all and they nodded enthusiastically. Holly disappeared and came back a moment later with Bob. There were more shots of the children clustered around the ever-patient reindeer and then Jimmy took a couple of Eliza leading Bob across the stage, as she had in the play, then of Holly with Bob, and then he started packing up. The children drifted back to their parents; Eliza hesitated then did the same. Edward sighed. He'd never seen her hesitate to come to him before.

He said his good nights, then he, Cressida and Eliza turned and walked to the door like the little family they had once been. He looked back once. Holly was deep in conversation with the Greaveys. He wished with all his heart that they were waiting for her, instead of leaving her behind. To think that he'd been on the verge of telling her that he thought she was special. He thought he may even have been about to ask her out to dinner. *Way to pick your moments, dude!*

'Cressida?' Edward's mother nipped round to block their way, her crutches not slowing her down. 'Edward may be mincing his words in front of Eliza but I'm cut from a different cloth. I come from a different generation. So hear this, young lady. You're a spoiled brat. A prima donna. You always were, and you've got worse. You're selfish and badly behaved and you're not good enough for my granddaughter. You made her life hell. You'd better not do it again.'

As if she were dealing with pushy paparazzi, Cressida ducked her head and pulled on her tinted glasses.

Edward hustled. 'OK, thanks, Mum. I'll call you tomorrow.'

But Sarah Sutton wasn't finished. 'And…' she cried, reaching up to pluck off Cressida's glasses and look her right in the eyes, 'you were *never* good enough for my son.'

CHAPTER FORTY-THREE

Holly

Getting home was a horrible anti-climax. Holly threw her bag onto a chair and herself onto the sofa and groaned. She'd made peace with her solitary life over the past weeks and had come to take real pleasure in her home. She'd learned to enjoy her own company and to relish her small luxuries and daily habits. But this was a special occasion and she wanted to spend it with special people. It wasn't company per se she craved – she wouldn't give thanks for a crowded pub full of acquaintances just now – but she wanted to be with people she cared about. After a long, busy day of running around, of being surrounded by children *like some sort of modern-day Maria von Trapp*, of colour and excitement, this silence, this stillness, was too great a contrast. It was disorienting.

Leaving Cressida's dramatic arrival aside, it had been a triumph. Parents and children happy. Evie Greavey's parents beside themselves, apologising for their earlier behaviour, Evie shining like a star. Holly's play had done exactly what she'd hoped it would do – move people, make them shed a tear and laugh too. More than one mother had said to her tonight that she'd been too stressed to feel Christmassy, juggling preparations and normal life. 'But I feel Christmassy now,' she heard over and over again. 'You're a miracle worker, Miss Hanwell.' It was wonderful.

But she *couldn't* leave Cressida aside, could she? It seemed that Eliza's miracle had been cancelled out all too soon. It had been so moving to see her up there on the stage, knowing the fears that had plagued her, and knowing that she, Holly, had played some small part in helping Eliza change her mind. And for five minutes afterwards, Eliza had been *happy*. Holly could see it, *feel* it, even from across the hall. When she'd gone to talk to them, she could practically feel sparkles jumping off Eliza and landing on everyone around her. In her tissue-shedding, droopy-tinselled, wonky, spotty dress, she had the magnificence of a small queen. But by the time Cressida was done flouncing around and making pronouncements, Eliza had wilted. Reverted in minutes to the child Holly had first met, the damp squib. It made Holly so mad that she couldn't stop thinking about it. How could a parent be so self-centred?

Holly got up and paced for a while, fury bubbling inside her. It showed no signs of subsiding so she put some soothing classical music on and made a mug of chamomile tea, then returned to her seat, tucked her feet up under a cushion and tried breathing deeply. Still mad.

What a splendid little play… A very nice effort indeed. Patronising witch! But it wasn't Cressida's good opinion that mattered to Holly, it was Eliza. And Edward. He too had looked absolutely flabbergasted. Well, you would, wouldn't you? It was the last thing he deserved after the tough couple of months he'd had, and holding it all together for Eliza, and acing that presentation. The Suttons should have been celebrating the play *and* the presentation.

And *she* should have been at Christmas House with them, drinking hot chocolate in front of a toasty fire, instead of sitting here alone trying to kid herself that she had *any* chance of relaxing tonight. She'd bet a thousand pounds Cressida wouldn't ask Edward a single thing about his work. But there *she* was with the people who were fast becoming Holly's favourite people even though *she* didn't really know the first thing about them.

Just because of some accident of biology, she thought it was her God-given right. *There's no time like the present, darling. I want to celebrate with Eliza. Shall we all go home together?*

Edward hadn't looked happy at all. And yet, as well as feeling truly sorry for him, Holly also felt… worried. Worried about something that wasn't really her business to worry about. Whether he and Cressida might… It was sure to be horrible between them at first, but later, when they'd sorted things out, Cressida would say it was too late to leave (Holly had no doubt that Cressida would say that)… then Edward might look at the woman he had once loved so much, the mother of his beloved daughter and… well, Cressida was heavenly-looking; no one could deny that. If she really was serious about wanting a relationship with Eliza, if she were to spend more time in Britain, then a relationship of *some* sort with Edward had to follow. There had been that quick hug, the warmth in his invitation to join them, that had made her think maybe… No. Surely not. *What had he been about to say to her earlier?*

Holly knew she was pretty. Beautiful, even, sometimes. Plenty of people told her so, and she had mirrors. But she was real-world pretty; although blessed in the looks department, she was still very much an ordinary woman, with frizzy hair when it rained and round cheeks when she grinned and a tendency to get very red in the face when she was excited. Whereas Cressida looked as if she'd just tumbled down – gracefully – from Mount Olympus.

Holly sighed. In some ways it didn't seem likely, Edward and Cressida. Certainly, there had been no love lost between them this evening. But they had history, and Cressida obviously had qualities, besides the obvious, that had made him love her and marry her. *I'm about to leave with my family.* She'd been away a long time. Perhaps she was ready for another change.

Could he resist her if she was? Would he even want to? Was Cressida genuine? Could she make them happy? Questions kept diving at Holly like greedy seagulls and she had no way of knowing the answers to them. Now more than ever she needed to set her feelings for Edward aside, along with her wish that it was she and not Cressida who was Eliza's mother. She was only a new friend of theirs, only Eliza's teacher. She would always be there for them if they needed her, but she had to step back and let matters take their course.

There was *one* thing she could do for them, though, she thought suddenly. Something that might, if it worked, cancel out some of the effects of Cressida turning up like an exploding bomb. It was late but she knew that Jimmy would still be up, finishing his story, faffing about online. Whenever she had to contact him, his WhatsApp invariably showed that he was last active at some horrendous time in the small hours. He was a night owl if ever there was one. She pulled her phone from her bag, unable to help hoping there would be a text from Edward, something along the lines of, *Sorry about tonight. Rain check on our celebrations?* But nothing. Naturally. He had his hands full.

Holly brought up Jimmy's number, hit call and gazed around as it rang out. Her home was so cosy and pretty. Butter-yellow walls, glowing in the lamplight. A huge raspberry-pink beanbag under the window. The soft, saffron sofa and the toe-wrigglingly soft sheepskin rug spread before it. Bookshelves and candles and framed photos of Holly laughing with her parents and friends. She wished she could invite Edward and Eliza over to see it.

'Holly, babe, what's up? What a night, eh? Any other A-listers turn up? Scarlett Johansson? Tom Cruise?'

'No, thank goodness. Thanks for coming tonight, Jimmy. How's the story coming?'

'Oh fine, fine. I haven't finished yet but the night is young.'

Holly shuffled to a more upright position on the sofa. 'Good. Look, Jimmy, I need to ask you the most almighty favour. I have no right to ask you and you can certainly tell me there's no chance in hell. But it's this. Please don't print anything about Cressida Carr.' Not waiting for what she was sure would be his outraged response, she barrelled into an explanation about Eliza's trauma when her mother left and how much Eliza and Edward hated the fuss and drama that Cressida's celebrity caused. 'They're just lovely people, Jimmy, and Eliza's such a special child. I know it's an enormous ask but they've already been through so much.'

When she finally stopped talking there was a pause and she checked her phone screen to see whether Jimmy was still on the line. Then he said, 'I'm not writing a damn word about that woman, Holly Hanwell. What do you take me for?'

He *wasn't*? 'A journalist, Jimmy. I take you for a journalist. Don't get me wrong, you're a good guy, I *know* that about you, but you have to do your job, right? Report on local news. This is news, isn't it?'

'Holly, I saw that little girl's face. I don't know what's going on in that family and I don't want to, but no one there was very happy. I was sent to cover the pageant. Something inspiring, Christmassy and quirky – that's the brief my boss gave me. Jeez, Holly, that singing kid, your little friend in her weird outfit, Bob the reindeer... I got that in spades, didn't I, without her madamship showing up. So chillax.'

'Jimmy, after tonight, I'm something of an authority on angels and let me tell you, that's what you are. What if your boss finds out that *Cressida Carr*, for heaven's sake, turned up and you wrote nothing about it?'

'I'll tell him I didn't see her.'

Holly laughed and almost choked on her chamomile tea. 'Jimmy, she was pretty damn noticeable. How could you *possibly* have not seen her?'

'Had a bit too much mulled wine, didn't I? Distracted by the bloody reindeer. No one at the office thinks I'm a saint, Holly.'

'Well, I do. Thank you, Jimmy, you're a star.'

'Happy Christmas, Holly.'

She wished him a happy Christmas then hung up, cradling her phone and smiling. A journalist with a heart; who'd have thought it? Everyone who'd been there tonight knew that Cressida was Eliza's mother now. But at least, thanks to Jimmy, Eliza would only be in the news for the right reasons. At least it wouldn't *add* to the gossip and fascination that was bound to surround them for a while.

Holly pointed the remote at the TV and started scrolling through Netflix. There was no point going to bed yet – sleep was far away. She noticed a Cressida film that she hadn't seen and hovered over it for a minute. But no. That would be masochistic. She didn't want to spend two hours watching that woman. She'd caught a few words from Edward's mother's parting shot – she hadn't exactly been keeping her voice down – and Sarah Sutton was right all the way. Cressida didn't deserve Eliza *or* Edward.

CHAPTER FORTY-FOUR

Edward

On the drive home, Edward explained in more detail to Eliza how all this had come about. How Cressida had taken him by surprise at the office, and how he'd been determined that nothing should upset his daughter before the pageant.

'I get it, Daddy, I do. I would have said yes – about seeing her I mean – so don't worry. It's bad timing, though, isn't it? We wanted to have fun tonight. I wanted Holly to come back with us and celebrate.'

'We'll have our celebration with Holly, don't worry,' he reassured her. 'It's not off, only postponed.'

He drove slowly, so that Cressida could follow them home in her shiny blue hire car. Just as well; he was so shaken from the highs and now unexpected low of the day that he needed to be careful. He was glad when they arrived, though also dreading having Cressida with them inside their haven.

The Lotus pulled up beside them and Cressida stepped onto the gravel as if it were a podium. She exclaimed very unconvincingly over the house and how 'characterful' it was. (It was, but Cressida made it sound like a bad thing.) Inside, they trailed after him into the kitchen and he noted how Eliza didn't offer to show her mother her room. He tried not to react when Cressida commented on the cobwebs and the outdated kitchen units, rather than the welcoming glow in the hallway or the shadowy stretch of garden. Edward heated milk and threw a pizza in the oven in a daze, half listening while Eliza and Cressida sat at the kitchen table chatting – or rather Cressida chatted and Eliza responded.

All three of them tried their very best to be celebratory and make the rest of the evening about Eliza. 'A career-defining performance!' exclaimed Cressida. 'Miss Sutton at her cinematic best!' She was trying to joke and be kind, but the movie-review parlance went straight over Eliza's head and Edward noticed that Eliza didn't display one iota of the enthusiasm she had when Holly had visited. He did what he could to ease the conversation and guide them back to one another, reminding Eliza of things Cressida used to do when they all lived together and filling Cressida in on some of the developments in Eliza's life since she left.

Then he showed Cressida into the lounge and left her by the fire while he tucked Eliza in all by himself. By that point she was so tired her eyes were drooping, so he promised they could talk about whatever she wanted in the morning and kissed her good night.

When he got back to the lounge, Cressida had turned off the light and was sitting in the almost-dark. She turned her face up to him with a bright smile. 'Don't you just love firelight?' she said. 'It's my absolute favourite. Reuben and I have a wonderful fireplace in our house in LA. One of those big old stone ones you could stand a man in. You know, like you see in movies set on ranches? I've been missing it since I've been in London. I'm staying in a hotel – very grand, very soulless.'

'It must be very strange working away from home for so long,' said Edward, refraining from asking if she ever stood Reuben in their fireplace when he pissed her off.

'Yeah, it's hard. But at least I'm closer to you guys – geographically I mean – and it's given me the chance to see Eliza. She's such a precious little girl, Edward.'

'She is.' For a moment Edward felt a moment of accord with her. Even so, he switched the light back on. He didn't want to sit in the romantic shadows with his ex-wife. Cressida wriggled luxuriously like a cat and patted the sofa beside her. Edward threw himself into an armchair.

'But couldn't you do something with her?' wondered Cressida with a frown.

Edward laughed. 'Like what? Put her to work on a farm? Use her as a hatstand?'

'Ha ha. With her appearance, I mean. She's pretty, Edward.'

I know she's pretty, he thought indignantly. *I see her every day.*

'Well, she *would* be,' Cressida pressed on, laughing, 'sprung as she is from the loins of you and me. But you don't dress her as if she is. She could really go places with looks like that.'

Oh my God, thought Edward and couldn't come up with a single word to say for a moment. The firelight danced on the walls and across the brimming bookcase. He gathered himself. 'Cressida, I *don't* dress her; she dresses herself. Her clothes are the clothes she likes. She chooses them.'

'Well, there's your mistake! As if a child knows. Of course, you're a man, so you don't know either, but *someone* has to know better for her. Can't your mother help?'

'You sound just *like* my mother,' said Edward, which he knew would infuriate her. 'She doesn't understand how independent Eliza is either. She's not a child, Cressida. I mean, she is, but she's not *just* a child. She's a… a whole person. She has her own ideas. She *chooses*, and not just her clothes. If you tried to dress her up as a girly girl, she wouldn't be happy. And you're right, she *will* go places – there's not a doubt in my mind about that. But not because she's pretty, because she's bright and special and has more integrity in her little finger than most people have in their entire—'

'Alright, alright,' Cressida cut in soothingly. 'I didn't mean to upset you, Edward. I'm not implying you haven't done a great job with her. It's just, you know, coming from my world, I can't help perceiving things in those terms.'

'Of course. But I don't want her to grow up trading on her looks, thinking she has to be pleasing to the eye to be worth anything. I don't want beauty to be a currency for her. She always *will* be pleasing to the eye, of course, but that's by the by.'

'In this world?' scoffed Cressida. 'That's never by the by. I'm sorry, I'm being cynical. I'm sorry about this evening, Edward. It's been a long time since I've been around normal people, where me flying in and out isn't the greatest thing that could possibly happen. I'm rusty.'

'I get that. We live in very different worlds now, Cressida.'

'Yes,' she sighed, looking around the room. 'We do. You know, this is really a lovely room, Edward. You could make it look quite spectacular with the right decor. A chandelier. A white carpet. Some chrome.'

Involuntarily, Edward thought of Holly's suggestions, the warmth and colour and softness she'd described, and felt a tug. That was the room he wanted. The sort of life he wanted. He leaned forward, his hands clasped in front of him. 'Let me ask you a quick question. Two. Are you thinking of cutting back on work or stopping altogether?'

'No!' Cressida looked horrified.

'And are you planning to make more British films, work over here more?'

'Noooo. I mean, I wouldn't rule out another in the future, but as it stands, this is a one-off.'

'OK, so, Cressida, what are we going to *do*? I don't want to keep you away from Eliza, I hope you know that, but realistically, how will it work? There's no way she's coming out to LA alone so what are we looking at if you still want to see more of her? Will you make time to come here between films? Will you be content to wait until I can take enough leave to bring her to LA? Will you actually phone and write a bit more between times so she has a bit of continuity?'

Cressida took a deep breath but not before he caught the flash of panic that darted across her face. She nodded slowly. 'Good questions, Edward. Good questions. I guess, yes, if you could bring her to LA some time it would be better than nothing. We have a huge house and you could both stay—'

'I'm not staying with you and Reuben, Cressida. That's weird. I think I'm a pretty modern guy but no. I'll stay in a hotel.'

'And Eliza?'

'I would think she'd stay with me at first. I could bring her to you every day. Then, once she feels comfortable with you, and if she likes Reuben, then it's up to her. She could stay with you for a bit. And what about you coming here to see her?'

'Well, you see, I do get time off between films. Sometimes a month, sometimes two or three. But I *need* that time, Edward. Making a movie is… intense. It's draining. Often I'm shooting on location for weeks or months. In between is my grounding time, my regrouping time. It's when I can reconnect with Reuben and see my friends and have total downtime in a spa or just do normal things, you know, like shopping. Those are the things that recharge me so that I can go and do what I do all over again. If I used that time to fly over here and be away from all those things… well, Edward, I'd never be at *home*.' She uncrossed her long legs and tucked them up around herself, mermaid-style. Her beautiful face was overcast by a gentle frown.

He could see it was just dawning on her and gritted his teeth in frustration but forced himself to stay calm. 'That makes total sense. I can see why that wouldn't work for you. But then what *do* you suggest? I'm willing to accommodate anything you can think of apart from Eliza travelling alone and missing school and whatnot. You must have had some ideas, Cressida, or surely you wouldn't have just shown up at my workplace, at Eliza's school, disrupting everything? When we've spoken lately, you've said how much you regret the way you handled things with her and how you've been longing to see her, to re-establish a relationship. I understand that. But *how*? What did you have in mind?'

'Oh, Edward.' She looked away from him and fiddled with her rings – stunning rings with diamonds and crystals and beautifully wrought gold and silver. He remembered the days when she just wore the plain gold wedding band he'd slid onto her finger. He waited.

At last she sighed. 'OK, look. I didn't have a plan. I was working in London; I thought a couple of times how you guys were nearby. The more I thought of it, the more I wanted to see Eliza. It grew and grew until I showed up at your office that day. I thought… I don't know. It was stupid.'

'What?'

'I thought maybe *you'd* have a solution. Like, maybe you'd offer to move out to LA. I know, I know, don't freak out, I realise that's insane, but I wasn't thinking. I just *missed* her all of a sudden. And you always did have solutions, you know? When I got that part when I was pregnant, you were all like, "Do both!" And when I got the shot in Hollywood, you told me to go for it; you said you'd take care of Eliza and keep everything ticking over for as long as it took. And you did.'

'And you left me.' He couldn't help himself.

'I *know*. Anyway, I just thought there must be some way, and that you would help me find it.'

Edward laughed mirthlessly and spread his hands in exasperation. 'Well, I'm *trying*. But it does sound awfully as if you want to know Eliza but you don't want to make one alteration in your life that would allow that to happen. And I get it, I'm not having a go. But, Cressida, for God's sake, we have to be realistic. We have to look at the actual circumstances and work with those.'

She mumbled something, wearing the face of a chastised child.

'Sorry, I didn't catch that,' said Edward. But she just shook her head, her glossy hair gleaming. He was pretty sure that what she'd said was, *I'm not so good at that*. But that was becoming pretty clear; he didn't need her to spell it out.

Edward felt exhausted. Somehow it was nearly midnight. 'Cressida, you have to go. I've had a *really* long day. Not that you've asked *anything* about me, but I had a major presentation this morning. I didn't sleep properly last night and I need to go to bed. So one last time. What do you *want*?'

'I'll figure it out, Edward. I'll think about it all night. My goodness, is that really the time? Listen, can I stay the night? I *really* don't fancy the long drive back to London in the dark.'

Edward was taken aback. He hadn't expected that. Her face was imploring and she *did* look tired… But no. 'Have you thought for one minute about the message it would send to Eliza if she comes down to breakfast in the morning and finds you here?'

She hadn't. So with a lot of sighing and grumpy shuffling on the sofa, she tried phoning her assistant to book a car to pick her up. 'I'll sort out some way to come back for the Lotus tomorrow,' she told Edward while the phone rang. Her assistant didn't pick up, prompting Cressida to leave a peremptory-sounding voicemail.

'No joy!' she said, looking at Edward expectantly. Unwilling to have her lingering here indefinitely, Edward booked a car using his company's twenty-four-hour service and they were there within ten minutes.

'It's a bit small,' she said when she saw the black Ford Galaxy.

Edward laughed. It was too late and it was all too surreal. All he wanted in the world was silence and his bed. 'It probably won't be what you're used to,' he agreed, 'but it'll get you back safely and save you the drive. Good night, Cressida.'

CHAPTER FORTY-FIVE

Holly

Holly woke from a sleep patchy with weird dreams, feeling grouchy and disappointed in life. The day after the pageant was usually a happy, giddy sort of one, but she already knew that this one was going to be a huge struggle. She'd hardly slept from the adrenaline of the performance and preoccupation with the Suttons. She hadn't drifted off until two and now it was only… she fumbled for the switch of her bedside lamp and squinted at the clock. Six. Her alarm was set for 6.30 a.m. So if that hadn't woken her, what had? She'd been dreaming of woodpeckers.

She groaned and rolled over. Oh to stay in bed all day, feeling sorry for herself. It all flooded back. The pageant. Edward. *Cressida*.

Then she heard the woodpecker again. In December? On a residential street? And actually, woodpeckers didn't *make* a slow, steady noise like that. Well, whatever it was, Holly was too sleepy to care. There, it had stopped.

But it started again. Tap, tap, tap. An odd, out-of-place sound for six on a Thursday morning on her quiet little street. Eventually, curiosity bested sloth and she swung her legs out of bed, into the cold air. The heating hadn't even come on yet. She pulled back the curtain just an inch or two and peered out. It was still dark as a chasm, with no stars, but the street light helpfully illuminated an odd scene taking place on her own front lawn. Well, not so much a lawn as a patch really. It seemed that several small signs had sprung up like mushrooms – then her tired eyes and bleary brain registered that a figure was stooped over one of them, knocking it into the grass with a mallet. Tap, tap, tap. It was a very soft noise. If she'd been deeply asleep, it wouldn't have woken her. She frowned. The figure was swaddled in a long, padded anorak, the hood pulled up.

She gently dropped the curtain into place, pulled on her thick dressing gown and ran downstairs, all without turning on any lights. Conveniently, her fur-lined boots were in the hall so she stuck her feet into them and hesitated just behind the front door. Tap, tap, tap. *Gotcha!*

She turned the key in the lock and wrenched the door open in one swift move. The security light above her head flashed on and the anoraked figure looked up, startled. The hood fell down. And there was Phyllis. At 6.15 a.m., wielding a mallet. 'Bugger!' she cried. 'Caught in the act.'

'I should say so.' Holly stepped out into a darkness snapping with cold. 'And what *is* the act exactly?' There were five signposts in all, saying things like: *Santa stop here*; *I'm on the nice list*; *Mince pies inside*, and so on. Holly burst out laughing. 'Phyllis, you're a crazy lady, you know that?'

Phyllis wrinkled her nose and scratched her head. 'So my sons tell me.'

'I can't believe it's been you, all along. You *lied* to me!'

'Outright, blatant lies when needed,' Phyllis agreed.

'For God's sake come inside and have a quick coffee before I have to get ready for work. And explain yourself, woman.'

Phyllis followed her in, stashed her mallet on the hall table and kept her coat on while Holly fiddled with the heating. The little house rapidly lost its chill, humming and clicking. 'Why on earth have you been *doing* all this?' Holly asked, putting the kettle to boil. 'I thought I had a stalker!' Outside the kitchen window, the garden was still a dark square.

Phyllis grinned. 'You didn't seem very worried about it. If you had, I would've told you. It started off with the wreath. There's this gorgeous florist in London where I always get mine and I just thought it would be neighbourly to get one for you, because you're new. You weren't here when I brought it round so I thought I'd stick it up for you, save you a job. I came over later to explain but that's when I saw you crying, so I thought it wasn't the time. Then I knew something was wrong, so I got the tree to cheer you up and it went on from there really. You were so sad. I wanted to be your Christmas fairy.'

Holly shook her head, stirred the coffees, then gave Phyllis an enormous hug. 'Bless you for that. It really was weird at first, but then I just sort of got used to it, I suppose. I hadn't been feeling Christmassy at all, but even so it was nice having some pretty things to put up. And you do have the loveliest taste, Phyllis. Very classy. Apart from the lawn signs.'

Phyllis cackled. 'Those are a little joke, and the last in the series, I promise. Did you really not guess it was me?'

'I wondered at first, but then you lied to my face! And when you put the fairy lights through my letter box, I heard it and ran straight out, but you'd gone. I didn't know you could move so fast.'

'Oh, that wasn't me; it was my grandson, Stuart. I sent him over and told him to scarper the second he'd posted them. My son did warn me I was acting like a psychopath…'

Holly grinned. 'Thank you. It has cheered me up, and I needed that.'

'Not anymore, though. Not with handsome Edward on the scene and the pageant last night. I'll say it again, it was *wonderful*, dear.'

'Oh.' Holly drooped. For just a moment she'd forgotten last night. 'Phyllis, you missed some big excitement after you left. Guess who showed up?'

Phyllis spread her hands, leaning against the radiator.

'Cressida Carr.'

'*What*? Good God. What was she doing there?'

'Causing trouble. Look, I can't tell you it all now or it'll take forever and I'll be late for work. I need to get in the shower. Are you around tonight?'

'Come over for dinner and tell me *everything*.'

When Phyllis had gone, Holly flew around conducting her usual routine but without her usual zest. The temporary diversion had cheered her, but it didn't change the fact that Cressida had turned up and gone home with Edward. Uncharacteristically, she was running a little late and it was just starting to get light when she was ready to leave. She looked out of her back upstairs window while she buttoned her coat and saw that the acer tree was finally completely bare. She sighed. What an anti-climax. It was very hard to feel excited about new beginnings this morning.

Then she arrived at work to find an email from Mr Buckthorn explaining that Eliza wouldn't be at school because she'd be spending the day with her mother. Desolation flooded through her. That sounded promising – for them. But she couldn't bear the thought of a whole day without seeing Eliza, especially *this* day, which would be spent pretty much entirely rehashing the pageant, of which Eliza was one of the undisputed stars. Holly knew her feelings didn't bode well for the two-week holiday ahead, let alone next year when Eliza would move up to Mrs Conroy's class. Much as she loved the children, she'd never let herself get this attached before. Was she becoming unprofessional?

Only the children kept her from being sunk in gloom all day long. Them, and a text from Edward during afternoon break. It told her what she already knew, that Eliza was out with her mum. And he suggested a coffee when 'all this' was over, which was encouraging too. But who knew when it would be over, or what 'over' would look like? Though at least she knew that he hadn't forgotten her. Holly texted a reply.

That would be great – just let me know. Thanks for the update and good luck!

She sent it, then hesitated. There was so much more she wanted to say. Edward had confided in her – a lot. He and Cressida were, after all, divorced. And if Cressida *was* stepping back into the Suttons' lives – flawless, luminous, notorious – Holly didn't just want to fade away. There were things she wanted him to know, as he negotiated his new way forward. That she was over Alex – *so* over him. That she thought Edward was the loveliest man she had ever met. And that she would always be their friend, but she wished it could be more. She began typing.

Edward, I know you have a lot going on just now. I hope you know I'm here for you, no matter what. But I just wanted you to know that you and Eliza are very special to me. Getting to know you both has given me something to feel happy about, and I think that you're…

The school bell rang for the last session of the day. Holly jumped and deleted the whole thing.

CHAPTER FORTY-SIX

Edward

Thursday evening found Edward pacing back and forth, back and forth across the kitchen, much like a morning several weeks ago. This time, the cause of his anguish was not his own mother, but Eliza's. Eliza was missing school, just this once, and Cressida had taken her out for the day; they were due back any moment. How had they fared? Would they have become the greatest of friends in just one day? Would it have been an unmitigated disaster? Was Eliza *alright*?

Last night, during the ten-minute wait for the car to arrive, Cressida had somehow persuaded him to let her spend the next day with Eliza. To what end, he wasn't sure, since she couldn't seem to see a way forward, but she'd been very imploring and at one point she'd actually clasped her hands together and said, 'Just one day, Edward. Then no matter what happens, at least we'll have had that.' Oscar-worthy.

That was how he came to find himself spending the day alone, watching three of her films back-to-back. Why? A stupid way to spend his day off, really, but he wanted to scan them for clues about her. It hadn't helped, of course. In one she was a prostitute, in the next a secret agent and then last she was dying of leukaemia. She was utterly convincing in all of them; it seemed the only role she wasn't too good at was that of a mother. He had to conclude that the only real thing of Cressida that was in the films was her consummate acting ability.

He found himself thinking back to when he'd met her, when she was twenty-one. She'd been so vibrant and fey, so impulsive and determined. Combined with her beauty, it had been an intoxicating combination. It was easy to remember why he'd fallen for her. Fast forward all these years and she hadn't really changed that much. Yes, the exterior was like some sort of Photoshopped version of Cressida, but she hadn't grown up. *At all!* Motherhood hadn't changed her, success hadn't changed her, supposedly seeing the error of her ways hadn't changed her. All the traits that had charmed and enticed him, untempered by any life wisdom or empathy, weren't beguiling anymore. They were just annoying.

On reflection, he should have stuck to his guns and insisted they start off with a shorter outing, or that he go with them. But Cressida had a knack of railroading you. And Eliza had agreed to it, of course… But he couldn't help thinking of how she was always so unfailingly considerate of others. He'd *told* her she could say no, but would she really have felt that she could? Children internalised their own private set of rules and there was nothing harder than the feeling that you were disappointing your own mother. Edward knew that better than anyone.

In retrospect, he couldn't help thinking that when they'd left that morning in the metallic blue Lotus, Eliza had had the air of someone going to an interview for a job they didn't really want, rather than a child gleeful at the prospect of an exciting day out. Cressida wanted to take her to the film set to meet the other actors and see how she worked and had promised that she would royally spoil her daughter. It was an amazing opportunity for anyone.

The worst of it was that there was a part of Edward that didn't *want* it to have worked out. Of course he didn't want Eliza to have had a miserable day, but he didn't want them becoming instant best friends either; he still didn't feel at all sure about Cressida, and he missed, after just one day, the way things used to be. But that was selfish. If Eliza could have a decent relationship with her mum, she should.

He forced himself to stop pacing and filled the kettle in case Cressida wanted a *tisane* – that's what she called it, not herbal tea – when she got back. He checked his watch – five to four. They were due back by four at the latest. The last time he'd looked, approximately four hours ago, it had been ten to four. How was time passing this slowly? The day had been agony.

Spending the day alone, watching Cressida's films, was hardly how he'd planned to spend this first day after the pageant and the presentation, but he was too tired after an intensely busy and emotional few days to turn to something useful. Snacking on the sofa was all he was good for. His mind was on overload after the previous night.

In between the second and third films, he'd texted Holly. What he'd really wanted to do was meet up with her and kill a bit of this endless, awful day with all its uncertainties. But she was at work and besides, he'd be dreadful company, tense and distracted; he'd leaned on her enough already.

Congrats again on last night – it was wonderful. Eliza's out for the day with her mother!!! I'm home alone going out of my mind. If you're up for it, I hope we can have a coffee when all this is over.

Her response had come quickly. *That would be great – just let me know. Thanks for the update and good luck!*

It had made him smile. It was nice to have someone you could reach out to and feel a connection with, even on the craziest of days. He'd typed another text.

It means a lot to have your support. You're a really special person. I hope you know how much I value knowing you. I can't wait for all this to be over so that we can…

So that we can what? he'd wondered. So that he could start hanging out with her again because nothing made him happier. So that he could enjoy their friendship, and his deepening feelings, without his ex-wife hanging over them like a spectre. He couldn't say that. He'd deleted the text and grabbed the remote control.

Now, hours later, his ears straining for the sound of the car, he was jittery as hell so he grabbed his phone and texted her again: *Expecting them back any minute. Climbing the walls. How's your day been?*

Before a reply came through, he heard the welcome sound of the gravel crunching and nearly jumped out of his skin before he flew to the door. The glittering blue car pulled to a stop and there was a small pause before first one door and then the other opened. Two sets of shoes appeared on the gravel – small purple Doc Martens on one side, burgundy stilettos on the other. It almost made him smile. They were so different, but that didn't mean they couldn't be great friends.

'Welcome, welcome!' he heard himself cry and wondered why he sounded like the MC of a comedy club. He held his arms out and Eliza charged into them, gravel skittering. She threw herself at him with one of her whole-body leaps and he held her tight, her purple boots dangling in the air for a long, thankful moment. Then he put her down so he could look at her. Cressida was hesitating by the car but he'd get to her in a minute.

Eliza looked fine. She wasn't tearful or agitated or anything like that. Neither was she her usual exuberant self. Normally by the time she'd been home ten whole seconds, she was chattering non-stop and he'd be getting dizzy trying to keep up. 'How are you, Lizzie-Loops? How was the day?'

'I'm fine. It was nice,' she said. She *was* fine, he could see that, but also, the day hadn't been a raging success. Rightly or wrongly, Edward felt great relief on both counts.

'Do you want to go inside and get settled in? I'll get some biscuits out – how about that?'

'The lemon ones!' She brightened up a bit.

'Sure thing. Welcome home, Lizzie.'

She ran indoors and he looked up. Cressida was wearing a dusky-pink sheath dress with a cream coat and her burgundy boots, with matching burgundy bag, gloves and scarf. Standing beside the Lotus, she could have been posing for a photo shoot. The wind whipped her dark hair around her face and the bare laburnum shivered in the wind. Beyond them, the woods waited, brimming with their own secret life.

'Cressida, how are you?'

'I'm fine, Edward. Absolutely fine.'

'Are you coming in? Cup of coffee? Tisane?'

He couldn't read her body language; she appeared to wilt and stiffen at the same time. 'Sure. Can you give me a hand with these…?'

She started pulling enormous quantities of bags from the boot. He didn't even know how she'd fitted them in there; Lotuses weren't really about the carrying capacity. He grabbed a few handles from her and frowned. 'Cressida, what's up? You look weird. Are you OK?'

She glanced towards the house to check there was no sign of Eliza. 'Edward, I can't do this.'

'What? Drink tea?'

'No,' she hissed. 'That bit I can do. Motherhood, not so much.'

'Oh, Cressida. Are you *kidding*?'

She scuffed the gravel with a pointed burgundy toe. 'Don't hate me! It's really hard, Edward. Conversation is… well it's not what I'm used to. And when we were on the set… it was just awful.'

'Eliza misbehaved? That's not like her.'

'No, she was perfectly good. And perfectly polite. And she answered anyone who spoke to her and sat quietly when she needed to and said thank you for everything. Everyone said what a model child she was, how good and quiet and trouble-free.'

'Oh I see. That doesn't sound like her either.'

'It doesn't sound like any child, Edward, even *I* know that. She was miserable. No, she wasn't miserable; she was just bored. I'm her *mother* and I'm a *huge star* and we were on a film set and she met *Lane van der Hahn* and she was bored. She kept talking about *foxes*! How can she be my daughter? I'm desperate for a drink and the loo before I go, Edward, but I can't face any more time with her today. I need to regroup, like right now.'

Edward laughed and put an arm round her, accidentally whacking her with a Hamleys bag as he did so. 'Sorry, Cressida, come in. Have a quick break before you drive back. It'll be fine, I promise.'

She leaned against him for a minute and he could feel her relief. She wanted someone to take charge; she wanted him to make everything work out, as he always had. And for the first time in the last two weeks, he knew that he could.

While Cressida freshened herself up in the bathroom, Edward found Eliza in the lounge and told her that her mother was coming in for a drink. Eliza gave a little sigh then said, 'OK, Daddy.'

He smiled. 'Don't worry, Lizzie-Hat. She won't stay long. And then you and I are going to light the fire, crack open that big box of chocolates I was saving for Christmas Eve and you're going to tell me all about your day – the good, the bad and the ugly, OK?'

'Even the bits I didn't enjoy?'

'*All* the bits. Now have you got any homework to do for half an hour?'

'You want me out of the way while you talk to Mummy.' Eliza grinned with a flash of her usual perspicacity.

'Yes, not to put too fine a point on it.'

'I don't have any homework. But I could watch a film for a bit.'

'Perfect. I'll set you up with Netflix if you want. There are some great kids' films on there but it's really hard to work out how to use it and which remote and so on. Took me ages.'

Eliza looked amused. 'Daddy, it's *easy*. I worked it out the minute we had it.'

'Of course you did.' Edward re-boiled the kettle, silently apologising to the environment as he did so and provided Eliza with a healthy snack of carrots and hummus, cheese and oatcakes as well as the promised lemon biscuits. Seeing as dinner would basically be chocolate, he thought he should give her some nutrients. As he emerged from the lounge, carefully shutting the door behind him, he found Cressida descending the stairs with red-carpet grace.

'Eliza's gone to watch a film,' said Edward. 'We're in here.'

'Oh,' said Cressida when she stepped into the kitchen. 'What a dingy, depressing room this is.' Edward raised his eyebrows at her and she amended hurriedly: 'I mean, I don't mind at all, of course. I'm just thinking of you two having such a dreary little kitchen. It's not little for the UK, of course... just so shabby and old... I'm sorry, I'm not making it better, am I?'

'Cressida, here's your tea. Eliza and I have had some of our happiest moments in here. When we first arrived, we couldn't get the thermostat to work and we had no furniture. This was the warmest room then, and it's where we sat for every meal and every snack and every chat. We'd hear her foxes outside, and we'd laugh and we'd discuss all the important things, like where to spend Christmas. We'll get around to renovating it one day, but even now, it's my favourite room in the house.'

Cressida sank down at the kitchen table, wrapping her hands around her mug. 'I see. Well, I suppose I've just gotten used to very different things. Edward, we're poles apart. You and me, me and Eliza. How am I ever going to bridge that gap when I'm almost never here?'

Edward settled himself opposite her. 'You're not. That's just being pragmatic, Cressida. Look, I understand that you've had second thoughts about your choices and that you needed to come and see Eliza. But honestly, I think you had it right all those years ago when you sat me down in our flat and told me you were leaving. You said that you weren't a natural with children and that one day, when Eliza grew up, you'd be able to do lunch together, in Hollywood or London. Do you remember?'

She smiled and grimaced at the same time. 'I guess…'

'Well, I think that's how it's going to go. You're very different creatures, the two of you. I haven't talked to Eliza yet so I don't know what she wants, and I don't want us to make the whole decision without her. But I do think the two of you will find some common ground when she's older. When she's a teenager perhaps, heaven help me. For now, with you there and her here…'

'I know. It's just not going to work. To make a go of things with Eliza, I'd have to give up much more than I'm prep— than I'm able to.'

'I think so,' he said gently. 'But, Cressida, now that you've seen her, spent some time with her, can't you please keep in touch better? If we're agreeing that the two of you can't meet up on a regular basis, couldn't you at least video call her every week or fortnight? Couldn't you send the odd postcard from wherever you are on location so that she catches glimpses of your life, so she knows you do actually think of her?'

'I… I suppose so.'

'*Suppose* isn't good enough. You've turned up like a bomb going off. Now you realise it's not as simple as you thought, but you've *got* to follow through *somehow*, Cressida. If you hightail it back to America and she doesn't hear from you for another three or five years, she'll feel as though you came to see her and she was somehow disappointing. If there's any part of you that would like to have those ladies' lunches with her in the future, that's a sure way to ensure they never happen. Do you see?'

'Yes. I do. It's just that my memory's not great. I'm a very… in-the-moment sort of person. When I'm out there, well, it's easy to forget this other life ever existed.'

Edward looked around at the battered calendar hanging on the wall, scrawled upon with all the details of his and Eliza's life.

Their moments and memories. Infinitely precious. 'But Eliza *does* exist. Cressida, bring up your diary and put her name in every other Wednesday for a year or whatever it takes to make sure you remember. I'm not suggesting every single day. I'm not saying you have to talk for an hour. Five minutes, if that's all you have. I'm just saying, it has to be regular. You're the only mother she has.'

Cressida swallowed and nodded. 'Thanks for the tisane, Edward.'

'Cress, you know it's just a herbal teabag from Tesco, right?'

She stared at him and for a moment he thought she was going to cry, then she suddenly laughed. 'God, I'm awful, aren't I?'

'Little bit, yup.'

She stood, graceful as a swallow and looked around one last time, as if taking in an alien landscape. 'I'm going now. I've just heard today that I'm flying back tomorrow. So much sooner than I'd thought. I'll ring… on Christmas Day, shall I? I don't want to disturb your day; just to say hello.'

Edward stood up too. Already the daylight was fading and he didn't want the whole *I don't want to drive back in the dark* shenanigans to start up again. 'I think that would be great.'

'Those are' – she pointed to the masses of bags on the floor – 'presents for Eliza. I took her shopping after work. I think she thought I was a bit OTT, but I wanted her to remember today.'

'Trust me, she'll remember it. You don't have to *buy* her stuff, Cressida. Just don't *forget* her. Do you want me to wrap half of them so she can open them on Christmas Day? Then she'll have a little bit of you here even though you're not?'

'You'd do that? Yes, that would mean a lot to me. Thanks for everything, Edward.'

Cressida kissed Eliza goodbye, promised to phone and hugged Edward, then drove off in a cloud of Chanel and air kisses. They watched her go, Eliza leaning against his legs, Edward hugging her to him, and stood for a long while after she'd disappeared from view, the cold wind whistling around them and the landscape darkening rapidly. Edward could hardly believe that after the stress and fear of the last week and a half, it was over. Cressida was gone. Things could go back to normal. He didn't have to part with Eliza. But maybe she would have more contact with her mother now and that could only be a good thing. Cressida wasn't a *bad* person, he reflected, just utterly selfish and clueless. He closed his eyes and smiled. Life at Christmas House would carry on, grow and blossom just as they'd always dreamed it would. He could hardly believe how lucky he was.

'Daddy, I'm cold. And you promised we'd eat the chocolates.'

'You're right. Let's go in, Lizzie-Tops, and choc till we drop.'

CHAPTER FORTY-SEVEN

Eliza

Eliza snuggled up in bed that night feeling happier than she'd ever thought possible that morning. When her mother had arrived to take her out, Eliza had been really unhappy about missing school. Was there any other kid who preferred going to school than a treat day with their own mother? But everyone would be talking about the pageant – debriefing, Miss Hanwell had called it – and Eliza would miss it all. School was where Fats was. School was where Miss Hanwell was. All day long she'd struggled to have fun because she knew she was supposed to be, but really all she could think about was how she wanted to be with her dad, and Fatima, and Miss Hanwell and Aunty Pam.

The film set had been alright. It was quite interesting to see the big cameras and how many times the actors had to repeat their lines and how the director lost his temper gradually, gradually until at last, he exploded. Eliza decided she didn't ever want to have a job where it was OK for someone to yell at her like that. When she said so, her mother had looked surprised and said, 'But that's just what directors *do*, darling. It doesn't mean anything. Besides, they never yell at *me*.'

It was true. Her mother was very brilliant, that was obvious; she hardly ever had to redo her bits, and everybody loved her. They all called her 'sweetheart' and brought her skim lattes whenever she wanted. Everyone had exclaimed over Eliza too and brought her sweets and soup. It was obvious that none of them had ever heard of her and there was general amazement that Cressida Carr had a daughter in England. Eliza had wondered if she should feel sad that her mother never talked about her, but then she'd remembered that she never told anyone about her mother either, so maybe it was the same thing.

After the filming, they had gone shopping. Eliza enjoyed shopping with her dad because they stopped regularly for hot chocolate and they talked the whole time. With her mother, it had been harder because they didn't know what each other liked so Eliza had spent quite a lot of the time being bored but pretending not to be, which was quite tiring. She'd suspected her mother had felt just the same. Eliza knew that children had to have mothers, unless they were dead, of course, but she couldn't help wishing that sometimes you could just admit that things were fine as they were and save yourself all this work. By the time they were driving home, they'd run out of things to talk about altogether.

When her dad had spoken to her mother in the kitchen, Eliza had been a bit worried they were sorting out more days like this one. But then her mother had left, saying she was flying back to America the very next day. It seemed she would be gone as suddenly as she'd arrived.

Later, when her dad had asked her all about her day, and how she felt and what she wanted, Eliza could be honest, even about really hard things like this, because they knew each other so well. And then he'd explained that her mother had enjoyed seeing her very much and loved her very much, but because her life and work were still in America, they wouldn't be seeing her for a long time. He'd looked a bit worried, as if he thought Eliza would be upset, but she'd sagged against the back of the big squishy sofa and kicked up her heels in relief.

'Didn't you like your mum?' he'd asked.

Eliza had thought about that carefully. When she'd first showed up, Eliza had thought maybe she would hate her, and that hadn't made her feel good. But it had been different today. 'I *did* like her, I think. She didn't do anything mean, and she was trying very hard to give me a nice day, so that was a kind thing, wasn't it?'

'Yes, darling.'

'But she isn't… fun. She doesn't feel like home and I feel… *easier* when she's not here. She's happy in America, isn't she, Daddy? I don't want her to be unhappy. But she doesn't have to feel as if she's letting us down if she leaves us alone.'

He'd smiled. 'Eliza, you have such a way with words and such a gift for getting to the heart of things. She *is* happy in America and I think she's a little bit relieved that she's going back to her other life now. *I'm* a little bit relieved too, if I'm honest. I like it when it's just you and me. But any time you want to see more of your mother, you just let me know and we'll see how we can work it out, OK?'

'OK. Thanks, Daddy. I like it when it's just you and me too. But that doesn't mean you can't have a girlfriend if you want one, you know. As long as she's someone really nice.'

He'd guffawed with laughter and looked at her with twinkly eyes. 'Where on earth do you get such ideas from, Lizzie-Loops? Thanks for the permission; I'll bear it in mind.'

Now, lying snug in bed, Eliza felt joyous. It had been *interesting* seeing her mother, but Eliza was definitely glad she was gone now. Her dad had said she might be phoning a little bit more and Eliza didn't mind that. There was school tomorrow and it was the last day of term so there was going to be a party! Perhaps they'd still be talking about the pageant and Miss Hanwell would fill her in if she'd missed any exciting news. Her dad was going to work from home tomorrow so he would come to pick her up from school and after that – Christmas holidays! They had so many wonderful things planned – like a Christmas Day walk in the woods. Eliza hadn't seen a trace of the foxes for ages, not even footprints in the frost. They were going to visit her grandparents one day and that would be nice – one day wasn't too long. Even more exciting, her grandparents were coming here for a day. Eliza couldn't wait to show off Christmas House to them.

And they were hosting their first party on Christmas Eve – the nice vicar was coming and he was going to bring his wife and his daughter. Aunty Pam and her grumpy husband and Fats and her parents were coming too. And Eliza had decided to ask Miss Hanwell. Of course, when she'd told her dad he could have a girlfriend, Miss Hanwell was who she'd been thinking about.

She didn't think it had even crossed his mind but honestly, how much more perfect could you get? Miss Hanwell was pretty, kind, funny, clever and she smelled really nice. You could tell she really liked Eliza *and* her dad, and Eliza knew she didn't have a boyfriend or a husband because Lily Orton said so. Lily had also said that Miss Hanwell was spending Christmas alone – Eliza didn't know how she knew that. But that seemed sad and all wrong, so Eliza was sure she'd like to come to their party. Sometimes, though, adults could be really slow figuring things out so Eliza might have to give them a little nudge now and then, but otherwise, she would have to be patient. Her dad often left things to the last minute, like her costume. He'd get to it eventually.

CHAPTER FORTY-EIGHT

Holly

What a difference a day could make. Yesterday had been tough. Holly had gone straight to Phyllis's from work and poured out every last detail of Cressida's grand entrance. (Phyllis had been suitably scathing.) Today, Holly had slept better and Eliza was back in school, undiminished by her adventures. Holly had worried that it would be the subdued Eliza who would return, but instead she was just as she had been over recent weeks – exuberant and sociable. Holly listened carefully to the children's conversations but Cressida's appearance hadn't provoked any jealousy or unkindness, and only a small amount of interest.

'Your mum's a film star,' said Javai Anand.

'Yes,' said Eliza.

'Cool.'

Griff Heaton wanted to know if Cressida was going to make any films about space monsters and Eliza said she didn't know but would ask the next time she phoned. 'But she doesn't phone me very often at all,' she warned him, sounding matter-of-fact and not a bit upset.

'OK,' said Griff.

Lily Orton asked if Cressida got free samples of make-up and clothes, to which Eliza shrugged, then Lily invited Eliza to tea. If there was a little bit of opportunism at work there, Holly wasn't too worried. Lily had talked plenty to Eliza before all this and it was tea, not teasing. It was all good.

In the morning they did show and tell and Eliza brought a photograph of Blackberry and told everyone about how her father had rescued and healed him. In the afternoon, they had the end-of-term party with games, music and general merriment. When Eliza ran up to Holly at the end of school, Holly assumed she was going to wish her a merry Christmas. Her desk was wonderfully piled with cards and gifts from the children. But instead, Eliza said, 'Daddy's picking me up today. Come and say hello.'

Holly had an hour or so of paperwork to finish up before the holidays, but she could come back to that. She resisted the urge to fish her mirror out of her handbag. 'He's got a day off today?' she asked.

'Working from home.'

'Ah, I see. And how are you, lovely? Did you have a good day yesterday?'

Eliza shrugged. 'It was alright. I'd rather have been here, but it was interesting. We're having a little party at our house on Christmas Eve. I'll tell you all about it then if you'd like to come.'

Holly smiled. Another invitation from Eliza. It warmed her heart, but she would still really love an invitation that came from Edward. 'I'll talk to your dad and have a think about it,' she said. 'And you're alright, Eliza? You seemed a little shocked to see your mum on Wednesday evening and I just wanted to check it didn't upset you.'

'It did at the time,' said Eliza, 'but she was alright yesterday and she's gone back to America today so we're back to normal. I'm fine.'

'Oh, OK. That's good.' Holly resisted the urge to do a victory dance and followed Eliza's small figure down the corridor and across the yard, exchanging waves and hellos as they went. Edward was standing near the gate where David Kanumba's father was talking at him very intensely. His expression was fierce and he appeared very wound up; Holly wondered what they were talking about. Politics? Human rights? A local crime? When she reached them, she gathered it was football.

Then David ran over and Mr Kanumba's face melted into a beatific smile. *Parenthood*, thought Holly. *What a thing.* She smiled at Edward as the Kanumbas left for the holidays.

Cries of 'Goodbye! Merry Christmas! Have a lovely break!' drifted on the air like seagulls. This was a bittersweet occasion for Holly. It was wonderful to see so much happiness, and she was filled with a sense of satisfaction – it had been a successful term of which she could feel proud – but she still didn't relish the prospect of two weeks without work or family. *It is what it is*, she reminded herself. Two weeks was hardly a lifetime. She was doing so much better now and she was proud of that too.

'How was the last day?' asked Edward.

'It went very well. And how are you? Working from home today, I gather?'

'Yes. The plan was that I'd collect Lizzie then go back and do another couple of hours' work, but to be honest, I'm done for the day. It'll be dark in an hour. We're going to kick off the weekend with a tramp through the woods while there's still a bit of daylight.'

'That sounds wonderful.'

'Will you join us? Can you leave yet?'

Holly thought of the paperwork on her desk. She always finished it straight after school at the end of every term. It was part of her super-organised approach. But she could come in over the weekend to do it. Even if she left it till January, it wouldn't be the end of the world. The woods were a tempting prospect, and it was Edward who'd asked. 'You know what? I can. I just need to run in and get my bag. I'll follow you in my car.'

'Fantastic. See you at the house.'

Holly grabbed her bag and took a long look around her classroom. It *had* been a good term and she was lucky, she knew, to have a job she loved so much. The walls were covered in Christmassy artwork and she remembered Eliza's first day when the pictures had been fireworks. In January they would all come down, but then there would be World Religion Day, then Valentine's, Easter, Ramadan… a year marked with milestones, a cycle of celebration.

At Christmas House, Eliza and Edward were waiting. 'Yay, you made it!' cheered Eliza, jigging up and down. 'Let's go!'

Holly changed into wellies – fortunately she'd started keeping a pair in her car boot since moving to Hopley with its surrounding fields and her visits to Penny – and they plunged into the woods. The last couple of days had been very cold, and though the temperature had risen by a couple of degrees, there were still, here and there between the trees, frozen puddles like slabs of green butterscotch. They were easy to avoid, though, and there were plenty of soft, muddy pathways to follow. It was darker here too, with the trees throwing up bare arms to screen the light of the rising moon. The air was chalky with cold. Holly shivered; it felt mysterious and magical.

Eliza ran ahead, needing to let off some end-of-term steam; Edward and Holly followed slowly, and she heard all about Eliza's day with Cressida.

'She *says* she's going to phone more and send postcards,' Edward finished, 'but honestly I'm not holding my breath. She said she'd phone on Christmas Day but I haven't said that to Eliza. That way, if she does, great, and if she doesn't, nothing lost.'

'I do admire how you handled it,' admitted Holly. 'I'm not sure I could be so calm and gracious. And *generous*. You're very accepting of her… traits.'

'It's much easier now I know I'm not going to have to change my whole life after all. By the time I spoke to Cressida last night, she'd realised what she knew all those years ago, that she's just not good at all this…' He waved his hand around vaguely. 'You know, normal life, regular people, being a mother. She's good at acting – brilliant in fact. She's good at being a star and following her heart and inspiring and entertaining people.'

'Those are good things,' said Holly thoughtfully. 'Maybe someday when Eliza's older she'll benefit from having a mother with those gifts.'

'That's what I think.'

'Eliza said that she flew out today? She doesn't seem sad. And you? Are you OK? Seeing her didn't bring up any… old feelings?'

'Oh God no! We're both fine. We're as we want to be, me and Eliza. You know, she said last night that seeing her mother had been *interesting*. I would have gone with stressful, crazy-making, infuriating… but now that it's over I agree. It *was* interesting. I mean, I used to be head over heels with her, but now I can see her as I saw her then *and* as I see her now, one overlaid on top of the other, like different layers of life colliding. It was… affirming, I suppose. That's a word they use a lot these days, isn't it?'

Holly nodded. 'I'm glad you're both OK.' That was an understatement. She hoped her relief wasn't written all over her face.

'We're better than OK. Oh, and do you know what else Eliza told me? She told me I'm allowed to get a girlfriend, but only if it's someone *really* nice.'

Holly burst out laughing, amused and a little nervous. 'She did? Wow. So did you have anyone in mind?'

Edward stopped and looked serious. 'Only one person sprang to mind, but I'm not sure if the timing's quite right.'

Holly stopped too. 'Oh really? Anyone I know?' Her stomach turned over as she looked up into his kind face. The woods sighed and crackled with spells around them.

'Holly, I love being friends with you. And I really, really don't want to mess that up…'

Holly's breath caught as she waited to see what he'd say next.

'But I'd be lying if I said I *only* thought of you platonically. You're… you're beautiful. And you bring everything to life around you like the… the goddess of spring or something.'

Holly stared at him in disbelief. 'No one's ever compared me to a goddess before.'

'Well, they should.' Edward made as if to reach out and touch her but drew his hand back, uncertain. 'I like you a lot. But you might not feel the same. Plus, we haven't even been on a date, because you can't count an outing with an eight-year-old. It's more like family time, like we've skipped ten steps ahead. So I don't know how that works. And you, you're coming to terms with a lot of stuff. It's not even a year since you broke up with someone you thought you were going to marry. So maybe all of this isn't even on your radar. I'm happy just to carry on being friends, if that's all you want, I really am. I'd still like more opportunities to enjoy your company, starting with… I wanted to invite you to a little Christmas Eve drinks party at ours, if you're free. But I thought, if we're going to be spending time together, you should know that I have a bit of an agenda. Full disclosure.'

Holly smiled and felt her smile grow until it stretched ear to ear. Thoughts and questions chased each other through her with the exuberance of butterflies in summertime but she tried to stay calm. 'Thank you for telling me. You know what? I have a bit of an agenda too.'

'You do? You don't want to run a mile?'

'I feel the same, Edward. I think you're just lovely. I have for a while. I just didn't want you to think I was trying to muscle in on your family.'

'Oh please, I'd love you to muscle in on my family. Muscle away!'

Holly looked at her wellies, now smeared with sticky mud that didn't seem to know whether it was melting or freezing, and she felt very much the same way. 'I'm not normally one for rushing into things,' she said, 'but just so you know, I don't need more time to get over Alex. I've had almost a year without him now and honestly, I feel that's more than enough. The baby thing is harder, but that's a situation that's not going to change. Even so, it's probably sensible to take it slowly. I'm very… attached to Eliza, as I'm sure you've seen. I don't want that fact to put pressure on us.'

'I appreciate that. And she's crazy about you, so…' They gazed at each other a long moment and then he bent his head towards her. She felt light and airy, as if she was drifting closer to him…

At that moment Eliza came charging down the mulchy track towards them. 'Come on!' she gasped, her face rosy, her grey eyes shining, her hair flyaway under her red bobble hat. 'Why are you just *standing* there? I just saw a squirrel and a magpie and I heard an owl. I'm sure it was an owl. But I thought they only came out at night… it's almost night, though, isn't it? No foxes, though. I'm going to see if I can see the owl.' She turned and flew off again, disappearing into the trees.

'Not running like that, she won't,' muttered Edward. 'How is she so like a baby elephant when she's so small?'

'Will you say anything to Eliza?' asked Holly. 'Do you suppose it's… you and me… crossed her mind?'

'I don't think so. I guess I should say something, yes. We always talk about everything, the two of us. And I want to be able to… I don't know, take you out for dinner, without lying to her. God, Holly, since we came here, I've had more serious conversations with her than in the whole eight years before.'

'And what will you say exactly?'

'Well,' said Edward thoughtfully, 'that we're friends, definitely. That we think we'd like to be more than friends, but that we don't want to rush into anything so she mustn't jump to any conclusions if we start spending a bit more time together. Does that sound good?'

Holly nodded. 'Perfect. I know it's a bit tricky, figuring out how to do this, with Eliza, and my job and not getting ahead of ourselves, but… I like it, Edward.'

'Me too. Shall we?' He held out his hand in its big sheepskin glove to her and Holly, clad in pink woolly gloves, reached out and took it. The comfort and joy of holding his hand ballooned through her and the pride on his face made him look as if he'd been given a rare treasure. Then they set off through the woods together, enjoying the winter, and the wonder of it all.

Half an hour later, they were heading for home and it was almost completely dark. Holly was glad to hang on to Edward's hand as they stumbled back, and Edward insisted Eliza stay close. 'We cut it a bit too fine, Lizzie,' he said. 'Luckily we know the woods well, but we shouldn't risk getting lost in the dark.'

When they reached the edge of the woods and the boundary of Christmas House, it seemed lighter again – a purplish, misty dusk. 'Mulled wine?' suggested Edward. 'I got some in because I know you love it.'

Holly felt a surge of complete and utter contentment travel through her. She hadn't felt this right in a long, long time.

Then Eliza gasped and grabbed them both to jerk them to a halt. 'Look!' she whispered, pointing. Her face was alight, her eyes so wide they looked like pools of silver-grey ice.

Ahead of them, Christmas House looked warm and welcoming under a sickle moon, a pool of soft yellow light from the outside lamp spilling over the doorstep and part of the garden. On the lawn was a family of foxes. Three of them tumbled and twirled in the shadows like burnished Catherine wheels while a fourth looked on as if standing guard. Holly froze, and beside her, Edward stilled completely.

'Do you think it's Blackberry's family?' whispered Eliza, coming to lean against Holly. Holly laid an arm around her shoulders.

'I don't know, Lizzie-Loops; it could be,' whispered Edward.

Just then, the watchful fox turned to look at them with shrewd yellow eyes. Holly held her breath, sure that they'd run away, but they didn't. They continued to box each other and tussle.

'Daddy, take a photo. Quick!'

Edward patted his pockets and groaned. 'I'm sorry, Lizzie-Boots, I've left my phone at home.'

'Miss Hanwell?'

'I'm so sorry, Eliza, but mine's in the car. And you can call me Holly, if you like, when we're not in school.'

Eliza grinned and gave her a quick hug. Despite the cold, Christmassy evening, Holly felt her insides melt like ice cream in the sun. 'Fetch my phone,' said Holly, handing over her car keys. 'It's in the door pocket on the driver side.'

Eliza darted off, lifting her knees in a cartoon-like parody of stealth so as not to frighten off the foxes. They watched her go, stifling laughter, and when she reached the car, Edward turned to Holly. She looked up into his grey eyes, full of stars and shadows on this most magical night, and felt herself melt all over again as he bent his head and kissed her on the lips. He smelled of fresh air and woodsmoke, and his mouth was soft and warm. Of necessity, it was a brief kiss – Eliza was already hurrying back to them – but it brimmed with promises. Holly couldn't stop herself standing on tiptoe to follow it with a quick peck on his cheek – stubble, aftershave – then Eliza was back.

Holly took a number of photos of the foxes for her, then slipped her phone into her pocket. Edward immediately took her hand again.

'Thank you, Holly,' said Eliza, then she sighed. 'We were right about this house, weren't we, Daddy? We were right to come here, even though Granny thought we were mad.'

'You know what, Eliza? We definitely were.'

Holly could hear the satisfaction in his voice, and the three of them continued to watch the foxes play as the night gathered around them.

A LETTER FROM TRACY

I wanted to say a huge thank you for choosing to read *The Little Christmas House*. If you enjoyed it and want to keep up to date with my latest releases, just sign up at the following link. Your email address will never be shared and you can unsubscribe at any time.

www.bookouture.com/tracy-rees

This story has been with me a *long* time – twenty-four years or so! It began life as a short story I wrote when I was in my twenties, living in London and dreaming of being a writer whilst working in an office publishing medical textbooks. Back then, it focused entirely on whether Eliza would be in the pageant, and some sections were written from Blackberry's point of view! It never won me any competitions and I still have the original printed sheaf of A4 pages, yellowing a bit now with ancientness!

Since then, I've done many different jobs and written many different books; however, Edward, Eliza and Holly (and Blackberry!) have stayed with me through the years, insisting there was more to their story and that I should write it in a longer form. So it was a treat and a pleasure to have the opportunity to revisit my old friends as a published author and give them a proper book of their own.

I've also always wanted to write a Christmas novel, so it's been wonderful to write something centred around that magical time of year, when collaboration, connectedness and cooperation make the season special. It was fun working in all the lovely festive details (although somewhat confusing when spring came and the hedgerows started blooming, and I was still writing about tinsel and mulled wine!). And it was lovely to travel again to my little fictional town of Hopley, which featured in my first Bookouture book, *Hidden Secrets at the Little Village Church*. I was glad that Edward and Eliza, as newcomers, found support and welcome from the established residents! I hope that readers of *Hidden Secrets* will have enjoyed recognising some characters from that story.

I do hope that you'll join me for my next book, which will take place in a new town by the sea, and which will be out in 2022. Meanwhile, if you enjoyed reading *The Little Christmas House*, I would be very grateful if you could write a review. I'd love to hear what you think, and it makes such a difference to new readers discovering my books for the first time.

If you have any questions or comments, please do get in touch with me via Twitter, as I love chatting to my readers.

All best wishes,
Tracy

@AuthorTracyRees

ACKNOWLEDGEMENTS

First of all, a huge thank you to you, my readers, for choosing to read this story. For an author there's nothing like the feeling that all the lonely hours of scribbling have translated into someone else's enjoyment. And thank you to all the book reviewers and bloggers who do such wonderful work and create such a buzzy, positive book community.

This book has been doubly blessed with editors. Thank you to Kathryn Taussig for taking it on and early editorial input – amazing as always. And thank you to Natasha Harding for all your support – of my story and my wellbeing. Hugely appreciated. Your feedback has been so valuable and your eye for detail is a wonder. You're both a joy to work with.

Big thanks go to the whole amazing team at Bookouture: Peta Nightingale, Kim Nash, Sarah Hardy, Saidah Graham, Kelsie Marsden, Alexandra Holmes and everyone else who has worked on this title. Also to designer Debbie Clement for a lovely, Christmassy cover, Laura Kincaid for copyedits and saving the timeline and Becca Allen for proof reads.

Thank you, Mum and Dad, for always believing in me. This story has been with me a long time, and the desire to write books even longer than that. You've always supported and encouraged me and your enthusiasm for my writing means the world to me.

And thank you to all my friends, too many to list by name, but each of you so special and important to me. Merry Christmas!

Lightning Source UK Ltd.
Milton Keynes UK
UKHW011115151021
392259UK00001B/143